THE MEN FROM ECHO CREEK

N.R. WALKER

Copyright

Cover Artist: Reese Dante
Editor: Boho Editing
Publisher: BlueHeart Press
The Men From Echo Creek © 2024 N.R. Walker

Warning

Intended for an 18+ audience only. This book is intended for an adult audience. It contains graphic language, explicit content, and adult situations.

Trademarks

All trademarks are the property of their respective owners.

Blurb

In the winter of 1882, a boy from the mountains has to prove himself a man.

When Albie Bramwell's father died, he was left with two thousand hectares of mountain to farm, and little help to run it. Abandoned by all but two of his workers, the whole town of Alpine Falls called him too young to run the farm alone.

Young, yes. At just nineteen, he was determined to prove them wrong. Even if it killed him.

In search of a new life, Percy Collins found himself in a small mountain town where he ran into a man not much older than himself and scored a job at Echo Creek. A property *full of misfits,* or so the townsfolk had called it. But what Percy found was a home.

What Albie found was something he never thought possible. A man to love, and a man to share his dreams.

But times were tough, the winter harsh, and money scarce. Albie and Percy would need to do more than prove themselves worthy. They'd need to not only prove themselves better than anyone else. They'd need to prove it twice.

THE MEN FROM
ECHO CREEK

N.R. WALKER

CHAPTER ONE

THE FREEZING WIND HOWLED THROUGH THE
Snowy Mountains, biting and chilling to the bone.
Cold and stoic faces stood around the graveside, hats
low, coat collars pulled up. "A good man is laid to rest,"
Father Michael said. "On this here day, in the year of
1882 of the Good Lord. Respected by all who knew
him, Arthur Bramwell, may he rest in peace."

Albie Bramwell stood at the foot of his father's
grave, the damp winter air doing little to soothe the
burn of his aching heart. *Fitting,* he thought, *that the
sun wouldn't shine on this day.* The low, dark clouds
clung to the highlands, the trees, and the homestead as
if their gloom sympathised with Albie's loss.

Not even the eucalypt shared their scent on the
breeze. Out of respect or heartbreak, Albie dared not
guess.

These mountains were forever changed now, as was the man who called them home.

He was alone now, his father taken far too soon by a logging accident. Echo Creek was now his farm to run. And he would, like his father had. Built from nothing but hard work in even harder times. Albie would forge on like his father would want him to. Expect him to, more to the point.

Stop with the foolishness, boy, his father would have said. *Chin up and get back to work.*

A hand clapped on Albie's shoulder, snapping him from his memories. He turned to find Des behind him, his hat in his hands. In all the years Des had been Arthur's leading stockman, Albie had seldom seen him remove his hat.

Albie noticed then the wagons were leaving, folks from the town heading home before the weather truly set in. "The men would like a word," Des said, a scowl in place. "Best get it over with."

Four stockmen stood in a nervous circle, and Albie noticed a little too late that their horses were tethered to the railing and packed with their gear. The eldest of them, Fitzgerald, a tall, brusque man who had worked for Arthur Bramwell for ten years, raised his bearded chin. "We are sorry for the loss of your father, Albie. He was a good, good man," he said. "But these are no parts for a boy to call his own. We wish you well, son, but our time here is done. We'll be seeking work elsewhere."

Albie couldn't believe his ears. "You would leave me now, of all days?"

Williams tipped his hat. "These mountains have broken men twice your age. If you want some advice, go to the valley and earn your keep. Put your head down and learn from the men who know what it takes to live up here."

"You need to do your time, boy," another added. "And come back a man."

Albie clenched his jaw, his anger bubbling with indignation and grief. "I have two thousand hectares of mountains to farm, and you would see me fail because you think I'm not a man! My father thought me a man. Man enough to give the orders in his absence, and none of you would have dared question me then, but now you think I'm not capable?" He pointed his finger at them. "You lot can get the hell off my property. If you doubt me, then I don't want you here. And that goes for anyone who thinks I'm not man enough."

Not man enough . . . Albie couldn't believe what he was hearing. It was pure disbelief that these men, whom he'd known for years, would abandon him on the day of his father's funeral. The four men walked toward their horses without another word. Their heads down in shame.

As they should, Albie thought.

Albie turned to Des, and Robert, who stood behind Des. "If you think I'm not capable, feel free to join them."

Des looked Albie right in the eye. "I stood by your father, and he was good to me. I'll stand by you."

Albie then looked at Robert. He was a weedy man who'd found himself in trouble with the bottle and the law, but Albie's father had sorted him out and given him a job. He was good with horses and a hard worker, and he'd always been good to Albie. "I'm staying," he said.

Albie lifted his chin in pride and defiance. "I might not be my father, but I was raised in these mountains. It's all I've ever known. And I will prove those bastards wrong."

Marcy and Evalyn appeared on the veranda, dressed in their Sunday clothes, heads bowed. "Ain't nothing personal," Marcy said. "I wish—"

"Come along," Fitzgerald called out to his wife.

Marcy gave Albie a sympathetic look. "I'm sorry, Albie. There's enough supper to last awhile. I made sure of it."

Albie should have known that Marcy and Evalyn would leave with their men. It was only right.

"Thank you."

Evalyn was teary. "Sorry, Albie."

"Wagon's leaving," Williams called out, his horse turning under his hard reins, and both women hurried along.

That left them four stockmen down and without a cook or a housemaid.

The three men stood there by the veranda and

watched them ride down to the property gates. Albie was furious and hurt, but he refused to show it. He had no clue what he would do, or where to even start, but he was in charge now. He was the boss. At just nineteen years of age, freshly orphaned, and shot into a role he wasn't sure he could handle. But he had no choice.

"Right then," Albie said. "Let's get to work."

FOUR DAYS LATER, Albie saddled Minnie in the stable before daybreak. Minnie was a chestnut mare, barely fourteen hands high, a mountain pony through and through. More mountain goat than horse, Albie's father had once said with a laugh. But if any man was only as good as his horse, as the saying went, then Albie was confident. She was as smart as she was sure-footed, and Albie trusted her with his life. When you were riding flat strap, chasing cattle down the slopes, dodging trees and rocks, that trust was the difference between life and death.

These mountains rarely afforded second chances.

Des appeared, not quite awake yet, and began to ready Ox. The tall black gelding was, or rather, had been, Albie's father's horse. Albie was still struggling with thinking of his father in the past tense. Ox had been a bit skittish as a colt and took a firm hand to yield, but he was a good stock horse: as strong as his name suggested.

Albie was riding to town, and for the two-day return trip, he would ride Minnie and tether Ox behind. Ox would serve as the pack horse. Albie had a few matters to attend to in town and a list of supplies to bring back. It was a half-day's ride into Alpine Falls following the narrow road down the mountains, and Albie had made this journey countless times.

The plan was to see his lawyer, collect all the supplies, stay overnight, and return home by midday the following day. He also planned on putting the word out for any men who were looking for work.

He wasn't optimistic, but it couldn't hurt.

No doubt word had gotten out about Fitzgerald and his men leaving, and Albie had to wonder what rumours had followed. He'd never cared for the town life. There were too many people and too much fuss for his liking, but this trip couldn't be put off any longer. He was, after all, the man in charge now.

Des finished putting the saddlebags on Ox and took the bridle in hand. "You ready?"

Albie double-checked the girth strap and gave a nod. "Yes. I'll be back around noon tomorrow. There's enough stew and damper to last the night, and fresh eggs if you collect 'em."

Des grumped and led Ox out of the stable. "Robert can fetch the eggs," he drawled, his deep voice as stoic as he was. "I'll worry about the horses and cattle."

Albie put his foot in the stirrup and hoisted himself up into the saddle. Minnie tossed her head to the side and Albie tightened the reins and gave her a nudge. "Come on, girl."

Once they were outside, the sun was turning night into day along the mountain ridge that lined the eastern sky. Des tethered Ox to Minnie, and with a tip of his hat, Albie said, "You're in charge, Des."

"Got it . . . boss." The man almost smiled like he found something funny in calling him boss. But then he frowned. "Watch the crossing."

Watch the crossing was something Albie's father had said whenever Albie had gone down the mountain, and hearing Des say it now sent a pang of grief through him that made it hard for Albie to breathe. The best he could manage was a nod, and with another nudge to Minnie, he rode down the long entrance and out his property gate.

The trek down the mountain was cold, damp, and peaceful. The winter mist clung to the slopes like a shawl, the smell of wet earth and eucalypt the perfume that would always remind Albie of home.

He'd been a small boy on childish adventures in these parts, pretending to be a bushranger, climbing trees, and building lean-tos from bark. He'd been a teen, taking off on horseback when his father allowed, spending time by himself trying to get away from it all, giving himself time to think . . .

He loved these mountains.

The birds, the trees, the winds, they knew his stories. They knew his secrets.

And so he rode. The trip was mostly a chore for everyone else, but Albie didn't mind it one bit. It gave him uninterrupted head-clearing time, and by the time he rode into Alpine Falls, he was determined to do everything on his list, already eager to get back home.

The township of Alpine Falls was a decent size. Stores and saloons with verandas lined the dirt street that became mud with the hint of rain. Posts to tether horses dotted the streets, troughs of water, and people milling about with important business that Albie never much cared for. The tannery reeked, the bullock trains did too, noise and foul language spilled from the saloons, children ran and yelled, and it was all too loud and busy for Albie's liking.

He rode past the saddler's store, the bank, and the barbers, and a few of the townsfolk nodded his way. He tipped his hat and offered no more than a smile until he found the place he was looking for.

First stop was to see Mr Bill Flannigan. He had helped Albie's father over the years, and Bill had told Albie at the funeral he'd need to come to town to sign the paperwork to transfer the title deeds over to his name. It was easy enough.

"Ah, the man from Echo Creek," Flannigan said, greeting him warmly the way he used to greet his father.

The man from Echo Creek…

The reminder was a little too raw and it seared Albie with fresh grief, right where he stood.

Flannigan seemed to notice and regretted his choice of words. "It's good to see you, Albie."

"Likewise," Albie replied. He hadn't realised how much he'd needed to see a friendly face.

A handshake, further apologies and condolences at the loss of a good man, and Flannigan quickly explained how the ownership of Echo Creek now rested on Albie's shoulders.

At just nineteen, Albie was the owner of two thousand hectares of mountain country. He should have felt pride or something—men twice his age rarely had what he did—but all Albie felt was loss and a huge weight of responsibility. His father's passing had left him with quite the burden, and he'd have given it all back to have his father alive again.

Albie couldn't read too well: he'd never had much time for school, but he could read well enough. His name, his father's estate, and the deeds to Echo Creek. That was all he needed to know.

And so, with a scribble of a blue fountain pen, it was done.

Albie had perhaps expected more. He wasn't sure what exactly he expected more of, but when Mr Flannigan congratulated him and said it was done, Albie felt . . . empty. Sad, and a little lost.

And very much alone.

Deciding he should eat and find a bed for the night, Albie rode to the hotel he'd stayed at before. The saloon was always loud and rowdy, but the food was good and the rooms were clean. He slid down from his horse and tied her to the railing just as a dog came from nowhere, barking and snapping at his horses.

Albie held onto Minnie's reins as he tried to kick at the still-barking dog, yelling at it to get lost. It snapped at his ankle and Minnie shied away, but Ox pulled and stomped, and Albie tried to calm both his horses. Then the feral dog snapped at Ox's hind fetlock and the big horse kicked and pulled, his tether coming free.

He reared up, his eyes wild, all while the dog still barked. People stood by and watched, and Albie grasped for Ox's tether, but Ox pulled back, out of reach. He neighed and stomped at the dog, ready to bolt. The crowd scattered, and Minnie jacked up now as well, and Albie was about to lose control of both horses in front of everyone . . .

Until someone raced in from behind, quick as a whip, and grabbed Ox's tether. Albie was so busy trying to calm Minnie and get rid of the menace dog, he hadn't realised just how fast Ox had quietened.

"Woah, boy," the man said, talking calm and gentle, holding the tether near the bridle—holding strong but talking sweet—and he soon had Ox under control. The dog had been scared away, and all that was left was the chatter of the spectators, the hard breathing of the horses, and Albie's hammering heart.

It was then the man turned around and walked Ox back toward him. He looked no older than Albie. He had straight blondish hair, a little longer than men normally wore. He had blue eyes and a roguish smile. His white shirt wasn't too clean, his brown pants not much better, his boots were well-worn, and his muscled forearms were that of a horseman.

"He almost got away from ya," he said, handing the tether to Albie. "Fine-looking horse it is."

"Thank you," Albie said, still a little breathless. He gave Ox a reassuring pat and did a quick once over. He was, thankfully, fine. "That blasted dog."

"Nuisance dog, it is," the man said. "It's with the last bullock team that came through. Reckon they'll be gone tonight." He ran his hand through his dirty blond hair and licked his lips, and Albie was taken aback by just how handsome the man in front of him was. He'd only dreamed of such men, and even then, his dreams didn't quite do this man justice.

It took a moment for Albie to remember his manners. "I'm indebted to you."

"It was no problem at all, mister."

Albie stuck out his hand. "The name's Albie Bramwell."

The man smiled, all roguish and charming. His grip was firm and warm, but his eyes were like blue fire. "Nice to meet you, Albie. I'm Percy Collins."

CHAPTER TWO

PERCY HAD HEARD THE COMMOTION OUTSIDE THE
saloon and, like everyone else, went to investigate. A
man and his two horses were being rounded up by that
nuisance dog that had bit at the horses' hooves the
night before. People were gathered around watching,
unsure of what to do. Perhaps frightened by the size of
the unsettled horse or the aggressive dog.

Fools, Percy thought. *Don't just stand there!*

But stand there, they did.

The dog was savage, and the black horse was big.
Percy couldn't deny the scene was intimidating, especially given the horse was rearing up, braying, and kicking. It wasn't the horse's fault, nor was it the horse
owner's fault either. That stupid dog snapped at
horses' hooves, and it would serve itself right if it were
kicked in the head.

Before Percy could stop himself, he ran into the

middle of it all and grabbed the black horse's reins. It took all his strength to hold him, every muscle straining, and at least someone had the sense to hunt the dog away with a broom.

The crowd gathered around them muttered and whispered, and Percy calmed the horse with soft words and gentle strokes, leading it back to his owner. He was young, not much older than Percy, if he were to guess. He was tall, had short brown hair, tanned skin, and light brown eyes, and Percy had to make himself not stare.

So very handsome.

Don't get caught staring . . .

"He almost got away from ya," he said, handing the tether to the owner. "Fine-looking horse it is."

And it was. At least sixteen hands, black as night, bright eyes.

"Thank you," the man said, still a little breathless. He gave the big horse a reassuring pat and did a quick once over. "That blasted dog . . ."

"Nuisance dog, it is," Percy said. "It's with the last bullock team that came through. Reckon they'll be gone tonight." He ran his hand through his hair and Percy caught the man's eye for the briefest flicker before he looked away.

"I'm indebted to you," the man said.

"It was no problem at all, mister."

He stuck out his hand. "The name's Albie Bramwell."

Percy smiled as he took his hand to shake. His grip was strong, but his eyes . . . there was a flicker of something, held for a beat too long. Percy had to make himself speak. "Nice to meet you, Albie. I'm Percy Collins."

"Well, Percy Collins, you know how to handle a horse." He took the reins from him. "Ox here is as strong as his name suggests."

Ox. That made Percy smile. "Great name. And yes, born and raised around horses. Could ride before I could walk."

Albie smiled at that, then pointed his chin to the railing outside the saloon. He began to tether them to it. "I need to see about a room for the night. Thank you again."

"Oh, right then," Percy said. "I might see you around. I'm staying here too. Looking for work if you know of anything." He wasn't normally so brazen but he was getting desperate. His money was running low.

Albie looked him up and down, then pulled his hat low to hide his eyes. "If I hear of anything . . ."

Albie disappeared up the steps and into the saloon, and Percy stood there a moment watching the doors swinging in his wake.

Most of the crowd of onlookers were gone now, the few still standing there with not much else better to do, apparently. They were the pretentious kind in fine suits that looked down their noses at the likes of Percy.

If only they knew he was once like them, with the clean tailored clothes . . .

"That's the Bramwell kid," he heard one of the men say. "I recognise his old man's horse. Shame what happened to Arthur. He was a good man."

"Hm." The other man nodded, pursing his lips. "I heard his men upped and left him. Wouldn't work for a kid. Can't say I blame 'em. Des Blackwell stayed on though. And that Robert Fuller."

The sour-faced man snorted. "A cripple and a drunk. A farm of misfits."

"Des is a good man," he said. "Cripple or no, he's loyal to a fault." He shook his head. "It'll be to his detriment. How long do you reckon before the kid loses it all?"

"A few months, maybe."

Percy didn't mean to eavesdrop, but it was difficult not to overhear.

"It'll be worthless soon enough, and McAllister will buy the place for pennies. And that's if the mountains don't kill the boy first."

Albie came back out and he was staring at the two men. Percy could only guess he'd heard part of their conversation, or all of it, and from the way they'd straightened up, the two men guessed as much too. Albie tipped his hat to them but said nothing.

He untied his horses and gave the men a scathing look as he turned them and walked them to the side of the saloon. Percy couldn't help but smile as they went on their way. And he had to wonder about this Albie Bramwell; his reputation preceded him. He had his own property? At his age?

It must have been quite the story for the people in the town to be talking about it.

But his men had left him, which meant maybe he did need some help. A farmhand or a stable hand, Percy didn't care at this point. So, with that in mind, he followed Albie around the side of the saloon, no doubt taking his horses to the stables.

He went in, the smell of horse sweat and dung was cloying and familiar, and sure enough, Albie was tending to his horses in the end stall. He was taking the saddle off Ox and startled when Percy cleared his throat.

"Oh, I wasn't expecting company," he said, dumping the saddle onto the rail.

"I just wanted to say not to let the likes of those men bother you," Percy said. "Can't mind their business, apparently."

Albie gave a wry smile as he took the bridle off Ox and gave his neck a pat. "I don't care what they think." Then he looked around. "Are you here for something?"

Percy glanced behind him, embarrassed at being caught following him. "My horse is across the stall. I was just coming to check on him," he lied. He'd checked on him not too long ago. He went to the stall and his horse, Bandit, came to nudge him. He smiled as he stroked his neck. "I couldn't help but overhear what they said," he said, still patting Bandit and not looking Albie's way. "That your men quit on you."

There was only silence in response, and when Percy turned around, Albie took a shovel of horse dung and slumped it against the wall. "That's what I think of that."

Percy hadn't meant to upset him, but the horse-dung analogy was fair. "At least manure's useful. Great for garden beds."

Albie put the shovel away and wiped his forehead with the back of his hand, and Percy'd be damned, but Albie smiled in a way that Percy had to blink a few times to clear his mind from the dangerous places it took him. "I, uh, yeah, sorry. I just wanted to say that if you need a farmhand or a stable hand, or anything, that I'm looking for work. I've got a purse of silver that's getting lighter every day, but I don't need much pay. Just a roof over my head and one or two squares a day."

Albie looked Percy up and down. "You're on your own?"

Percy nodded and ran his hand through his hair, trying to straighten it some. "I am. I'm eighteen, a grown man, and I'm a hard worker. I have my own horse, and I'd be no trouble."

Albie stared, and what he was thinking, Percy had no clue.

"I've got some errands to run today," he said, dusting his hands on his pants. "I best get them done." And with that, he turned and walked out.

Percy gave Bandit a frown. "Had to try, didn't I?"

Percy would rather not eat at all if it meant he didn't have to sell his horse. He refused to even consider it. Bandit was all he had in the world, and he'd be damned if he ever went back to his family with his tail between his legs.

Bandit snorted and nodded his head up and down. At least it drew a smile out of Percy.

"Yeah, you and me," he said. "We'll be okay. Even if we have to sleep under the stars. And if you eat grass, it can't be that bad. Maybe I could try it—"

He felt eyes on him, so he turned and found Albie at the stable doors. "Forgot my wallet," he said, coming back in.

He went into his stall and came back out a moment later, patting his pocket down. "So," he said, that dangerous smile on his handsome face. "You talk to your horse often?"

"All the time," Percy admitted. "He's a real good listener. Never complains."

Albie's smile grew enough to show his teeth. He licked his bottom lip, and Percy had to blink again. He cleared his throat and wiped his hands on his shirt. "I'll let you get to running your errands," Percy said, and it was Percy who walked out this time, the fresh air enough to clear his mind.

Dangerous thoughts, indeed.

It wasn't proper to think of men that way. At least

not in front of them. He could save his dirty thoughts for later, in the privacy of his room.

Of sun-kissed skin and syrup-coloured eyes, of a crooked smile.

And with a deep breath, he went back down to the bullock yards, hoping to score himself a few shillings for mucking out.

———

PERCY DIDN'T THINK MUCH ELSE of Albie Bramwell that day until he got back to the saloon. He was filthy dirty and starving hungry, so he set about washing up before he went in search of food. The boarding rooms above the saloon were small and mostly bare. A single bed and a dresser with a basin on top, jugs of water to be collected from the communal laundry-washroom.

His shirt was splattered with bullock dung, so he took it off and washed his face, cleaning himself up the best he could. His pants were a mess, but the least he could do was wash his shirt. And when that was done, he took the basin of filthy water to dispose of in the washroom. He walked out of his room and ran smack-bang into Albie Bramwell. The dirty water splashed his shirt.

"Oh, I'm sorry," Percy said, taking a step back, trying not to spill any more water. He held the basin with one arm and stupidly tried to pat Albie's shirt.

Albie took his wrist and stopped him. "Ah, it's . . . it's okay," he said, brushing himself.

"No, it's dirty water. If you need me to clean your shirt, I've just washed mine so it's no bother—"

"I didn't bring a spare," Albie said. "I'm only staying one night. Be gone in the morning. It's fine. It'll dry." Then he made a face. "Well, it'll stink, but it'll dry."

Percy felt bad. "I am sorry. I was mucking out the bullock lots, and it's messy work, so I wanted to clean up before I ate something. The saloon cook will hunt me out if I stink up her kitchen."

Albie did that dangerous smirk again. "It's fine. And I know the cook. She's not that mean. The barmaid, on the other hand . . . She's the one to watch."

Percy smiled at him. He was actually talking to him, joking even. He felt like a foolish boy in the company of this man, and it was unnerving. He felt *a lot of things* in the company of this man that were unnerving . . .

"Do you always leave your room without a shirt?" Albie asked.

Percy looked down at himself. He was wearing an undershirt. It wasn't like he had no shirt on at all. He was about to say as much when he noticed Albie smiling. "I'll be sure to dress appropriately when I go downstairs," Percy said.

Albie smirked, pulled his hat down, and brushed past him. "See that you do."

Percy stood in the hallway, his heart hammering, his belly full of butterflies. The water in his basin sloshed a little and it reminded him of what he was supposed to be doing.

A short time later, he went downstairs in search of food. And yes, he had on a proper shirt. One of his best shirts, actually. Not that he had many. But let's see what Albie Bramwell thought of him now.

What he thought of him was not much apparently, because, for the next hour or so, Albie sat there and talked to Elsie, the barmaid. Looking too comfortable and he even laughed, and she touched his shoulder, leaving him to eat his stew and bread.

He'd said he knew her, so Percy shouldn't have been surprised.

No, he wasn't surprised.

He was jealous and disappointed, which made no sense on either part. Because Percy had never met another man like himself. That had impure thoughts of other men. They all only had eyes for women, which was fine and understandable, and oh, how Percy sometimes wished he did too. His life would be so much easier. He'd still be at home, getting married as his parents had wanted. But he wasn't, and he couldn't lie to himself or to the poor girl he was supposed to marry—

"What business is it of yours?" Albie said.

Percy whipped his head around to see a man

standing at Albie's table. He'd seen this man around town before, though he didn't know his name.

"Because you're a boy, Bramwell."

"I'll not have my father's name sullied because you don't think me worthy," Albie said, standing up. He was a fraction taller than the other man but not as wide. The other man looked hard-worn and strong. Though that didn't seem to worry Albie because he wasn't backing down. He stared him dead in the eye, fierce as anything. "The deeds are mine, my father's family name is mine, and you'll need to take both over my cold, dead body."

The man grabbed Albie's shirt and Percy was up and off his seat without thinking. He stood between them, staring at the man whose name he still didn't know. "You don't get to call him a boy, then try and fight him. Unless you only fight boys? If you fight men, *like a real man,* then admit that's what you consider him. You don't get it both ways."

Elsie was there then, with her shoulders back, spine straight, voice stern. "Peter Winnicott, I'll not have any of this nonsense in this bar, you hear? You want to start something, take it outside."

Albie raised his chin as if he was okay with that, but Percy pushed him back. "No, there'll be no fighting." He gave Elsie an apologetic nod. "Sorry."

Peter Winnicott grunted and grumbled, giving Percy a scathing glare as he turned and walked away, and Percy's breath left him in a rush.

"I didn't need your help," Albie said.

"You were about to need a doctor," Percy murmured. "You're welcome, by the way."

Albie straightened his shirt, collecting himself with a few deep breaths. "If he only fights men then admit that's what you consider him, huh?"

Percy winced. "Yeah. Sorry. But this whole *boy nonsense* really yanks my chain," he grumbled. "I get nothing but condescending, scornful—" He had to stop himself from ranting, but he knew all too well the prejudice Albie faced because he faced it too. "I'm a grown man, as much as any of them. Same as you. I'm not a child anymore."

Albie studied Percy for a long second, and Percy could barely make himself meet his gaze. He was mad now. Mad for Albie, mad for himself.

Until Albie smirked. "I can't offer much in the way of wages just yet, but I've got the work for you and a roof over your head and a stable for your horse if you want it. I'm leaving after breakfast. If you want the job, you'll be ready when I am."

Percy grinned, feeling true happiness and a glimmer of hope for the first time in far too long. "Absolutely. I'll be there. You won't be disappointed. I promise."

CHAPTER THREE

ALBIE WALKED INTO THE DINING AREA OF THE hotel to the smell of a fresh wood fire and baking bread. "Morning," Elsie said, greeting him warmly. "Trust you slept well?"

"I did, thank you. Just letting you know I'll be off now," he furthered, putting the large stash of his wares on a table. "Just wanted to say thanks."

Clara came out from the kitchen holding a small brown paper parcel. She was timid, always had been, but Elsie gave her a reassuring nod, and Clara handed the parcel to Albie. "For your travels," she said, her voice quiet.

Elsie gave her a proud smile, and Albie had often wondered about the two of them. Where one was, the other was never far behind. Clara was the quiet and meek little mouse and Elsie was the fierce, protective cat. He'd never dared to question their relationship, though he did wonder if perhaps they only had eyes for each other.

The same way he only had eyes for men.

He looked in the wrapped parcel to find two thick cuts of fresh bread, still warm from the oven. "Two? I don't need two," he said, starting to pat down his pockets for some coin.

Elsie put her hand on his arm. "One for you, one for your travelling partner," she said, giving a pointed glance to the far window. Sure enough, there was Percy with his horse, fixing his saddle.

He's on time, anyway. Always a good sign.

"Say," Albie began. "What do you know of him?"

"That he's eighteen, not from around here. Said he was new to town, been here a week or two now, and looking for work," Elsie replied. Then her voice lowered. "What else I can tell ya is that he's polite, well-spoken, and the boy's got manners. Never tried to lay a hand on me or any of the girls here. Doesn't grope or ogle them up and down in that filthy way the men around here do."

Albie put his hand to his chest. "I've never—"

"No, you haven't," she replied. "Your daddy raised you well."

The mention of Albie's father opened the wound of grief afresh, ragged and aching. He gave a nod, and he could see that Elsie regretted the reference. She gave him a nudge. "Maybe you and young Percy have more in common than you—"

At that moment, Percy came out of the stable leading Minnie and Ox . . .

"What in the devil?" Albie said, rushing out the back. He was about to ask Percy what on earth he thought he was doing with his horses when Percy spotted him and gave him a wide, charming grin.

"Morning, Mr Bramwell," he said. "You said you needed to leave early, so I thought I'd see to your horses. Saddled and ready, even gave them some fresh hay and water. Ox is a cheeky thing, isn't he? Tried to eat my hat." Percy fixed his hat again, still grinning, his eyes bright. He came over to where Albie, Elsie, and Clara were at the door. "Did you have your supplies? Let me get them packed away for you."

Albie wasn't sure what to say. He hadn't been prepared for cheerfulness this early in the morning. The sun wasn't even fully up yet, but Percy's eagerness had taken Albie by surprise.

Not to mention that roguish smile . . .

Elsie held the door open. "On the table there," she said.

Percy disappeared inside and came back out a second later carrying everything Albie had purchased the day before. He'd kept it in his room overnight, save anyone with light fingers the trouble of attempting to steal it from the stable.

And then Percy began to load up Ox's saddlebags with the flour, sugar, and salt and the two sacks of grains and seeds. Of course, Ox tried to nudge Percy's hat off his head, a habit of Ox's and a trait Albie had seen his father's stable hands try and whip out of him. But Percy only laughed and admonished him with a rub on the neck and a threat of no hay for his supper.

Albie wasn't sure what to make of Percy.

Agreeing to hire him would either be a godsend . . . or from the way the morning sun caught the blond of his hair as he fixed his hat and how the sound of his laughter made Albie's stomach swoop, maybe it would be a disaster.

Albie felt Elsie's eyes on him and when he made himself stop looking at Percy, he found Elsie smiling at him. "A turn of good luck, it seems," she said, holding his gaze a beat too long.

Had he been staring too long? Had he given himself away? What was she saying before? Maybe they had something in common? He wasn't sure.

He cleared his throat. "Good luck?"

"Yeah. He seems a hard worker," she said. "And you'll have someone your own age up there. Have you ever had anyone your own age at the farm?"

"Uh, no," Albie admitted. "Never. Just farmhands, loggers, workers. Cranky old men, most of 'em."

Elsie smiled, looking where Percy was fixing the saddle bag straps. She was pleased, it seemed. "I know you've got a lot on your shoulders, Albie. But it's okay to let yourself be young too."

He wasn't entirely sure what she meant by that, and he certainly wasn't about to ask. Instead, he tipped his hat. "Best get going," he said. "Thanks again for the hospitality. Friendly faces in this town are few and far between."

"Be safe now, ya hear?"

"If you're ever up my way, call in," Albie offered. He wasn't sure why, it just seemed the appropriate thing to say. It's what the owners of rural properties said, right? Now that he was the owner, he should think of these things. "I'm short a cook and a maid now, so if you're ever looking for a change of pace." He gestured to the parcel of bread he was still holding and gave Clara a smile. "You can bake bread in my kitchen anytime."

Then he realised how that might have sounded and he quickly followed it up with a bit of a joke. "No, no, nothing untoward, truly. Because the bread I made could have been sold to the mason, and Des's attempt was worse. The rate we're eating up there, we'll be as lean as McAllister's cattle."

Elsie laughed. "Go on," she shooed him away. "And don't you listen to those naysayers."

He gave both ladies a nod, and he caught the way Elsie slipped her arm around Clara as she walked her back inside. Albie's earlier suspicion might have been correct, but then again, he was so unfamiliar with the way women were, he couldn't be sure.

Maybe affection between them was common. The only women he'd known were the wives of the farmhands, Marcy and Evalyn, and they'd not been affectionate with each other. Not that Albie had noticed, anyway.

Not that he'd ever looked.

"Mr Bramwell," Percy said. He stood at the steps of the veranda, looking up at him, cautious now. "Everything right?"

Right. Yes.

He gave a nod.

He stashed the bread in his saddlebag and checked the reins and how Percy had secured Ox's tether to Minnie's saddle. He'd done a good job.

"You doubting me, sir?"

Albie looked at him then. "Don't call me that," he said. "A name reserved for my father whenever I was in trouble."

Percy made a face and bowed his head. "Sorry, Mr Bramwell."

Albie slipped his foot into the stirrup and hoisted himself up into his saddle. Minnie shook her mane as Albie shifted in his seat, both of them getting comfortable.

Percy slung himself onto his horse effortlessly.

"I can't fault your horsemanship," Albie said. "Though perhaps we can lose the use of *Mister* Bramwell. You were fine calling me Albie yesterday."

"You weren't my boss yesterday."

Well, Albie couldn't fault that either.

With a sigh, he pulled on the reins and nudged Minnie to begin the long trek home. It was funny how he could miss his home after just one night.

They rode in silence through the town. The streets were quiet, only the faint banging from the blacksmith and the early morning chatter between store owners who stopped to watch Albie leave.

He knew the whole town would know before lunch he'd gone back home with a new worker in tow. He didn't care what they thought, though he knew very little about his new employee.

Albie knew Percy was willing and able and that he'd stood up to the likes of Peter Winnicott in the saloon. When Winnicott had affronted Albie, Percy was quick to put himself right in the middle. He'd stopped the fight with quick-witted reason, and that told Albie that Percy was no fool.

In the one day he'd known him, he'd learned Percy was smart, loyal, good with horses, and willing to work.

That was all he needed to know. For now, anyway.

Albie didn't care about Percy's smile, or the way his laughter hung in the air, or the way his blue eyes caught the sunshine. Or why a young and capable, educated man was on his own.

Orphaned, most likely, Albie reasoned.

Not unlike himself.

"So that fella in the saloon last night," Percy said. They were out of town now, headed up Flagstaff Road, headed up into the high country. "Winnicott? Is that what Elsie called him?"

"Hm. Peter Winnicott."

"What's his problem?"

"The problem of half the men in these parts. I'm too young, they reckon. According to them, a man needs to prove himself; gotta earn the right to run cattle and horses in the mountains like they did."

"That's a load of wallop," Percy said, "Sounds to me like they're scared you'll make it look easy."

That made Albie laugh. "Easy? Nothing about these mountains is easy."

"But you love it."

Albie smiled, taking in the cool morning air, fresh eucalypt, and damp earth. The sounds of the crickets and birds.

"I've never known anything else," Albie said. "Never wanted anything else."

Percy was quiet for a bit, seemingly happy with that answer.

"I never asked to run my place alone," Albie volunteered. "Those men act like it was my choice, like I wanted to be on my own." He couldn't keep the bite from his tone. The emotion, the hurt. But it also made him so mad he could spit. "I'd give it all away in a heartbeat to have my father alive again. For even just one day."

Percy winced. "I'm sorry to hear about your father."

The look on Elsie's face had been similar.

"It's fine. Sorry," Albie mumbled. "It's not your

fault. I . . ." He sighed. He should what? Be stoic and not talk about his grief?

Probably.

That's what mountain men did, right?

With the quick memory of Elsie's face, he remembered something else. He reached into his saddle pack. "Here," he said, handing a piece of bread out to Percy. "Clara cooked this fresh this morning."

He took it gratefully and bit into it with a grin. Then he groaned and his eyes rolled closed, and Albie was stuck . . . stuck staring, the look of pleasure on Percy's face, the sound he'd made.

"Sorry," Percy said with a laugh, covering his mouth. "This is good bread."

Albie made himself look ahead and he shifted in his saddle, his pants suddenly a little tight. Damn it. He bit into his bread, and yes, it was good.

Percy was, thankfully, oblivious. "Say . . . if you're short-staffed at the moment, dare I ask if you got any staff that can cook?"

Albie couldn't help but smile, and he squinted at Percy in the sunlight breaking through the trees. "Well, me."

His whole face brightened as if he found that hilarious. "You're the cook?"

"Well, I try."

"Are you any good?"

"Heavens, no," he replied with a laugh. "I'm terrible."

Percy's laughter rang down through the valley. "Well, you might have to add that to my list of duties."

"*You* can cook?"

"Better than you by the sounds of it," he replied. Then he froze. "I mean, if you'd like me to, Mr Bramwell. I didn't mean . . . I never meant to offend—"

Albie dismissed him with a wave of his hand. "It's quite all right. But for the love of all the heavens above, please call me Albie."

CHAPTER FOUR

PERCY KNEW THE HIGHLANDS WERE SUPPOSED TO be pretty. People talked about the wildness and how remote and isolating it was, how dangerous it was, but they'd also said there were views that had to be seen to be believed. Misty mountains, tall gum trees, and from the very top, how you could almost see the whole world.

None of what he'd heard did it justice.

The road came to a clearing fronted by a moss-covered post and rail gate with the name Bramwell painted on it in faded white, and a driveway that led down a sweeping pasture to a farmhouse. There were outbuildings and stables, by the looks of it, but the house itself was modest, with a veranda and steps, a shingled roof with wisps of smoke from the stone chimney. It stood proud on the rise, and it made Percy smile.

It looked welcoming and homely. Warm.

Albie leaned down and unlocked the gate, shoving it open enough for them to pass in single file. A move so well-practised, Percy could guess, that he must have done it a thousand times.

"Home," Albie said. "Never a sight like it."

He dropped his reins and slid down from Minnie, closing the gate behind them. He fixed the lock, and when he turned around, he found Minnie headed for home, Ox dutifully following.

Percy laughed, Albie's expression too funny to ignore.

"Oh, she's a right sod," Albie said.

Percy gave Bandit a nudge and he quickly caught up to Minnie, taking her reins. He held them up for Albie to see. "She's telling you to stop dawdling."

Albie climbed back up onto Minnie and he took the reins from Percy, scowling. "No, she's telling me there's hay in that stable, that's what she's telling me."

"Well, it would be rude to keep a lady waiting," Percy said, still grinning.

Albie huffed indignantly, though Percy could have sworn he was trying not to smile. He could tell Albie was a serious young man, astute and perhaps a little short-tempered. But he also saw a flicker of a sense of humour threatening to reveal itself every so often, and for that briefest moment, Albie looked his age.

Just nineteen, and all this land was his.

And what a beautiful place it was.

Two barking dogs came out to greet them, followed

by a man with a limp who stopped when he saw it was Albie. He was a solid man, with forearms like a brute. Mid-thirties, if Percy were to guess, with short curly hair the colour of mud.

He smiled at Albie. "Good to have you back, Albie," he said, then gave Percy a cautious nod. "I didn't expect you to have company."

Albie slid down off Minnie, so Percy did the same and came around for introductions. "Des, this is Percy Collins," Albie said. "He's starting here today. Percy, Des is the foreman. Do everything he asks—" He paused with the hint of a smile. "—before he asks it."

Des smiled at that, a familiar exchange between them that Percy assumed was an inside joke. Nonetheless, Percy held out his hand, nervous and wanting to make a good impression. "Nice to meet you, sir."

Des gave him a measured pause before shaking his hand. "Likewise. But how about we drop the sir?"

Percy gave him a grin, relieved. "Yes, si . . . Des."

Albie chuckled, then looked around. "Everything in order?"

"As it should be," Des said. "Took the liberty of getting your fire going. My knee tells me there's a southerly coming. Rain and cold. Robert's down checking the yearlings."

"Good, good," Albie said. "Percy, you can get set up in the bunk quarters with the men." He nodded over to the outbuildings where a smaller house stood at the end. "Hope you don't mind the sound of snoring."

"Oh hey," Des said, admonishing him. "Be away with that."

Albie laughed and the sound of it, the smile on his face, Percy couldn't help but feel the pull of a thread in his chest, tugging at something unfamiliar yet welcome. Warm and lovely.

And forbidden.

"Let's get these goods unpacked," Albie said, pulling at the buckle on Ox's saddlebag.

"You get everything on your list?" Des asked as he helped.

Percy could see now that Des didn't limp as such, more that his right leg just didn't bend too well.

Albie put the bags of seeds on the veranda of the house, Des grabbed the flour, sugar, and salt, and Percy rushed to help with the last few things. "Why don't you two talk business—the market sales have come forward, remember—and I'll tend to the horses," Percy offered. "Then when you're done, Des can show me which bunk is mine and show me what needs doing." He took the reins to Minnie and Bandit, with Ox still tethered. "Any stable in particular you want 'em?"

Albie gave him a pleased nod. "Whichever's clean and empty," he said. Then he and Des carried their bags and sacks inside the house.

Percy felt the breeze bite and he looked skyward. The clouds were low and dark, and slowly rolling in. Des's knee was right, he thought. "Come on then," he said to the horses. "Let's get you out of this."

He busied himself with the horses. He slung the saddles over the rail and hung the bridles and halters up on the hooks on the wall. He made sure they had fresh hay and water, and he even took a few minutes to brush them down.

Ox took his hat again, waving it like a joke. Minnie was happy with her feed, and Bandit . . . well, Percy took an extra minute with him. "You like it here?" he asked him. "Seems nice so far, huh? Away from the dirty looks in town, and the air's so clean up here it almost hurts to breathe." He brushed his mane. "We'll do just fine up here, I reckon. Just fine, you and me."

"You always talk to your horse?" Des asked from the door.

Percy hadn't heard him come in, and he started a little, followed quickly by a rush of foolishness. "I do, yeah," Percy admitted. "Mostly 'cause he never argues."

Des snorted, taking in the neatly arranged saddles and how each horse was fed and happy. Pleased, he threw a glance toward the door. "I'll show ya to your quarters."

THE BUNK QUARTERS were basically one large room with six single beds, a table, and a wood fire. The walls were wooden planks, same as the floor. The roof was tin. The windows were covered with uneven strips of fabric for curtains, and an old sheet on a rope divided the room for privacy. But it was warm and dry, and it sure beat sleeping outside.

"That's mine. That's Roberts," Des said, pointing to the two beds at opposite ends of the room. "The divider was for when we had married folks here but they're gone now. We kept the privacy curtain 'cause we could. Pick any other bed you want. It won't bother me or Robert none, whichever you pick."

Percy opted for one in the middle against the far wall and put his rucksack on the foot of the bed. "This is great, thank you."

"Albie said you're good with horses," Des said.

"Uh, yeah. Born and raised around them." He couldn't help but feel a little scrutinised, as if this was a test on Albie's behalf. "But I can do most anything around the farm if you need. I'm not afraid of hard work."

Des studied him for another long second. "We'll see about that."

CHAPTER FIVE

"DON'T YOU THINK YOU SHOULD TELL HIM TO stop?" Albie asked from the window. He sipped his mug of tea.

"Nah," Des replied. "I reckon we should see how long it takes before he stops all on his own."

So far, in the first few hours of Percy's arrival, he'd mucked the stables, rotated the feed hay in the loft with a pitchfork, fed the pigs, covered the chickens from the cold, and now he'd chopped enough firewood to last them a week.

"He takes pride in his work," Des said. "I'll give him that. Got those stables in neater order than you, and that's no small feat."

Just then Percy came inside with his arms full of chopped wood. His nose was red, as were his fingers. "I rotated the wood," he said, kneeling by the fire to stack the wood. "This is from the driest of the lot. And the rains are about to hit. Those clouds are real dark. Never seen 'em so low. Or is it because we're up so high? Feels like I'm walking in them."

"Because you are." Albie poured some hot tea into a mug, and when Percy stood up and turned to face him, Albie handed him the mug. "You've done enough for today, and you're cold and damp to the bone. Warm yourself by the fire. Have you got an oilskin coat? You'll need it up here."

Percy wrapped his fingers around the warm mug and sighed as he sipped it. "Thank you. I appreciate this. And no, I don't. Have another coat, that is."

Albie pursed his lips and tried not to be mad about it. The weather in the mountains had claimed more lives than most, and to be ill-prepared was foolish. But he reminded himself that Percy wasn't from here.

He didn't know where he was from, exactly. The qualifier of 'from down south' could have meant anywhere.

"Stay here," he said, urging Percy to sit in the seat closest to the fire. He disappeared into his room and came out with his old oilskin coat and gloves. "Here," he began. "They're not fancy by any means, and I grew out of them before I could wear them through. But it's a damn sight warmer than the one you have on now."

Percy put his mug of tea down and stood up. "Oh, I don't need to be a bother. I mean, you don't have to—"

"I'll not have you catch your death on my farm," he barked, quickly taking Percy's coat off him. Yes, he knew Percy was a little shorter than him, his pants only held up by his suspenders because he was so lean. Maybe too lean. And he remembered that he'd over-heard Percy say he'd perhaps have to eat grass with his horse . . .

Albie put that out of his mind for now and helped Percy into his old coat. "Here, try this on." He slid his arms through, then tugged the front to see the fit of it. "It fits anyhow. And like I said, I outgrew it so it was of no use to me. At least you'll be warm and dry."

Albie picked up Percy's damp coat and hung it by the fire. It was a fine coat. Maybe it had even been expensive at some point, but it was no match for winter in the highlands. "This will serve you best in warmer months, but you'll wear this one in winter." He turned back to Percy and flattened the lapel at Percy's collarbone, ignoring the realisation that he'd just touched him in a manner not usually fit for a man . . .

Ignoring how Percy was watching him with those big blue, imploring eyes and ignoring the prettiest blush he'd ever seen . . .

"Right then," Des said loudly, making them both startle. "Robert's back. I'll go explain the new horse in the stable and tell him to wash up for supper."

"Yes, please. And thank you," Albie said, remem-bering his place.

He was the boss now; he needed to act like it.

Des closed the door behind him and Albie, needing

some distance between him and Percy, turned for the kitchen. "Supper's in thirty minutes," he announced.

"Oh," Percy said, bringing his mug of tea with him over to the stove. He peered into the pot of stew. "Did you cook this?"

"I did."

"I thought you said you couldn't cook."

"I can't."

"Smells good to me."

Albie looked him up and down. Aside from how much Albie liked to see his coat on him, he could really see now just how lean Percy was. "A belly full of stew and bread is just what you need," he said. "Warm you right up."

Percy grinned behind his mug of tea. "I think I'm gonna like it here."

"You proved yourself this afternoon." Albie uncovered the risen dough and poked at it, unsure of why, only that he'd seen Marcy do it.

"You can so cook," Percy said. "Look at you."

He wiped his hand on his pants. "I don't even know what it's supposed to look like. Only that I saw Marcy make it and that's what she used to do. Poke it, then flour a tray and put it in the oven. I don't know how it's supposed to look. Should it sink or bounce back when I poke it?"

Percy clearly found that funny. "Who's Marcy?"

"One of the wives of the men who worked for my father. There were two, Marcy and Evalyn. They took care of all household duties." He shrugged. "Now it's just me."

"Well, now you got me too."

Albie wasn't prepared for the thrill at his words or the warmth of his smile, his eyes. He had to collect himself. "Can you make a damper?"

He made a face. "I can try."

"Tomorrow. It'll be your turn. So, no laughing at mine until you've had a go." Albie floured the tray like he'd seen Marcy do. Then he plopped the dough onto it and slid it into the wood stove. "Be kind to us," he said.

Percy laughed but he straightened up when Albie shot him a look.

"Yes, be kind to us," Percy echoed, raising his mug of tea like an offering to the stove.

Albie hated that he wanted to laugh.

No, he hated that he felt he couldn't.

That, as the boss, he should keep a professional distance. And as a grieving son, he felt guilty for finding a glimmer of happiness when his father was dead.

Albie frowned. "Right then," he said, taking a step back. "I need to get the table ready. You should go get cleaned up for dinner. We're not high society by any means, but we shall keep the table manners my father insisted upon."

Percy nodded and, seeing his mug was empty, he was unsure what to do with it. Albie took it, and Percy offered a smile. "Thank you. For the tea, and the coat."

Albie gave him a stern nod as his reply, then went about his business in the kitchen.

It was a trivial thing, setting the table and expecting manners, but it was something Albie felt strongly about.

In all his years growing up, the likes of Des and Robert never ate at the dinner table in the main house. None of the staff did. They ate in their quarters, and Albie and his father ate in the house.

But after the funeral, when it was just Albie, Des, and Robert, it made sense that they'd eat together. Albie insisted they eat in the house with him, and he could tell himself all the lies he wanted: that it was for morale, that it was easier, that it made sense, given there were just three of them.

But the truth was, Albie didn't want to eat alone.

He couldn't bear the thought of sitting at the dining table next to his father's empty chair.

It sat empty still.

Though Albie was certain Des saw through him, and perhaps Robert hadn't been too keen on the idea and Des had insisted, for Albie's sake.

So every night they cleaned up, hands and faces washed, hats off, and using manners as if there were a lady in the house. A far cry from how they spoke in the yards.

Albie liked it though, he had to admit. And he reckoned his father would like it too.

When the three men came in, Albie was serving up plates of stew on the table. The damper was done, slightly burned on one side, and the stew was more potatoes and gravy than beef.

It wasn't anything like what Marcy could cook, but he was proud of it. He'd made it from scratch, without any lessons or guidance, and he was providing food for his hard-working men.

Des, Robert, and Percy all took off their coats, brushing drops of water from their hair, and Percy's smile was wide, made even brighter by his clean face. "Sure smells good," he said.

His smile was contagious.

And breathtaking.

When they went to the table, Albie noticed Des steer Percy away from his father's seat, for which he was grateful. That also meant that Percy now sat beside Albie, and he was kinda grateful for that too.

Percy literally sat on his hands to stop himself from eating before he was allowed, and Des seemed to approve of that. As the foreman, he was responsible for all staff, and that included Percy. He'd probably given him a stern talking to before they'd come in, but Percy clearly had manners.

He was hungry, though, and underfed.

"Please, eat," Albie said.

The only sound for a long while was cutlery

scraping plates. The stew wasn't terrible. It wasn't exactly great, but they sopped up the gravy with the damper, and it mustn't have been too bad if the cleared plates were anything to go by.

If you're hungry enough, you'll eat anything, his father used to say when he was a young boy, turning his nose up at vegetables.

It was true. As he got older and started growing, Albie had been grateful for any food on the table.

Percy patted his belly. "Thank you for the meal. It was . . . good."

That didn't sound honest. "Good?"

He gave him that blinding grin. "I like my damper well-done."

Robert covered his laughter with a cough, and Des fought a smile, even though he grumbled at Percy to watch his manners.

"It's fine," Albie said. He could appreciate humour, and honestly, a laugh with the men felt good. "Percy's cooking the damper for tomorrow's dinner. So if it's a charred lump of coal, we can sit here and watch him eat it."

Percy wasn't even concerned. He just chuckled. "It'll be the best coal I ever eat." Then his eyes met Albie's. "And I was only pulling your leg. Your cooking was fine, and I appreciate the meal. So, thank you."

Albie was a little embarrassed at the direct praise, especially in front of the other two. "We'll see if you're still so grateful after your first full day tomorrow."

"So, Percy," Robert said after a few seconds of silence. "You're not from around here. Where you from?"

Percy sipped his water, and it was perhaps the first hint of anything *but* confidence Albie had seen in him. He swallowed hard. "Uh, down south," he replied. "Down Kiama way."

Kiama.

Hm. Interesting.

"What brings you up this way?" Robert asked. "Most people are heading toward the gold towns, not away from them."

Percy blinked slowly, his smile not quite sitting right. "Wanted to make it on my own. I'd heard stories of the mountains, and I'm not cut out for the likes of Sydney."

It was clearly not a comfortable subject for Percy, and Albie wanted to protect him somehow, for reasons he didn't quite understand. "I was never cut out for the big smoke," Albie announced. "I went once, when I was ten. Too many people. And we saw a boy get hauled off by the bobbies for pickpocketing. Right in front of us, he was. A boy younger than me. I couldn't believe it."

"Your dad talked of that for years," Des said, smiling fondly. "I think he thought it was good for you to see, so you wouldn't steal anything from anyone."

Albie chuckled. "Except that time I stole the

apples. Remember that? He whipped my backside for that."

"You stole apples? From who?" Percy asked, his eyes wide and his genuine smile back in place.

"From the cook," Albie said. "Old Mrs West. She came to help out when my mother passed away. She was as wide as she was tall and cranky as a bull."

"Oh, she wasn't that bad," Des said.

"She was mean to me," Albie said.

"Because you stole her apples," Des replied. Then he looked at Percy. "Weren't even for him."

That wasn't exactly true. "One was for me, one for my pony."

"Ah, Buck the grade pony. Now *that* thing was mean."

"Because you didn't give him apples," Albie replied with a grin.

Des smiled fondly and let out a sigh. "Well, we should be going."

"Oh," Percy said, taking his plate and reaching for Albie's. "Let me clean up."

Albie stopped him. "Leave it. I'll take care of it. It's . . ." he steeled himself but went with honesty. "It gives me something to do. You guys go on. Breakfast at six."

They stood up and put their coats on as Albie began clearing away. He didn't miss the way Percy stopped at the door for a beat, watching him, before Des ushered him along.

He spent the next hour or so cleaning up, taking his time, because keeping busy beat acknowledging the silence. The hole in his world where his father had once been.

He'd have sat by the fire and filled in his ledgers, which Albie had yet to look at.

Now that he'd been to town, signed the deeds, and made everything official, there was no putting it off.

But not tonight.

He put more wood on the fire, got himself ready for bed, and blew out the lantern.

He lay there, staring at the ceiling in his quiet house. And for the first night in over a week, his thoughts didn't drift to his father or to the funeral. Or to the men who'd abandoned him when he'd needed them most.

He could recall the words they'd said, feeling the anger burn behind his ribs just as hot as the moment they'd said it.

But tonight, as the storm blew and rains fell, as he sank into sleep, he thought of all he had to do tomorrow, and he reminded himself he'd need to cook enough breakfast for four people, not three.

And then his mind wandered to Percy. To how hard he'd worked all afternoon. To how his nose was pink with the cold and what it felt like to undress him and help him into the bigger coat. To those blue eyes. And as sleep claimed him, a certain smile and pale skin with flushed cheeks lingered at the edges of his mind.

CHAPTER SIX

WHEN ALBIE HAD SAID HE HOPED PERCY LIKED snoring, he wasn't kidding. Both Des and Robert snored so loud it was like he had competing logging teams at either end of the room.

Needless to say, he didn't sleep much.

But the bed was warm and dry in spite of the rain outside, and Percy had a good feeling about his job here. Both Des and Robert were decent fellows. He recalled what those two gossiping men in town had said about the two men who'd stayed with Albie. A cripple and a drunk.

Well, yes, Des had a pronounced limp but he wasn't crippled, and Robert never touched a drop all night. He drank water with dinner and made tea over the fire before bed.

Proof, for Percy, that those men in town had no clue about the truth.

And sure, what Albie lacked in age and experience, he made up for with grit and determination. He had a fire under him to prove his worth, and Percy liked that about him.

Percy liked a lot of things about Albie . . .

The way he'd fitted his coat to him and squeezed his hand to feel how cold he was. How warm his touch had been.

And that blasted smile.

Visions of which plagued his mind while Des and Robert snored the night away. Or maybe he'd have slept some if he hadn't been thinking so hard about Albie . . .

Percy was up before the sun. No point in lying in bed when there was work to be done. He slipped his boots on as quietly as he could, pulled his hat down, shrugged into Albie's warm coat, and went outside.

It had rained all right.

The skies were still cloudy, sunrise doing its best to break through, but at least it wasn't raining now. Percy trudged through the mud to the stables to check on the horses first thing.

The stables were dry, the horses content. He fixed them some hay and carried buckets of water up from the well, sliding a few times in the icy mud underfoot.

When that was done, he collected the eggs from the coop and knocked on Albie's back door.

Albie opened the door, confused and alarmed. He

was dressed, thankfully. The sun was almost up now, so he'd assumed Albie would be awake.

He held his upturned hat full of eggs. "I collected the eggs already, but my boots are all muddy. I don't want to come inside."

Albie blinked a few times, then shook his head and finally looked down at Percy's feet. "Give me this," he said, taking the hat. "Take your boots off. Are you trying to die up here? You'll catch your death if your feet get wet in winter."

Percy pulled his boots off, showing holes in his socks at the big toes. He walked to the edge of the veranda and clapped his boots together to get rid of most of the mud.

Albie looked annoyed. "Come inside and bring them by the fire."

The house was exactly as he'd left it last night. Modest, meagre old furniture. But boy, it sure felt like a home.

Albie put the eggs on the table and stirred a pot on the stove. "You're up early," he said, not looking at him.

Percy grimaced anyway. "You weren't wrong about the snoring."

Albie shot him a look. He kind of smiled, kind of didn't. "Loud, huh?"

"I'll get used to it," he replied, smiling. "Can I help with anything in here?"

Albie looked around the kitchen. "Uh. You could set the table."

"Sure!" Percy made himself busy doing that, then tidied up the firewood beside the fire where a few logs had tumbled.

"I hope you like porridge."

"Love it," Percy said. "Especially in winter. Nothing better than a bowl of hot porridge on a cold morning."

"Well, you might want to wait until you taste it," Albie said. Then he took another damper out of the oven and slid it onto the stovetop.

Percy couldn't help himself. "Oh, you cooked it medium today."

Albie shot him another look, but it was followed by a grin. "Don't forget who's cooking it at dinner time."

Percy smiled right back at him, his belly full of butterflies. "Already looking forward to it. Everybody needs some charcoal in their diet."

The front door burst open, and Des stopped when he saw Percy. "Oh, there you are," he said. "Thought you'd done a runner when your bed weren't slept in." He stepped back outside and hollered to Robert. "Found him!"

When he came back inside, he acknowledged Albie with a nod. "Morning. Sorry for the intrusion. Thought we mighta had a quitter."

"A quitter?" Percy cried. "I ain't ever quit on a job yet."

"He's already been and collected the eggs," Albie said, nodding to the hat on the counter.

"And the horses," Percy added. "And I checked on the pigs and the dogs."

Robert came inside, a little out of breath. He gave Percy a nod before he spoke to Des and Albie. "Went to see if his horse was still there, and they've already been fed and got fresh water."

"I took it from the well, just like you said," Percy said to Des.

Des eyed him. "You allergic to sleeping or something?"

"He's allergic to snoring," Albie said, taking the pot of porridge to the table.

Percy groaned, wishing Albie hadn't told them. "I'll get used to it," he said. He brought the damper over as Albie fixed the hot tea. "Better to be busy anyway," he said, trying to pick up the mood. "If I'm helping make dinner tonight, I need to make sure all my chores are squared away early, right?"

Albie took his seat, as did Des and Robert, so Percy did the same.

He had to admit the porridge wasn't the best-looking gruel he'd ever seen, and it certainly wasn't the tastiest. But it was hot and enough to fill his belly, and for that, he'd always be grateful.

He'd gone hungry too many times in the last few months to not appreciate any food he was offered.

Not to mention sitting at a table where he actually felt welcome.

"What have you got me doing today?" Percy asked

Des when they were done eating and enjoying the last of their tea.

"We need to bring up the cattle herd from the southern end," he said. "If they're gonna go to market."

Percy couldn't help but grin. "For real?"

Des frowned at his excitement. "You ever worked with cattle before?"

"Well, no. I've worked with sheep."

"Sheep?" Albie asked.

Percy managed a nod, his breakfast suddenly feeling like a lump in his belly. "I grew up on a sheep farm," he admitted. "I'm guessing they can't be too different from cattle."

Robert laughed. "Oh, this should be good."

Albie made a face. "More importantly, has your horse ever worked with cattle before? In the mountains?"

Percy felt all eyes on him. "Uh, no? I, ah, I don't think so."

Albie turned to Des. "Put him on Minnie."

Des gave a hard nod and Percy tried to object, but Albie wasn't having it. "Minnie's part mountain goat, I'm sure of it. She knows what to do, especially around cattle. Until your horse gets used to it, you'll ride her."

That was Boss Albie speaking, so Percy didn't argue again.

"When we bring the cattle into the yards," Des said. "We bring your horse into the fold. He'll learn soon enough."

Percy felt better then, and he afforded Des a grateful smile. "Of course."

With that settled and breakfast had, it was time to get to work. Albie was staying at the house. He had business matters to work on, apparently, though Percy kinda got the feeling this was more of a test on Percy.

Maybe Albie wanted to see how he worked under Des, how he followed orders and used his head.

Percy couldn't blame him for that. It was fair. He'd have to prove himself for a while yet, he reasoned. He gave Bandit a scratch before climbing up on Minnie and following Des and Robert out.

The ground was mud, the air was biting cold and clean. The sun was barely recognisable behind the low grey clouds, and the further they got from the homestead, the steeper the terrain got.

Des and Robert were cautious on their horses, never pushing too hard, letting them set the pace. There were craggy boulders of granite everywhere, the whole area thick with trees, shrubs, and long grass.

Until it flattened out a little and there were some well-trodden muddy paths through the bush, which they then followed until, sure enough, Percy spotted his first cow.

A Hereford.

"Look," he said, pointing.

Des nodded further up ahead and there was half a herd.

Percy was so excited. This was magical.

"I'll go left," Robert said, steering his horse off the muddy path.

"Come on," Des said, nudging his horse to the right. "Percy, you're with me. Let Minnie do the work. Don't fight her."

"Okay," he said eagerly.

Now, he had been born and raised on a sheep farm, and yes, he'd seen horsemen work flocks of sheep. He could manage along with the best of them, even as young as thirteen, he was out there working the sheep with grown men.

But he ain't ever worked cattle, and truth be told, he wasn't sure exactly what Des had meant about letting Minnie do the work. A rider was always the one in charge. But he didn't doubt Albie or Des. And he might not have known how to work cattle, but he knew horses.

And some were smarter than people. So if they said to put Minnie in charge, that's what he'd do.

And oh boy.

It was all he could do to hold on.

She turned on a dime, cutting cattle in and out, rounding them up, always keeping the advantage and never stopping, until they had the herd heading for home.

Percy grinned the whole way back, despite the sleet and misty rain and the freezing cold.

It was hard work. He was panting and muscle-sore. But he'd loved every minute of it.

When they got back to the homestead, Albie was at the front paddock, gate open, and the cattle funnelled through. Except one cow tried to break away; Minnie darted for it, and it quickly fell back into line. Percy laughed and cheered. "Best day ever!"

Albie shook his head, but it did get a smile out of him, and he headed back to the house.

Des ordered the horses back to the stable. "I'll tend to the horses," Percy volunteered. He slid down off Minnie and took the reins of Des' horse. "Leave them with me."

They did, and a short while later, he had all horses unsaddled, brushed, and safely in their stables with some fresh hay as a reward. Then he went in search of Des.

"Albie wants to see you," Des said.

So he went in search of Albie. Found him inside, clanging pans in the kitchen, but there were books strewn across the table. Well, he didn't find Albie so much as his backend poking out, his head in the bottom shelves, muttering and cussing to himself.

He admired the view for half a second before he cleared his throat. "You wanted to see me?" Percy asked.

Albie donked his head on the shelf and stood up, rubbing the spot. "Ow."

"I'm sorry, I didn't mean to startle you. I wasn't being quiet or nothing. You were just . . ." He gave a pointed nod to the bottom shelf. "Busy."

"I was looking for . . . never mind," he said. Clearly, he wasn't in the best mood. "You enjoyed your morning," he noted, walking past Percy to the table where he began to tidy up the books. "Des said you did well, considering."

Considering he'd never done it before.

"I think I can give full credit to your horse," Percy replied. "I just had to hang on. Des said to trust her, and he was right. Is your head all right? You banged it pretty hard."

That gave Albie some pause and he sighed, settling on a smile. "It's fine, thank you."

They stared at each other for a moment until Percy's heart squeezed. He let out a breath. "Des said you wanted to see me."

"Ah, yes." Albie turned away, seemingly annoyed again. "If you want to make the damper for tonight, you'll need to get started."

"Oh, of course." Percy hadn't realised the time. He couldn't help but notice the edge to Albie's clipped tone or the way he was handling those books. "Is everything good?"

"Yes, of course, it's just . . ." Albie shook his head. "It's nothing."

"It is something," Percy pushed. "You can tell me. I won't tell Des or Robert."

Albie looked at him then, his eyes fierce, but something in them gave way, defeated. "I'm not very good with this stuff," he blurted out, frowning at the books he held. "This was my father's business. He understood it. The percentages and taxes and stock prices. I can't make heads nor tails of it. I've wasted a whole day. I can barely—" He stopped there, mad at himself again.

"You can barely what?" Percy asked quietly.

Albie swallowed. "My mother taught me to read," he said quietly. "And I was six years old when she died. My father tried to pick up where she left, and old Mrs West tried, though she had no patience for children. And I tried to keep going with it, teaching myself. I would read my father's papers at night, to try and improve, but I thought I'd have time . . . before I'd have to do this myself." He pushed the books as if it were their fault. Then he raised his chin, defiant. "I can read enough to get by. To sign papers or order stock at the store. I can do basic sums to know the price . . ."

"But finance ledgers are hard," Percy said gently.

"I can run this place. I can round up cattle and plant crops. I can keep horses and that out there"—he said, gesturing to the door—"is easy. But this . . ." He stacked the books neatly again. "This is not."

"I can teach you," Percy said. "To read. Properly, that is. And maths." He shrugged. "Just between you and me. No one else has to know."

Albie stared at him for a long beat. "You know how to read?"

Percy nodded. "I went to school."

"School? A real school?"

He smiled sadly and nodded again. "I did."

"Where did you come from? You said Kiama," Albie said quietly. His eyes bored into Percy's as if he was trying to put puzzle pieces together. "Or perhaps a better question is why did you leave?"

"Because . . ." Percy began, his stomach a tight knot. He wasn't sure what he could say, or how to answer honestly but not give anything away. "I left for me."

Robert burst through the door with barely a knock. "Albie, we got company."

Company?

"Who is it?" he asked, going to the door to see for himself.

"Two men on horses," Robert said.

Des came walking down the veranda, slower with his bad leg. "Looks like one of McAllister's men."

Albie seethed, his gaze narrowing.

Percy had heard the name McAllister in certain circles from his time in town. He was wealthy, powerful. When he spoke, men listened.

So this couldn't possibly be good.

Percy saw the two men approach the house. They never got off their horses, so Albie stepped out onto the veranda. Robert stood by the window, watching, Des on the veranda beside Albie, and Percy stood in the doorway.

"Albie," one of the men said. He pulled a letter from his coat pocket. "From Mr McAllister."

Albie studied him for a minute before he took a

step forward. Percy was quick to stop him, instead stepping off the veranda to retrieve the letter on Albie's behalf.

The man's smile wasn't a friendly one.

The second man tipped his hat. "Des."

"Williams," Des replied flatly.

Albie crossed his arms. "I see you found yourself a new job."

"No hard feelings," Williams said, though the smug look on his face told Percy otherwise. He could guess that perhaps Williams was one of the men who'd walked out after Albie's father's funeral.

"No hard feelings at all," Albie said coolly.

They turned their horses, hard on the reins, which Percy didn't care for. And when they'd gone a few yards, Williams nodded to the cattle. "Good luck at the saleyards next week," he said, and they both laughed as they trotted up the drive.

Albie seethed at their backs, and Percy handed him the letter.

Robert headed toward the stable. "I don't trust them not to leave the gate open," he yelled, taking off to run for his horse. He came back out on his horse a second later, bareback, still fixing the bridle as they took off up the driveway.

The three of them went inside, all eyes on Albie as he opened the letter.

He unfolded the heavy paper, and Percy could see

it was the fancy kind, the writing elegant calligraphy in blue ink.

Albie frowned at it.

"To Albie Bramwell," he read out loud.

"In t . . . times of . . ." He squinted at the letter, then looked up, furious. "His writing is not legible. How does he expect anyone to read this?"

He eyed the fire and then the letter and took a step toward it, but before he could toss it into the flames, Percy stopped him with a gentle hand on his arm.

"Let me try," he said gently. Then he felt the need to shrug and explain. "My grandfather's handwriting was like that. I can try to read it if you want. Then if you decide to burn it, I won't stop you."

Albie growled and thrust the letter toward Percy. He took it and began to read aloud.

In times of grief, we sometimes cannot see clearly. But when the clouds of mourning clear, truths often come to light. I hope you can see now the truth of your situation, young Albie. It is not your doing, simply a situation you find yourself in.

McAllister Holdings hereby offers Albert Bramwell the reputable sum of five thousand pounds for the title deeds to Echo Creek.

Your father was a good man. I trust you'll honour his memory and do what is right. These mountains make mockeries out of lesser men. Don't let your father's name be one of them.

Signed, Royce McAllister.

Percy swallowed hard and looked up then. Des was shaking his head, but Albie . . . Albie was seething fire.

"I will do no such thing," he said, his voice low. Then the bubble of anger burst and he went for his coat. "I'll go and tell McAllister exactly what I think of his offer—"

Percy stopped him, again holding his arm. Des blocked the door. "Albie, no," Des said.

Percy agreed. "You can't go there. You can't go onto his land and declare war on a powerful man in his own house."

"Yet he can come onto mine—" he cried.

"Prove you're the better man," Percy tried again.

"Percy's right," Des added. "Going over there now would be like walking into a snake pit." He shook his head. "He'll only make things more miserable for you, and you don't want him as your enemy." He patted his bad leg. "Trust me."

Albie's breath left him in a rush, deflated. "How dare he think he can insult me like that. Insult my father. He wants to talk about honouring my father, then he should do the same."

"The likes of McAllister honour nothing but money and greed," Des said quietly. "He's after a reaction, Albie. Don't give him what he wants."

Percy only realised then that he still had his hand on Albie's arm. He let go, missing the touch immediately.

"Give him the opposite of what he wants," Percy

suggested. "Reply to his letter, thanking him for his kind words during this difficult time. Thank him for the generous offer but you believe the best way to honour your father is to prove you are the man he raised."

Albie's eyes met Percy's. Honesty and understanding stared back at him, pools of warmth Percy wanted to get lost in.

"Being overly nice to him will piss him off because it proves you won't stoop to his level," Percy added. "And then you prove you are worthy by working hard and taking those cattle to market this week. Not next week, those lying cowards. Did you hear what they said?"

Albie nodded, and Des looked between them. "You're sure the market's this week?"

Albie nodded. "There was talk of it coming forward."

"And signs at the bullock run," Percy added. "There's logging work out on the eastern pass. And I heard men talking about it in the bar. It's definitely this week."

"I don't trust them," Albie added quietly.

"We should leave tomorrow," Des added. "In case there's been another change."

Albie nodded. "Agreed."

Robert came back inside. "Gate was wide open."

"Those low belly snakes!" Albie said. "Any cattle get out?"

Robert shook his head. "No. Not that I could see. None of them were near the gates at all."

Albie gave him a pat on the arm in thanks. "We're going to leave tomorrow, take the cattle down the mountain."

Robert gave a hard nod. "I'll get us ready." And he was out the door again.

Des watched Albie for a long moment. "Keep your head down, Albie. You're doin' fine."

He followed Robert out, leaving Percy and Albie alone in the house.

"Are you all right?" Percy asked. He certainly didn't look it.

"My father tolerated McAllister for the same reason everyone else does. Because he has the power to ruin people, and McAllister knows it."

"It's a game the likes of him play," Percy offered. "It helps to know the rules, but you don't need to play his game."

"I can't be bought," he muttered. "And five thousand pounds."

It was a lot of money.

"It's insulting," Albie said, glaring at the fire. "My father's name is worth more than that."

Percy couldn't help it. He went to him and put his hand on his shoulder and gave him a squeeze before rubbing his upper arm. "Your name is worth more than that."

Albie's gaze cut to his, his eyes melting into him.

And they were too close, too alone, and Albie was far too . . .

Too tempting.

Percy swallowed hard and took a step back, and Albie shook his head as if he'd been caught in a trance.

"Damper," Percy said, his face burning. "Bread. Dinner. Did you still need me?"

Albie only seemed to remember . . . "Yes, right."

His cheeks were flushed pink too and Percy wished he hadn't noticed.

What did that mean?

Surely not . . .

Albie lifted the lid to the pot on the stove. "I've added carrot and more potatoes," he said, stirring it, staring at it, not looking at Percy. "The bowl to mix the flour is down there."

Percy found it on the bottom shelf, and Albie nodded to the sack of flour. He set about sifting the flour with salt. He added a dash of milk and some chunks of butter and began to knead it.

"Butter and milk?" Albie said.

Percy wasn't sure if he was horrified or offended. "Well, yes. Do you . . . do you not use that? Was I allowed to use the butter?"

Albie blinked and shrugged. "Well, yes. I mean, sure. I've just never . . ."

Percy laughed, kneading the dough with the heel of his hand, the same way he'd seen his mother and their staff do it a thousand times. "So all the damper you've made is just flour, salt, and water?"

Albie closed his mouth, his lips a tight line.

It made Percy laugh more.

He left the dough in a ball, wiped his hands, and found the cast-iron pot and lid.

"What are you doing with that?" Albie asked.

Percy floured it before dropping the ball of dough in it. "Making damper," he replied. Wasn't it obvious?

Then instead of placing it into the wood stove, he carried it into the living room and placed it on the edge of the wood fire.

"Uh." Albie stood there, clearly unsure. "We have an oven."

Percy raised his hand. "No making fun of it until you've tried it." He used the fire poker to turn the heavy iron pot one-quarter turn.

Albie's lips twitched as he fought a smile, then he sighed. "Thank you," he said. "For before. For reading that letter. I would have muddled through it if I had time, but with everyone watching, I . . ."

"It's fine. That fancy writing isn't easy to read," Percy allowed.

"You managed it."

"Practice."

"Your grandfather's writing? Is that what you said?"

Percy shrugged one shoulder. "I used to read his books and papers."

Albie's eyes met his once more. They were kind and a little determined. "One day you'll tell me about your life and what brought you here."

Percy swallowed but conceded a nod.

"And about you teaching me to read," Albie added quietly.

Percy grinned at him. "Starting tonight. After dinner. You can tell Des and Robert I'm cleaning up—"

Albie raised his hand in a stop fashion, but he did manage that half smile that Percy liked so much. "When we get back from the sales. Tonight, we'll need to get ready."

"Do we all go? Who stays behind to watch the place?"

"Des will stay," Albie said quietly. "His leg's no good on long trips unless we take the wagon, but we're droving the cattle, so . . . He'll stay behind. He treats this place as if it were his own, and I trust him. But you, me, and Robert will take the cattle."

Percy couldn't stop his grin. It sounded like an exciting adventure to him.

Albie sent him a disapproving frown. "You'll be on Minnie. I'll take Ox. He's not used to me so much but I'd rather you were with Minnie. I can't have you getting hurt."

Oh.

Percy wasn't sure if that was out of kindness, concern, or because he wasn't yet fully competent.

It's all out of concern, he reasoned as he turned the

pot in the fire another quarter turn. And it had been so long since someone had cared . . .

You're his employee, his responsibility, that's all there is to it.

"Ow, blast!" Albie cried from the kitchen.

Percy raced over, seeing him holding his wrist. "What is it?"

"Oh, nothing," he winced. "I caught my arm on the pot. It was foolish. I wasn't paying attention."

It didn't look like it was nothing. He looked to be in pain. "Let me see," Percy said, taking Albie's arm. He held it gently, seeing a red line burned across his wrist. "You caught it all right. Here, let's apply some butter. It's supposed to help."

Percy took a spoon and shaved off a sliver of butter, then applied it gently to Albie's arm. Still holding his wrist, now standing so close their bodies were almost touching.

"How do you know such things?" Albie asked quietly.

Percy looked up at his face and had to steady his breathing. His cheeks grew hot, his heart raced, and he had to make himself look away. "I've seen it done before," he murmured. "In the kitchen back home."

"Hm," Albie hummed, a low rumbling sound that set fire to Percy's loins. "Why are you blushing," he whispered.

Percy's eyes shot to his, fear and excitement blazing

in his veins, just as Des and Robert came through the
door.

Percy and Albie shot apart, Percy rushing over to
the fire to turn the damper the final quarter turn.

"Dinner's done," Albie said.

Percy wasn't game to turn around. "Damper is
almost ready," he mumbled.

The men sat down and Albie served up his stew,
waiting for Percy. Using the kitchen rags, he carefully
lifted the pot out from next to the fire and sat it atop the
stove. He took out the damper, hoping all hopes it
wasn't a failure.

It certainly looked good. Smelt good too. He
carried it over, steaming hot, and placed it in the
middle of the table. All three sets of eyes went from the
perfectly round damper to Percy.

"You made this?" Des asked.

"Oh, well, yes," Percy replied. "Let's see how it
tastes first." He took his seat next to Albie.

"Shall I?" Robert asked, his knife at the top of the
damper.

"Please," Percy said. "See if the knife can cut it. I
apologise in advance if it's no good."

The knife went through the damper like butter.

Steam rose, and the first slice came out clean. It
was baked, at least. Percy waited for the first taste tests,
not realising how his happiness hinged on their
approval . . . until Robert's eyes went wide and he
smiled as he chewed. Des sighed, his eyes closed as if

he were tasting a long-lost memory, and Albie gave Percy a nod of approval.

Percy could have just about burst.

"You can cook this every night," Robert said. "Breakfast too, no complaints."

"Oh," Percy replied, giving Albie an awkward smile. "I don't want to take someone's job."

Albie smirked as he ate another bite. "Believe me, I'll not be sad about it."

Percy noticed the red mark on Albie's arm then. "How's your arm?"

"Whadja do?" Des asked, instantly concerned.

"Cooking." Albie held his wrist up. "It'll be fine. Just a small burn."

Robert snorted. "Jeez, boss. You might wanna give the cooking job to Percy. Save yourself some serious injury."

Percy kept his head down and ate his dinner. He didn't mean for anything or anyone to belittle Albie's hard work. When the meal was done, Percy stayed to help clean up.

"Sorry if what they said offended you," Percy said, taking dirty plates to the kitchen.

"Offended me?" Albie's eyes were wide. "How on earth was I offended?"

"With the cooking." Percy took the mugs next. "I'm grateful for any food. I just want you to know, I don't care what you cook. I'll eat it and never say a bad word."

Albie stopped him with that damned smirk. "The other night you said my damper was well-done."

"Oh." Percy's face went red again, embarrassed this time. "That was a joke. I didn't mean any harm. I'm sorry if I—"

Albie patted Percy's upper arm, warm, gentle but firm. "It's fine. And I'm happy to hand over the cooking. I hate it. I'm not any good at it, and my time'd be better spent doing just about anything else. I'm sure Des and Robert would agree."

"I can do a damper, but I don't know about anything else. I mean, I could try. If you're giving me an order, I'll do whatever you say. If I poison everyone, I'd like it to be clear on the record that I said I wasn't any good at it."

Albie laughed. "You'll be fine. How about we see about it when we get back from taking the cattle to market?"

Percy gave a nod. "Okay." Then he remembered. "Now, about some reading lessons . . ."

Albie gave his shoulder a squeeze this time, the warmth of it sending a jolt through Percy's core. "Leave it for tonight. We've got an early start tomorrow. It can wait until we get back."

Percy stared up at him, lost to his brown eyes, to the smile tugging at his lips. And Albie stared straight back at him, his lips parted. They were so close . . .

Then Albie took a step back and cleared his throat. "You should go," he said, his voice sounding strained.

"Get some sleep before Des and Robert keep you awake all night."

"I can help you clean up," he said, taking a tray from the table.

"I said leave it," Albie shot back. He took the tray from Percy. "I'll see you in the morning."

Percy knew he'd crossed a line. He knew he shouldn't have been caught staring at Albie that way. He shouldn't have reacted that way.

But Hell be damned, Percy was attracted to him. A man, no less, as he'd always known he was attracted to men. But Albie, his boss. Albie who had shown him great kindness, who had given him a job and a place to live.

Albie who had warm hands and stars in his eyes, whose smile made Percy's knees weak.

He left with barely a nod, his mouth dry and his heart heavy.

Sleep didn't come again that night either, though this time it had nothing to do with the snoring.

CHAPTER SEVEN

ALBIE BARELY SLEPT A WINK.

His thoughts filled with a certain blond man. His smile, his deep blue eyes. The way he'd tended to the burn on Albie's wrist, the way he'd looked up at him, leaning in closer, slow-blinking and dreamy.

The way he'd blushed.

Albie had always known he'd never found attraction in the female form. Not that he'd had many to choose from, but the way the men talked about women and the way he'd seen Williams and Fitzgerald be with their wives—handsy and amorous—Albie had never had that inclination.

But when it came to men . . .

As a teen, he'd spent many days by himself in the scrub, daydreaming about his first kiss, his first time. And he tried to picture beautiful women. He tried to plant that seed in his head.

But the form kept morphing into a man.

Hard angles, rough hands, and as he got older, he imagined cocks and wet mouths, muscled backs, and a small, firm backside . . .

Now he imagined it was Percy.

And the way he'd looked at him, twice tonight, it didn't take much imagining.

How he'd looked up at him, blinking those pretty blue eyes, and licking his pink lips, leaning in as if he were drawn to Albie in the same way Albie was drawn to him.

He couldn't be though, right?

Albie knew what the church said, what the law said, about such matters. He knew such lusts should accompany shame and guilt.

But he couldn't make himself feel those things.

Not when he thought about Percy and what it would be like to touch him. Kiss him.

Shame and guilt didn't exist in his private thoughts, in the privacy of his room. When he found his hand reaching down into his drawers to relieve some pressure.

Oh, how he imagined Percy then.

He imagined kissing him, their tongues touching. He imagined their bodies pressed together, how he felt. Then he imagined it was Percy's hand on him, not his own, and he brought him to climax so fast, so hard.

He cleaned himself up and fell back into bed,

sleepy now. He smiled at the ceiling, into the darkness, and waited for the shame and guilt to creep over him.

But they never did.

ALBIE HAD BREAKFAST STARTED EARLY. A belly full of porridge would see them through until dinnertime. He expected Percy to join him early again and was disappointed when he didn't.

He came inside with Robert, both of them dressed and ready.

"Des is just finishing up with the horses," Robert said.

Albie was dishing up porridge and he tried to avoid looking at Percy, memories of his fantasies from last night a little fresh in his mind. It wasn't until they were all seated at the table that he looked up and saw Percy's face. He was clearly tired, as if he'd not slept at all, again.

Albie didn't say anything. Not in front of the others.

He didn't want them to think Percy was weak or not fit for being a farmhand.

But he ate well and was keen to get started, and it was an eagerness and excitement that made everyone smile.

Albie really liked that about him.

He was a mood-maker, that was for sure.

Soon enough, with the dogs at foot, and Des holding the gate, they herded the cattle out and onto the road.

"Be safe now, ya hear," Des said. "And watch the crossing."

Albie tipped his hat. "Be home tomorrow night. Go put your feet up for a bit."

Des laughed and closed the gate behind them.

Droving cattle down the mountain was never easy, and Albie hadn't ever done it without his father. Robert was well versed and could read the cattle well and the dogs helped with any strays, but Percy was green.

He kept to the right of the herd, Robert on the left. Percy was a quick study, watching everything Robert did and doing the same, and they were halfway down the mountain before Albie realised he'd been enjoying himself: the jokes, the thrill of droving. And he wasn't concerned for Percy at all. In fact, Percy was more than competent. It helped that Minnie was in charge, but he certainly knew how to handle a horse.

Percy was also funny and witty. Quick with a joke, and the sound of his laughter ringing through the valley made Albie's heart warm. Albie even caught Robert smiling a time or two.

It was the first time since his father's death that he felt any semblance of joy. The open air, being on horseback and droving the cattle. It was a nice reprieve, however brief, from the weight of grief he'd been carrying around with him.

It was slow going though, and it wasn't until late afternoon that they rode into Alpine Falls stockyards. Albie left Robert and Percy to get the herd corralled, and he went in search of John Bailey.

Mr Bailey was a stout man. He sported a long grey beard and a short temper, but he'd been good to Albie's father all these years, even attended his funeral. And Albie hoped he'd receive the same treatment.

He was met with a handshake and a tip of his hat. "Wondered if I'd see you this time," he said.

Albie was relieved. "Got a business to run," he said. "Bought down twenty head o'cattle." He nodded to the holding yard they were in, and Mr Bailey gave a nod.

He counted the stock himself and handed Albie the receipt. "Good, good," he said, busy and dismissive. "Market prices announced tomorrow. Come by to pick up your purse."

Albie gave a tip of his hat in return and walked back to where Robert and Percy were by their horses, letting them drink water, and he was sure he saw Percy sneak them a few bites of chaff.

He was pleased with himself for doing this on his own. He'd done it countless times with his father, but this was now him—Albie's business, Albie's responsibility—and he felt a true sense of accomplishment. Pride, even, that he'd managed his first drove to market.

He knew his father would be proud.

"All done?" Robert asked.

Albie couldn't help but grin. "Until tomorrow. Let's go find some grub."

They rode to the hotel, minus the yapping dog this time, thankfully. Percy held Ox's reins while Albie went inside to make arrangements. He found Elsie behind the bar, serving beer, and she smiled when she saw him. "Didn't think you'd be back so soon."

"Come down to the saleyards," he explained. "Gonna need three rooms if you have them."

She made a face. "Best I can do is one room, two beds. We're full with the meat market on. You're lucky you got in when you did."

One room, two beds would have to do. Sure beat sleeping in the stable.

"I'll take it."

He paid, and seeing she was too busy for any conversation, he told her he'd catch up later and went back out the front. Percy was all grin, but Robert seemed a little tense. "We all good?" Percy asked.

"One room is all they had, but it's ours. Two beds. I'll take the floor," he said.

"Nah, I can take it," Percy said. "As long as there's a roof, I've slept in worse."

Albie wasn't sure what to make of that, but Robert was already taking his horse around to the stables, so they followed. They got the horses and dogs settled in a stall, and Albie caught Robert looking back at the hotel a time or two.

Then he remembered . . .

The drink. He remembered how his father had once explained Robert's urge to drink was like an illness. Like a devil that called his name in the dark when no one else could hear it, only him.

"You good there?" Albie asked him quietly. "If you'd rather we went somewhere else . . ."

"No, I'm good. I just won't . . . I just won't be downstairs. It's not good for me."

Albie gave a nod. "We can eat up in the room, and tonight we'll play cards. Maybe teach Percy a thing or two about euchre, huh?"

Robert met his gaze. Grateful, a little embarrassed, and he nodded. "Sounds good. Sorry to be a—"

Albie clipped him on the shoulder with a hard knock. "No apologies. Now let's go find this room so we can eat."

The room was small, but there were two beds, and it was warm and dry. They'd make do. They freshened up, washed their hands and faces in the laundry room, then Albie and Percy went downstairs in search of food.

True to his word, he took their plates of stew and bread up to their room, the three of them sitting on the beds and scarfing it down. They were too hungry for pleasantries or manners.

"Kinda glad my father isn't here to see me eat like this," Albie said with his mouth already half full, shovelling in some bread and butter.

Robert laughed, which was the reaction he'd hoped for. "He'd have tanned your backside."

"I'd have had trouble sitting for a week." He smiled, briefly wondering if the happy memories of his father would always be accompanied by a pang of sadness.

"He'd have tanned mine too," Robert added, and that made Albie laugh.

Percy kept his head down, not even acknowledging their conversation, and Albie had to wonder what his real story was.

He caught Robert's gaze, and Robert shrugged. He didn't know either.

They finished their meal in silence then, and when their plates were empty, Albie stood up, holding his plate out. "Stack them and I'll take them down to the kitchen."

"I can help," Percy said, taking the empty jug and cups and not really asking.

They went down and handed the plates and silverware to the kitchen, then he took the drinkware back to the bar.

It wasn't as busy now, and Elsie afforded him a smile. "You boys looking after yourselves, I hope," she said.

"As best we can," Albie said with a smile.

"Good," she replied. She picked up a cup and polished it clean with her cloth. "Don't turn around," she whispered, looking at her polishing. "McAllister and his men are here."

Albie bristled but didn't turn around.

She murmured so no one else could hear, "They've already opened the rum so it might be best if you lot just stay upstairs."

Albie hated that it came to this. "That was our plan anyway. Robert's with us and he can't handle the lure of the drink, so we thought we'd stay in and play cards."

She smiled at him. "You're a good one, Albie Bramwell."

She got called away, but before they could turn and walk out, they were spotted. "Young Bramwell," McAllister's voice rang out.

A hush fell over the saloon. When McAllister spoke, people listened. And they all smiled whether they liked what he said or not, just to keep in his good graces.

It wasn't really Albie's style, but he wasn't a fool.

Albie turned to face him. He sat at some joined tables by the fire. There were five of them, Fitzgerald amongst them. Albie wondered where Williams was. They were clearly drinking. Maybe not fully drunk but well on their way.

Regardless, Albie took his hat off, something his father had always taught him to do. "Mr McAllister. It's good to see you again." He met the smug gazes of all the men. "Gentlemen."

He began to turn around to leave but McAllister raised his hand. "I believe you received my letter."

Blast.

He gave him a nod. "Yes, sir. I intended to reply when we returned."

"Tell me now, boy. What say we have a deal."

Albie took a breath to calm his nerves and to cool his temper. He noticed a few of them glanced at Percy who stood behind him, and Albie was grateful he was there.

Then he remembered how Percy had said he should reply to that letter, to give him a polite and respectful grown-up response, not an angry remark of a child.

Albie looked McAllister right in the eye. "Thank you for the offer. It's very generous of you, Mr McAllister. As was the advice you gave to make my father proud. A comfort during this difficult time, thank you." That was total horseshit, but this public pissing contest was a game two could play. He raised his chin a little. "But I believe the best way to honour my father is to prove I am the man he raised."

McAllister smiled but his jaw ticked. He knew this was a game and he knew Albie had played it well. In public, showed manners and respect. Anything that McAllister said now would only make him look bad.

"Don't let your pride get you killed, boy," Fitzgerald mumbled.

Albie bristled again but Percy mumbled behind

him. Not a word exactly, just a reminder. Don't give him a reaction.

So instead, Albie gave them a tight smile. "Good day, gentlemen."

They turned and walked out then, and Albie knew every pair of eyes were on them. They walked past the kitchen to go back upstairs when they heard a commotion.

"You can't be in here," Clara said. "Please don't."

Albie raced in to find a man trying to accost Clara, trying to hold her, grope her. She struggled and was clearly upset, scared.

"Come on," he said. "You know you want it."

"You there!" Albie yelled.

He turned around . . . and it was none other than Williams. He knew he'd have to be around here somewhere.

"This ain't your business, boy," Williams said, swaying, still trying to hold on to Clara.

"No, but it's mine," Elsie said, rushing in and pulling Clara free, shielding her. Elsie blazed fire at Williams. "You'll do well to leave right now before I have you thrown out. McAllister, come get one of your men."

There were men there now. Albie recognised faces but didn't know their names. McAllister's leading farmhand, a tall Irish man by the name of Bill Kelly came through the crowd like he was parting the Red Sea. He seethed at Williams and pointed his thumb in a get-lost motion, and Williams staggered out. He gave Albie a glare as he left but there was no heat in it.

Kelly tipped his hat to Elsie. "Apologies, ladies. Won't happen again."

"No, it won't," Elsie muttered, and the crowd dissipated.

Percy walked up to them, gently touching Clara's arm. "Are you all right?"

She was timid before this, even more so now. But she nodded, and Albie didn't miss how Elsie still had her arms around her. When it was just the four of them, she put her hand to Clara's cheek and straightened some wayward strands of hair. "You're fine now."

Clara nodded and gave her a sad smile, and Albie's heart skipped a beat.

He'd just witnessed a very private and tender moment between them, and it gave him butterflies. Two women! And he felt a rush of something . . . solidarity? Acknowledgement? Validation?

He wasn't sure.

But Percy ducked his head and Albie caught the colour of his cheeks before he went to the door to wait.

"If you're well," Albie said.

Clara gave him a nod. "I am. Thank you."

He gave a nod. "Any more trouble from that lot, you come find me."

He wasn't sure what he could do, but something was better than nothing. Elsie gave him a hard nod.

They went back upstairs to their room. Robert was sitting on the bed, a little agitated. "Everything right?"

"Ran into McAllister," Albie explained.

"What you said to him was perfect!" Percy said, his smile wide.

"I remembered what you told me to put in the letter I never wrote."

"You should have seen his face," Percy said, grinning to Robert. "He knew he couldn't say nothing back. Nothing to make him look good, anyway. I think Albie taught McAllister that integrity can't be bought."

"Fitzgerald's there," Albie said. "Sitting with McAllister like he's something special. And Williams." Albie spat the name. "Trying to have his way with Clara in the kitchen. The man's got a yellow streak in him as wide as the Snowy River."

Robert's expression was one of shock, but not surprise. "He always was a worm. Sorry I wasn't down there with ya."

Albie shook his head and tried to smile. "Best we stay up here tonight. If they're looking for trouble, they won't find it with us."

Robert gave him a clap on the shoulder. But he looked at Percy. "Ready for a lesson in euchre?"

Percy laughed. "Only if you think you're good enough."

THE THING about having such a late lunch was that it meant no need for dinner. Though Elsie knocked on their door at eight o'clock with a tray of bread and jam and another jug of water.

"As thanks," she said quietly. "From Clara."

"Much obliged," Albie said, taking the tray.

"Don't be telling anyone I gave you this," she whispered with a wink and disappeared down the hall.

It put an end to their euchre. Robert had beaten them both every game, though Percy wasn't too bad a player. It was good to pass the time anyway.

When the tray was empty, Robert went to the washrooms to clean up before bed.

"Is he good?" Percy asked. "With the drink?"

Albie nodded. "He was once the town drunk, if you can imagine it."

"Nooo," Percy whispered, disbelievingly.

"My dad gave him a job and got him sober. Hardest worker now. He's a good man, but I don't think it'd be a long step back into trouble for him." Albie shrugged. "Staying up here isn't ideal, but—"

"But it's the right thing to do," Percy said.

Robert came back in then, wiping his hands on the back of his pants. "What's the right thing to do?"

Percy stood up. "Going down to check the horses. That's the right thing to do. Won't be long."

Albie was about to argue, but Percy was right. "Here, take a lantern." He handed him one of the two lanterns in the room. "Don't be long. If anyone asks for trouble, don't answer 'em."

Percy's blue eyes and smile shone in the lantern light. "Yes, boss."

The hide of him.

Albie closed the door behind him.

"He seems a good lad," Robert said.

Albie nodded, trying not to give himself away. He had very impure thoughts about Percy just the night before, so . . .

"He is," Albie replied. "Don't know what his story is though. Has he said anything to you about his family?"

Robert shook his head. "And I didn't ask. If he wanted me to know, he'll tell me."

"Fair enough." Albie bit back a sigh. "Might go wash up too."

He went into the washroom and was glad to find it empty. He washed his face and scrubbed his hands but felt a sudden urge to go back to their room. He didn't want to get caught alone by any of McAllister's men, and he didn't want to miss Percy's return.

He slipped back into their room. Robert was lying on the bed, his eyes closed.

"Percy still not back?"

"Nope," Robert mumbled.

Albie sat on the edge of the bed because pacing seemed an overreaction, even though he *wanted* to pace.

Robert rolled over and faced the wall. "Albie?"

"Yes?"

"Thanks," he said quietly. "For tonight. You are your father's son."

Albie smiled at the back of his head, his whole chest filling with pride. It might have struck a tear as well, but he swallowed it down. "Any time."

Their door opened then and Percy came in, breathless.

Albie got to his feet. "Everything right?"

Percy seemed surprised by Albie's concern. "Yeah. It's all quiet down there now. Horses are fine. No one's getting into that stable because the dogs almost had me until they realised it was me."

Albie was relieved. "Good."

Percy looked over at Robert. "Is he asleep?" he whispered.

Albie nodded.

"It's just that he's not snoring," Percy added.

"I heard that," Robert grumbled, and both Percy and Albie laughed.

Percy lay on the floor, using Albie's coat as a pillow, his own coat as a blanket. Albie felt bad that Percy had to sleep on the floor. The poor man hadn't slept well since he'd joined them.

But they couldn't share a bed, could they?

He dared not suggest it, given the lurid direction his dreams had taken him last night.

So Albie lay on the bed, hands restless, staring at

the ceiling.

And then Robert began to snore.

Loudly.

Percy groaned. "There it is."

"It's awful, isn't it?" Albie replied.

"I considered the stable at about three o'clock this morning," Percy admitted.

"Oh, heavens," Albie whispered. "I'm sorry."

"What are you apologising for?" Percy asked. "It's not your fault."

Hm.

He wasn't sure that was true.

He was responsible for all their welfare now.

Percy rolled onto his side, and Albie assumed that was the end of their conversation. If he hadn't slept well these last few nights, and with the early start this morning, perhaps he'd manage some sleep tonight . . .

But then he tossed, and he turned. The wooden floor couldn't have been comfortable, but Robert's snoring was bad. Not to mention the muted snores coming from all the rooms.

He was just about to suggest he share his bed when Percy sat up.

"What are you doing?" Albie whispered.

"Might go check the horses again," Percy said.

No, he wasn't. He was going to sleep in the blasted stable.

Albie sat up. "Here, you take the bed." Not that he particularly wanted to sleep on the floor either. "Or we can share," he hedged. Then quickly added, "I'd rather you managed some sleep tonight, given you haven't slept well since you started with us. Lack of sleep makes for silly mistakes, and I can't have you injured or causing harm to my horses."

Yes, telling him it's a safety issue made sense. As his employer, it was his duty to look after his workers.

Right?

Percy looked up at him, his face silver in the dark. "Share?"

Albie cleared his throat. "Sure. It's just a bed for sleeping. Don't make a big deal of it. If you'd rather go sleep with the horses . . ."

Percy was up on the bed in a flash. He shoved his coat under his head and closed his eyes, smiling in the dark.

Well, then.

That settles that.

Albie lay back down slowly. He'd have thought maybe they'd have lain head to feet, but no. Percy lay with his head right next to Albie's, his eyes closed and that blasted smile that made Albie's heart stutter . . .

Albie was too scared to move, almost too scared to breathe.

He dared to peek at him, at his beautiful face in the dark. Percy was so close, and Albie took it all in—his hair, his eyebrows, his nose, his lips, committing each line to memory. He may never have this again, so he would cherish this moment forever. He would forgo all sleep to not miss one moment. To count breaths like wishes, no dream could compare.

The rush, the thrill of it. How his heart was racing, this emotion too much for his chest to contain.

Percy's lips parted, his breaths were deep and even, and Albie wanted to reach up and touch him. He wanted to trace every outline, map out every contour, every second.

But he wouldn't. As much as he wanted to, he couldn't. He had neither the confidence nor permission, though heaven help him, he wanted to—

Then Percy rolled toward him, the mattress sagging bringing his face even closer, his legs, his body.

Touching him.

Albie thought his heart might stop.

Percy mumbled in his sleep as if the devil himself was trying to tempt Albie, lure him in, closer, closer.

Then Percy snuggled in a little, then a lot, chasing comfort or warmth, Albie wasn't sure. But he moved his arm up, Percy quickly using it as a pillow. Percy's arms were folded up between them, his face almost in Albie's neck.

How Albie's thumping heart didn't wake Percy up, he'd never know.

How his heart didn't expire, Albie couldn't say. It sure felt as if it might. Knocking almost painfully against his ribs.

But he was lying in bed with a man in his arms.

That man was also asleep and unaware, but Albie gave himself this moment to treasure for all his days.

He'd never forget the feel of it. The warmth, the comfort, the strength.

Nothing had ever felt this good.

This right.

Albie lay there for what must have been hours, Robert's snoring an annoying metronome, but he didn't dare move. Percy was finally getting some much-needed sleep and he didn't want to disturb him.

At least that's what Albie told himself.

Until the lull of Percy's measured breaths, the warmth of his body, the weight of him, pulled Albie into sleep.

CHAPTER EIGHT

PERCY WOKE UP FAR TOO WARM AND FAR TOO comfortable. His body ached from not moving, and it took him a second to remember where he was.

In Alpine Falls, at the hotel.

In Albie's bed.

The source of the warmth was Albie. Wrapped around him like a blanket. Percy couldn't remember a time when he felt as safe as he did right then.

In the arms of a man.

Albie Bramwell, no less.

Handsome, strong, stubborn Albie.

His boss, no less.

But a man. Something he never thought he'd ever do. When Albie had suggested he take the bed or share with him, Percy wasn't letting that opportunity slip through his fingers.

Sharing a bed as children was common. He'd shared with his siblings most of his life. But as adults?

As grown men?

Never.

He closed his eyes and smiled, sinking into the safety, the impossibility, the dream . . .

Until someone in the room snorted and spluttered, scaring Percy half to death. He shot up, then saw it was Robert in the other bed, still asleep but not far from waking. Percy let out a huge breath of pure relief, and taking in the sight of Albie asleep one last time, Percy slipped out of bed.

It was almost morning. Daylight would be here soon enough, so he pulled on his boots and coat and went down to check on the horses.

He wasn't sure why he expected something bad to have happened. He just didn't trust McAllister's men to not try to hurt Albie any way they could.

But the horses and dogs were fine. Their saddles were right where he'd left them. Everything was exactly as it should be. All the other horses in the stables were docile, so Percy assumed he might have been the first one there. It was still before dawn, and with the amount of liquor those men had drunk the night before, he didn't think they'd be up for a while yet.

He set about saddling their three horses, and when he was done, feeling eyes on him, he turned to find Albie watching.

"Wondered where you got to," Albie said. His cheeks were pink, from embarrassment or the cold, Percy wasn't sure.

Would they talk of last night?

Would Albie bring it up?

Percy hoped he would and wouldn't in equal measure. Wanting to know his thoughts and fearing the words out loud all the same.

"Wanted to check on our lot," Percy replied. "I don't trust . . . some people."

Albie smirked, knowing exactly who those people were. "Me either. I'm grateful you came to check." He held up a dish of something that looked terrible. "Clara caught me on the way out. She said she saw you come out here. A little something for our dogs."

"Oh, good," Percy said. "For a second there, I thought you were going to say it was for me."

Albie laughed but fed the dogs, and with the few scraps remaining, he tossed them to the dogs in the stall across the way.

"I want to go to the store before the saleyard," Albie said.

The saleyards was on the way out of town, so that made sense. "After anything in particular?"

"Just more supplies. Then I figure I don't need to come back for a while."

"Good idea. Between the three of us, we can ration out the weight of it."

Albie smiled and stared as if he couldn't bring

himself to look away. Then he swallowed hard. "Uh . . . Did you sleep okay?"

So they were talking about it.

"Best night's sleep I've had in a long time," Percy admitted. "Thank you. I know I said the floor wasn't the worst thing I've slept on, but I dunno . . . maybe it was."

Albie's smile was brief. "You've slept in some less favourable places I take it."

Percy wasn't sure he wanted to admit this, but something told him to. That Albie deserved to know. "Outside. Under the stars isn't all it's cracked up to be. Well," he amended, "the stars are okay. But rain isn't, and winter up in these parts is no fun."

"Winter in these parts can kill a man," Albie said quietly. "I take it you have no family?"

Percy winced, the pain still too fresh. "I do. Kind of." He pulled the girth strap on Ox's saddle, then dropped his hands, not game to look at Albie. Too scared of what he'd see.

"But you left them," Albie offered, his voice warm and closer than it was before.

"I had to," Percy murmured. "I wasn't welcome. It's a long story . . ."

Albie was even closer now. Percy could feel the heat of his body behind him.

"I was supposed to be married," Percy said. "But I refused."

"Married?" Albie whispered.

Percy nodded. "It was all arranged. A wealthy family my father was securing leverage with. My father had lost a lot of money . . . That's a long story for another time, perhaps. But this business deal." He shrugged. "They had a daughter, but I refused."

"A wealthy daughter," Albie mused. "Why did you say no?"

Percy shot him a look then, their gazes locking, unable to hide anything.

You know why.

Percy couldn't bear the scrutiny. The honesty. It was too much, and he looked away. "It was no more than a business deal and I wanted no part of it. I would never marry someone I didn't love . . . couldn't ever love." He shook his head, swallowing the lump in his throat. "I was told to leave and not come back until I could see reason. Reality would prevail and impart some clarity, my father said. He'd provided a good life for me and my siblings, and I should have been respectful and . . ."

Albie put his hand on Percy's arm. "I'm sorry. How long have you been on your own?"

"Four months."

Albie winced then, as if this hurt to hear. Then he licked his lips, his voice barely a whisper. "When you said you couldn't ever love her . . ."

Percy's gaze caught Albie's, both of them wide-eyed and scared, too afraid to say the words out loud.

Words that couldn't ever be taken back. Words that could ruin a man.

"I tried to love her," Percy whispered, but then he shook his head. "She was pretty, and I tried to find something that appealed to me but . . . my dreams are not filled with the likes of her."

Albie blinked a few times, licking his lips as if his mouth had gone dry. "What are the likes you dream of?" His voice was so soft, so pained, gruff. "Perhaps they match my own."

Percy couldn't believe it.

Yes, he'd caught Albie looking his way a time or two, and they had slept in each other's arms last night . . .

But to hear it, to see the vulnerability in Albie's face, the fear in his eyes.

"If I had to choose," Percy whispered, his gaze falling to Albie's lips. "Between her bed and yours, I would choose yours."

Albie's breath left him in a woosh, just as a door slammed and men's voices came across from the hotel.

Albie and Percy separated, each pretending to be tending to a horse, fixing straps that didn't need fixing.

The two men who came in weren't McAllister's men. Albie called one of them by name, but Percy didn't retain it.

His mind was too busy reeling, his heart hammering, fingers trembling.

Had they just had that conversation?

Had Percy just admitted his deepest fears and secrets out loud?

And not to just anyone, but his boss?

He began to feel a little unwell, his stomach churning. He pushed the heel of his hand against his stomach and tried to breathe in deep. Albie caught him. "Are you ill?"

He shook his head quickly, taking a step back. "No. I'm fine. I'll bring the horses out. Is Robert ready?"

Albie gave a concerned nod, but there was sadness in his eyes too. "He was getting himself dressed when I left. I'll go fetch him and see about some bread and fruit for breakfast."

Percy nodded, and it was better not to meet Albie's gaze. So he ignored Albie, pretending the entire conversation hadn't even happened by making himself busy, so he began bringing the horses out. It was easier that way . . .

He didn't want to lose his job.

But he also didn't want to lose the friendship he'd newly forged with Albie. The first person in far too long to show him real kindness.

But oh boy, falling asleep in his arms had been the best night of his life.

He'd never experienced anything like it. It was heaven, and everything had felt right. Every doubt he'd had about himself was confirmed. Being with a man was what he truly wanted. Courting Emily at his parents' wishes had given him nothing but dread and a greasy belly. But the idea of being with Albie was all heart flutters, tummy butterflies, and warmed blood.

He needed to lie in his arms again. He wanted to know what it felt like to touch his skin, to feel his kiss. He longed to feel Albie's strong arms around him forever.

Though now, in the cold reality of daylight, he doubted he ever would again.

He was so conflicted, so torn. So devastated.

Mostly, he was terrified.

So closing himself off and getting back to work, making himself so busy Albie couldn't fire him was the only thing Percy could do.

He readied the dogs and horses, and when they'd gone to the store, Percy made sure to take all of Albie's wares and load the saddle bags. Oats, flour, sugar. Whatever Albie handed him, Percy took without question.

Without eye contact.

When they went to the stockyards, it seemed half the town was there. Crowded with people, horses, dogs, and noise.

Too much noise for Percy's liking.

"I'll stay with the horses," he declared, taking their reins.

It made sense that Robert would go with Albie anyway. Like it made sense for Percy to stay out of everyone's way and mind their horses and purchases, keeping his head down and out of trouble.

He didn't know how long they'd be so he stayed at the back of the lot by the trees so the horses and dogs could rest before the trek home. So he could get his thoughts together.

He couldn't believe what he'd told Albie in the stable. He couldn't believe he'd uttered those words out loud to anyone, let alone him. A man he'd shared a bed with, no less.

"If I had to choose between her bed and yours, I would choose yours."

Percy was mad at himself. Mad for being so foolish. Mad for hoping . . .

It was sometime later when Albie and Robert came back. Albie's jaw was clenched and he had murder in his eyes, and Robert gave Percy a quick shake of his head, silently telling him *not now*. They mounted up and rode out of the saleyards without a word and began the trip home.

Even though Percy was curious, he wasn't game to ask what happened. Business matters weren't his concern, and he didn't want to put himself in Albie's firing line.

As it was, Albie kept a tight hold on Ox's reins and he shifted in his saddle a time or two, clearly frustrated and angry. Percy had to wonder how long it'd take before Albie let some steam out, and he made it as far as the Flagstaff Road junction.

"That blasted McAllister," he seethed. "I expected no less from him, but I'd given more credit to John

Bailey than he's worth, apparently. The man's a coward."

"You did well," Robert said. "You kept your cool and Bailey knew you saw through him."

Saw through him?

"What happened?" Percy asked. He couldn't help it now they'd brought it up.

"Bailey gave Albie a lower price than the others," Robert explained. "Because McAllister told him to."

"What?" Percy cried. "That's not right!"

"There's no right or wrong with him," Albie said. "Only whatever he says goes. It's because I refused his offer yesterday in the saloon. I showed him up in public, being agreeable and polite when he wanted a fight."

"You showed him respect," Percy said.

"More than he deserved," Albie mumbled. "And never again. The way McAllister stood there today and watched with that smug smile on his face. He wants to see me fail, and I'll be damned if I let him."

There was that stubborn pride again. And for what it was worth, Percy loved to see it. Being determined and proud is what it took to survive in these mountains, Percy was sure of it.

"What did you say to Bailey?" he asked. "Was it a bad price?"

Albie sighed. "It wasn't terrible. It wasn't low enough that I'd take my stock back, but it wasn't the market price, and he knew it. He couldn't even look me in the eye."

"He told him thank you," Robert said. "He said he'd hoped for better. Bailey said that was the best price he could do, and Albie said no, not the price. He'd hoped better from the man his father had called a friend. Albie took his money, I tipped my hat, and we left."

Percy laughed. "You said that?" he asked Albie. "For real?"

Albie finally smiled. "Meant every word of it too. My father would be disgusted. That's what I should have told him."

"Nah," Robert said. "You did well. You were more a man today than the likes of any of them could ever be. Don't let 'em get to ya, Albie."

That made Albie smile, and the rest of the ride was easy then. The mood between them, anyway. The day was warm for winter, though there were dark clouds coming in, and Percy hoped it held off until they were home.

They arrived back at Echo Creek in the late afternoon, low clouds promising sleet. It was cold and bitter, which was an odd contrast because coming through those gates and riding down the drive to the house, Percy felt nothing but warmth in his bones.

Like coming home.

He wanted to belong here with his whole heart.

They unloaded the horses and Percy took them

into the stables. He didn't miss the wary glances from Albie, but he ignored them all the same.

Pretending nothing had happened—that he'd said nothing, that he'd admitted nothing—was the only way forward.

Then he went to check on the chickens and grab some more firewood, but Des had beaten him to it. So he decided cleaning up the bunk quarters was in order. Not that it was terrible but changing out of his now-damp clothes seemed like a good idea. Then he decided washing his dirty clothes and drying them by the fire while the place was empty was worth doing.

And that's where Des found him.

"There you are. Albie wanted to know if you're making damper again, which I gotta say, I hope you were," he said with a smile. Then he was looking around the now-tidy room. "Are you not getting worked hard enough you need to find extra?"

I'm avoiding someone . . .

"The chickens were done, and the firewood was too," Percy said. "Horses are all good, dogs are fed, and the vegetable garden is covered."

Des nodded slowly. "My knee told me this morning there was a cold snap coming. And I've been here two days by myself with nothing but time."

"What did you do to your knee?" Percy asked. "If you don't mind me asking."

"Was breaking in a horse that wasn't ready. Came off and broke it bad," he said, tapping the side of his knee. "I was workin' for McAllister at the time and I told him the horse weren't ready, so he told me he had no use for me not bein' able to walk right." He shrugged. "Albie's old man took me in. Said my mind for work was worth two able bodies."

"He sounds a lot like Albie."

Des nodded. "The apple, it never falls far."

No, it doesn't . . .

"So McAllister's always been a horse's behind, huh?"

That made Des laugh. "Oh, yeah. Driven by greed and spite." Des tapped his leg again. "He told the doc to take my leg off. I had to beg him not to. Though when the pain gets bad, I'm half tempted to take it off myself."

Oh, good heavens.

Percy shook his head. "If it ever gets that bad, you let me know. I'll do your work for ya so you can rest up."

Des smiled at him, then rubbing his hand over his stubble and looking back at the house, he sighed. "We better not be late. Don't reckon I wanna see if Albie's temper matches his father's."

Percy snorted. "No, we better not. Though as mad as he was, he kept his cool twice up against the likes of McAllister while we were in town. And his men. Got more guts than brains, I'd reckon."

Des laughed. "Been like it since he was a youngin'.

If he sets his mind to it, consider it gettin' done. Used to drive his old man mad."

Percy smiled, despite his heavy heart.

Albie was respected by everyone who knew him well enough, and Percy could easily see why. He liked him the second he saw him. He might have had different reasons—being so handsome and all—but the more he got to know Albie, the more he liked him.

And then last night happened, sharing a bed. And then this morning in the stable . . .

And now he had to go face him.

"Better get this damper made then, huh?" Percy said.

"Please. And maybe try saving the stew while you're in there. Don't tell him I said that."

Percy laughed. "I wouldn't dare."

He pulled on his coat and hurried across the yard and into the back door of the house, coming into the mudroom and then the kitchen, almost running into Albie.

"Here for damper duty," Percy said, trying on a smile he didn't truly feel.

Albie stopped, pan in hand. His eyes met Percy's, and he licked his lips. "Thank you. Or you could teach me how to make it, then you wouldn't have to worry about it again."

"I don't mind doing it," Percy said. "Though I should probably wash my hands first."

Albie winced. "Look, about this morning," he whispered. "I, uh—"

"There's nothing to be sorry for," Percy said quickly. He wanted to explain, to speak his truth, but no. He needed to put his head down and do what he was here for. "I'm just really grateful for this job and a place to stay, so if you don't mind, I'll start the damper. Des and Robert can't have a late supper."

Albie opened his mouth to say something, but the front door swung inward and Robert came in. "Albie, I think there's a newborn calf down."

"Oh, blast!" Albie turned and went for his coat and stopped, looking back at Percy.

"Go," he said. "I'll fix dinner. It's fine."

With a nod, he pulled his coat and hat on and ducked out the door.

Percy didn't dwell on the too-quiet house or the ache in his heart. He took the flour and put himself to work.

ROBERT AND ALBIE came in late, mostly wet and cold, and warmed themselves by the fire while Percy served up dinner. There was a calf and cow now in the stable.

Born before spring and unlikely to survive, but they'd do all they could to help it.

"Thank you," Albie said quietly as they sat down at

the table. Percy had set the table and fixed dinner, both damper and stew, and because Albie wasn't there to tell him not to, he'd made a little surprise for after.

Damper he could make, yes. As for the stew, he wasn't entirely sure . . . Albie had started it, but Percy had taken over, and he'd added a pinch of this and that, something he'd seen his mother do. And from the way everyone ate in silence, shovelling it in, he figured it wasn't too bad.

"And I made something else," he said, getting up. "For two reasons. One, a successful run down the mountain to the saleyard. No injuries, no illness, and Albie didn't punch McAllister in the mouth."

They laughed as Percy'd hoped they would. He took the special treat off the stove where it'd been cooling and put it in the middle of the table.

"What's the second reason?" Des asked.

"Well, the reason number two is," Percy said, taking the cover off the small pot, "that Albie wasn't here to stop me."

The three men at the table peered into the pot. "What's that?" Albie said.

"Sweets," Percy said. "Cocky's Joy my grandma used to call it. It's a sweet damper baked with treacle syrup."

It was only very small. Maybe one or two bites each and no more.

Percy could feel Albie's gaze on him, but he didn't

dare look. Instead, he cut the small sweetbread into quarters and scooped it out, each with some syrup on top.

"It wasn't much of the flour ration," Percy said, feeling the need to explain. "I thought it'd be nice, is all."

"And because I wasn't here to stop you," Albie said.

Percy looked at him then and found him smiling at him, his eyes soft. "Well, yes."

Robert made an obscene sound and both Percy and Albie turned to him. He had his eyes closed, savouring the flavour. And Des was shaking his head as he chewed, smiling.

It prompted Albie to taste it, and Percy did the same.

It wasn't as good as his grandma's, but oh boy, it was heavenly.

"Now Albie," Des said. "I got the utmost respect for you, and we sure do appreciate you taking on the cook's duty, but I think we can all agree that Percy should take over." He looked at Robert. "Right?"

Robert nodded. "Sorry, Albie, but he's got you beat. That was the best thing I've had in a long time."

Albie turned to Percy, still licking treacle from his lip.

"Oh, I don't want to take anyone's job," Percy said quickly. This was the last thing he needed today. "I'm not stepping on toes, or upsetting—"

"Dinners, yes," Albie said. "Let's see how you go with breakfast tomorrow. We'll see whose porridge is best, huh?"

Robert and Des both laughed, and Percy nodded, embarrassed. Or maybe it was how Albie smiled at him . . .

He needed to clear his head. He stood up and began stacking plates. "I'll get this squared away," he said.

"You don't have to do that," Albie began, but Percy was already on his way to the kitchen.

He already had some water boiling on the stove, so it was no trouble. And he wanted to keep busy. He needed to keep busy. And he could get all this squared away while the others finished their tea and talked of the trip into town, and by the time he was done, he could say goodnight and go to bed.

That was his plan, anyway.

And he almost had it. The kitchen was clean and Robert and Des were putting on their coats, so Percy went to join them.

"I'll see you in the morning then," he said to Albie, still avoiding eye contact. He had his coat, almost to the door, when Albie stood up.

"Percy," he said. "A word, please."

Percy's heart almost stopped, his belly in knots. He ducked his head, and while Des looked between them, he did no more than clap Percy on the shoulder and pulled the door closed behind him.

Percy stood by the door, half ready to bolt. He wanted to run, though he doubted he could get his feet to move. He held his coat, knuckles white, and blinked a few times, waiting for the axe to fall.

"About this morning," he whispered. "I didn't mean it, and I'm sorry. I won't say anything like it again. I really like this job, Albie, and I want to help as much as I can—"

Albie took the coat from Percy and hung it up on the coat rack. "I wasn't going to talk about that," he breathed.

"If it's about me taking over the cooking job, I didn't ask for that. Please don't—"

Albie surprised him by laughing. "You can have it. I hated it and was never any good at it, and you clearly are."

Percy looked up at him then. They were barely a foot apart, and Albie's height over him almost made Percy dizzy when he finally met his gaze.

Albie's eyes were soft and warm. He'd never seen him look like that at anyone else. As if it were a private look, just between them.

Then Albie was leaning in . . . or Percy was. Or perhaps it was the room spinning, or because Percy had forgotten how to breathe.

Albie blinked and straightened up, clearing his throat. He even managed a small step back, composed enough to speak. He straightened down his hair, then his shirt. "Uh. The other day," he said. "You said you could help me."

"Help with what?" Percy asked, barely a whisper, his brain a scrambled mess.

Albie smirked. "Reading. You said you could help me at reading."

Chapter Nine

"Oh." Percy blinked a few times, seemingly collecting himself. "Reading. Of course. Yes. I can. Uh, when? When did you want to start?"

Albie hadn't meant to corner him. It just so happened they had this conversation by the wall at the door. He'd not normally stand this close to anyone, but heaven help him . . .

Percy's pale skin and pink lips, his big blue eyes, and the prettiest blush he'd ever seen.

On a man, no less.

Albie wanted to touch it.

Oh, how he'd wanted to feel the heat of it under his touch. Percy's skin, all flushed like that. It reminded Albie of a springtime sunrise.

Poets and painters would create odes to the likes of it.

Albie almost did reach up and run his thumb across

Percy's cheek. He could so easily cup his cheek and tilt his face up for a kiss . . .

He had to stop himself and take a step back before he did exactly that.

"Tonight," Albie answered. "If you're not too tired. It's been a long day, and Des said you cleaned the bunkhouse and washed some clothes. Then you made dinner, so if you'd rather start tomorrow, that'd be fine as well."

"Tonight's fine," Percy said. "Maybe Des and Robert will be all snored out by the time we're done."

Albie smiled at that, then took some of his father's books and put them on the table. "I worried today that John Bailey was going to hand me something to read or make me sign something that I couldn't follow," Albie admitted. "He didn't, thankfully. I have the receipt for the sale and those numbers were easy enough."

"But you don't want to get caught," Percy said.

Albie nodded. "Right. I don't want the likes of McAllister knowing my weakness."

"Makes sense." He pulled out his seat at the table and Albie took his seat next to him.

It was a rush, sitting this close to him, both leaning in to read the book. A Bible of all things, not something Albie had ever followed closely, but words to read, nonetheless.

Albie dragged each finger across every line, slow and careful, sounding out any words he wasn't sure of.

Percy was patient and kind, encouraging, and gently correcting if Albie made a mistake.

And he'd smile when Albie sounded out a difficult word and got it right.

It made Albie want to get every word right from then on.

"You're doing really great," Percy said.

"Well, I'm sure I'm not, but thanks." Albie sighed, marked the page, and closed the book. "I do appreciate your help and not saying anything to the others . . ."

Percy gave a small nod. "Just so you know, what you said before," he said quietly. "It's not a weakness. Not being able to read. It's not a weakness, Albie. It's just that some folks aren't spared the opportunity. There's a difference."

That made Albie smile. Percy was so thoughtful, choosing his words carefully when many men didn't care. "True. After my mother died, I'd spend my days outside with no objections from my father. He was so busy, and he did try and make me read at night, but I wasn't interested. I should have listened."

Percy smiled sadly. "If I was given the choice to spend my days outside with the animals and exploring instead of being forced into a school desk, I'd have done the exact same."

Albie wasn't sure he should ask, but he was so curious. "Were your parents strict?"

"Oh, yes." His smile turned wry. "I caught the end of a belt many times."

"I'm sorry." Albie wasn't sure what else he could say.

"My parents are . . ." Percy frowned. "I was born into opportunity and privilege, and I'm grateful to an extent. But when I hear you speak of your father, with such admiration and love, I realise how vastly different we are. My father is more like McAllister."

"You said he lost a lot of money."

Percy nodded. "It was my mother's family that had money, sheep graziers and the like. My father never felt adequate—I'm sure my grandfather made it known—so when he'd heard of men making a fortune in the gold-fields, he . . ."

"Gold?"

Percy sighed. "Gold fever got hold of him and it almost ruined him. They almost lost the farm. My mother's father bailed him out of trouble, but he tried to save face by securing a deal with a new business partner."

"By you marrying their daughter."

Percy nodded sadly. "Yes."

Albie sighed. He wanted to touch Percy. To hold his hand, to rub his shoulder, but he stopped himself and his hand burned with the loss of it.

"Do you miss them?"

Percy looked across the room, but Albie could only guess he was seeing memories in his mind. "Yes, and no. I miss them, of course. I miss my brothers and sisters, but I don't miss what they insisted I become."

Albie knew parents arranged marriages all the time. It wasn't uncommon that they pushed courtships to see if romance blossomed. But what did Percy say?

It was no more than a business deal and I wanted no part of it. I would never marry someone I didn't love . . . couldn't ever love . . . my dreams are not filled with the likes of her.

And Albie had dared to ask what his dreams looked like. Perhaps they matched his own. And from the flicker of knowing and the flash of fear, Albie was certain of it.

And then Percy had said something that tilted Albie's whole world.

If I had to choose between her bed and yours, I would choose yours.

The way he'd looked at Albie's mouth, into his eyes . . . exposed and vulnerable.

Honest.

But then he'd retreated and had told him several times since that he appreciated his job, that he needed this job, fearful that Albie would fire him.

Albie would do no such thing.

In fact, Albie wanted to do the opposite.

He was desperate to know. Desperate to hope . . .

"I should get going," Percy said, standing up, his chair scraping the floor.

"Wait," Albie said, not sure what words would follow. He licked his lips and got to his feet. "Can we do this again tomorrow night?"

Percy wouldn't look at him, but he gave a nod. "Of course." He went to get his coat, so Albie followed him to the door.

"Look, Percy, I—" Percy opened his mouth to say something, but Albie raised his hand to stop him. "Please, let me say this." He tried to swallow but his mouth was too dry, so he licked his lips again. "You don't need to worry about your job here. You've more than proved yourself. I wouldn't turn you out over anything you've told me in confidence."

Percy's big eyes were so full of fear. His breaths were short and sharp.

"What you told me this morning in confidence," Albie murmured, "stays with me." He took a deep breath. "And I would hope that if I told you the same, you'd keep it to yourself."

Percy's eyes darted between Albie's, confused, searching for understanding. "Wh-what?"

Albie almost felt sick with nerves, and he wondered if his heart could physically stop from having a conversation such as this.

"Is this how you felt this morning?" Albie asked, putting his hand to his forehead, trying to breathe. "Because, oh boy."

"Are you ill?" Percy asked, concerned. Confused.

Albie barked out a laugh. "Uh, not really. I've never had anyone on this farm my own age, much less a man . . ." He wasn't sure how he managed to speak. "A man such as yourself."

Percy gasped, his voice barely a breath. "Such as . . . ? What do you mean, such as myself?"

"Beautiful," Albie whispered, his head swimming. "You're beautiful. And inclined to choose the bed of a man over that of a woman."

Percy's nostrils flared and he paled. His chest was heaving, irregular breaths, panicked.

It was a reaction Albie could relate to. This was the most intimate of secrets, and not one he thought he could ever share.

Until Percy.

Until Percy told him he'd choose Albie's bed over that of a woman's.

Albie had barely been able to think of anything else.

He put his hand over Percy's heart, his skin warm. "Breathe," he whispered, and Percy took a deep breath in, his cheeks flushed red. "Is that what you meant when you said that?" Albie asked quietly. "I've never met anyone who is inclined such as me, so forgive me if I . . ."

If I what?

Overstep?

Too late for that.

Percy blinked rapidly, still breathing hard. "I'm not . . . I'm not sure what . . . Albie, I . . ."

He looked stricken and torn, but then his eyes filled with tears and his chin wobbled. And he nodded.

And Albie did the only thing that felt right.

He pulled him into his arms and held him tight.

Percy was rigid, scared, until Albie rubbed his back. Then Percy relaxed into him, the tension melting away with each breath he took.

As if a great weight had been lifted from his shoulders.

"I tried not to be," Percy mumbled into Albie's chest.

"As did I," Albie agreed gently. "I spent days off in the mountains on my own trying to make sense of it. I knew deep in my bones that my heart never wanted a woman."

Percy pulled back then, looking up at Albie. He had tears running down his cheeks, his blue eyes disbelieving. "Is what you're saying true?"

Albie nodded.

Percy began to cry again. "I never thought I'd ever meet someone like me. I never thought I'd ever tell anyone. No one can know, Albie. It'd be the end of me—"

"Hey," Albie murmured. "We're keeping this secret together, yes? Our secret is the same, is it not?"

Percy nodded and he began to cry again, scrubbing his shirtsleeve across his cheeks. "I tried not to be like this," he murmured. "And I need this job, Albie. I don't have anywhere else to go."

Albie cupped Percy's face, wiping away another tear. His skin was warm and alabaster white; his lips were pink and parted just so . . .

"I told you before your job is safe here," he murmured, unable to drag his eyes from Percy's lips.

Oh, how he wanted to kiss him.

"Have you ever been kissed?" Albie asked, his voice barely a breath.

Percy gave the slightest shake of his head. "I kissed Emily Phillips' cheek once."

"Lucky Emily Phillips," Albie mumbled with a smile.

"It was terrible."

Albie chuckled at that. They were so close now, chests almost touching, and Albie's heart was thundering, every bone in his body buzzing. And yet, he was still struck by how beautiful Percy was. Even more so up this close. He had flecks of sapphire in his eyes and a faint spray of freckles on his nose.

But those lips . . . those pink lips would be the death of Albie, he was certain of it.

"I sure would like to kiss you right now," Albie whispered, leaning in closer, almost touching.

Percy gasped and his cheeks flushed the most beautiful shade of crimson.

"So beautiful," Albie murmured before he brushed his lips against Percy's. He'd never kissed anyone before, not outside of a dream, anyway. And he trembled with the excitement, the nerves. The thrill of it.

He pulled back, lightheaded and giddy. "Was that fine with you?"

Percy's eyes swam, and he slow-blinked as he

nodded. A whole palette of pinks spread across his cheeks, and it stole Albie's breath.

He traced his thumb across the warmth of Percy's cheekbone to see if it felt as warm as it looked.

It did, and Albie's heart squeezed. He had no words to describe how he felt in that moment or how utterly mesmerising Percy was. So instead, he lifted Percy's chin and kissed him again.

A little harder this time, daring to capture Percy's lips between his and opening their mouths just a little.

Enough to make Albie's pulse quicken, and he was almost overcome with the need to push Percy against the wall with his body, to feel every inch of him and devour his mouth, taste his tongue . . .

He pulled back abruptly, startled by his desire. How he even knew to do such things was beyond him, but his body somehow, most definitely, knew.

"Whew," he said, letting out a rush of air. He laughed at himself, licking the corner of his mouth. "I think I should stop before I'm unable to."

Percy slow-blinked again, his eyes dazed. "Oh," he said, breathless. Then he smiled and laughed. "Wow. Kissing Emily's cheek was never like that." He put his hand to his heart, and Albie put a hand to his own chest.

"You feel that too?"

Percy laughed and grabbed Albie's hand, sliding it over his breastbone. Then he stopped as if just realising what he'd done.

But Albie kept his hand right where it was. "I can feel it," he murmured.

Percy ducked his head. "I should go."

The last thing in the world Albie wanted at that moment was for this to end, but he knew Percy was right.

"Here, let me help you," he said, taking Percy's coat. He helped him into it, pulling the collar up for him. "Stay warm."

Percy gave a nod and slipped out the door into the dark. The wind was biting, carrying sleet in fierce flurries. When Percy disappeared off the end of the veranda, Albie closed the door and rested his forehead against the frame.

He took a moment to catch his breath, his heart still thundering.

He smiled, the risks and threat of Hell be damned.

This was a source of happiness, true happiness. The likes he'd never known, never dreamed possible.

And when he climbed into his bed, the sheets cold at first, he wished Percy was there with him. They could sleep like they had the night before, wrapped around each other, keeping each other warm.

Only now he could kiss him, and perhaps one day strip away their clothes and their inhibitions.

He fell asleep smiling, the glow of heat in his chest, the glow of something wonderful warming him all night long.

ALBIE WAS SURPRISED to see Percy up so early. He knocked on the back door and came inside with his hat full of eggs. His nose was red, his hair tousled by the wind, and he quickly stopped when he saw Albie.

He froze, then ducked his head, smiling, blushing.

"Oh," he said. "I wasn't sure what time I should . . . be here." He met Albie's gaze then, and Albie could see he was tired—dark circles under his eyes.

"You didn't sleep well again," Albie said. It wasn't a question.

"I'll be fine," he said, his piercing gaze meeting Albie's again. His eyes locked in on Albie like a key and turned Albie's belly to butterflies. "I'm still cooking breakfast, right?"

Right. Breakfast.

"Uh, yes, right." Albie took the pot and put it on the stove, unsure if he should mention last night, not wanting it to slip past him. "Look, uh," he began. "I just want you to know, about last night." But then he saw fear in Percy's eyes again, and it hurt to see. He put one hand on his arm, and he reached up to fix his wayward hair. Such an intimate thing to do, and Percy looked up at him with those big blue eyes, and Albie lost his resolve. "I don't regret it if that's what you're wondering."

"I wasn't wondering that," Percy whispered. "Should I have wondered that?"

Albie couldn't resist skimming the back of his fingers along Percy's jaw. "No. In fact, I'd like to do it again."

He wasn't sure where his bravado came from. He just couldn't bear to see the fear and uncertainty in Percy's eyes.

"Oh," Percy breathed. He blinked, dazed, and licked his lips. "You say such things that make me feel weak."

Albie laughed. "Your eyes make me weak," he said, scanning the depths of blue. Then his gaze drew down to his mouth. "Your lips . . . Heaven have mercy, your lips."

And then, right there in his kitchen, he lifted Percy's chin and kissed him again. Soft and sweet, his heart fluttering, his whole body alive.

Until Percy seemingly forgot he was holding a hat full of eggs and one toppled out and splatted on the floor.

"Oh!" He shot back a step. "Goodness."

Albie laughed and took the hat full of eggs. "I better take these."

"I should clean that up," Percy said. "What a waste. I'm sorry."

"It's fine," Albie said, bending to help him scoop up the mess on the floor. Albie wiped an old rag through it, and when he looked up, Percy was looking at him, his cupped hands full of broken shell.

And they both laughed.

"It was worth the egg," Albie said, putting it in the scraps bin for him.

Percy laughed again, his cheeks a glorious pink. "You talk as if you say these things all the time," he said quietly. "I'm not used to hearing it, and I'm certain no one should overhear you say such things to me."

"You make me braver than I've ever been," Albie said. He felt foolish for saying that, but it was the truth. "But you're right," he added, standing up. "I would never dare utter such things in the company of others. But when it's just you and me . . ." He smiled, embarrassed to admit this out loud. "I barely slept last night. I was so excited, nervous, and happy. I couldn't think of anything else but you."

Percy's smile was rueful. "I barely slept because of the snoring in my quarters. I was hoping I'd be used to it by now." He frowned, eyebrows knitting. "The night we slept at the hotel, in town, was the best night's sleep I've had in so long." He turned to the pot on the stove and looked inside it. It was empty, so he reached for the sack of oats. "I'm sure it'll pass. I'll sleep if I'm tired enough. Or maybe the stable might be better. There's a loft for the hay that wouldn't be so bad."

There he went again, mentioning sleeping in a barn.

"You can sleep with me," Albie said.

Percy went wide-eyed and his blush darkened. "Oh, I . . . I didn't . . . uh . . ."

Albie hadn't realised how that sounded, or what

he'd just offered. "I mean, you can sleep in the main house with me, not my bed. My father's room sits empty. I had no reason to take it until now, but I can if we need it. You can have my room." He swallowed hard, nervously feeling the need to explain. "It'd make sense if you'll be tending to meals and such, and if you'll be helping me with reading until late. So you don't have to cut across the yard when it's so bitter outside."

And then we can kiss again.

And maybe more . . .

Percy looked up at him, trying not to smile. "Are your motives pure, Albie Bramwell?"

Albie put his hand to his heart and lied. "Absolutely."

Percy saw right through him and laughed. "I'll consider it." He scooped out a cup of oats and put them into the pot. "It didn't help that my mind ran all night," he murmured. "Remembering my first kiss and how it felt."

A jolt of something hot and wonderful ran through Albie's whole body, and it made him laugh. "I want to do it again. I want to do nothing else." He shook his head, incredulous. "I fear you've awoken something in me."

Percy smiled at him, shyly, the colour on his cheeks rosy, and heaven help him, Albie needed to touch it again.

He found himself closing the distance between

them once more, this time pushing Percy's backside against the shelf, their faces impossibly close. He saw nothing but deep blue eyes, pink cheeks, and faint freckles. "Percy," he whispered.

This time it was Percy who slid his hand around Albie's neck and brought his face down for a kiss. But this was a different kiss . . . It wasn't so gentle, and they opened their mouths, breathing each other in. Percy slid his arms around Albie's waist, pulling him closer still.

Their tongues touched, and Albie's knees damned near buckled. His blood was on fire, and he needed to be closer, closer. He pressed up against him, pushing him against the shelf, and when their bodies met, when he felt Percy's arousal against his, they both gasped.

And froze.

Albie was so stunned, so incredibly aroused, he couldn't think straight.

Percy stepped aside, quickly turning away, running his hand in his hair. Albie had never felt so alive, yet Percy clearly didn't feel that way. He looked scared and conflicted.

Was it too much?

Perhaps.

He put a gentle hand on Percy's shoulder.

"I should go check on the newborn calf," Albie said quietly.

Percy nodded, not turning around. "Y-yes. Right. Good."

Albie knew he should give Percy some space, some time to think about what had just happened, and some distance so they could both simmer down. But he didn't want this to go unsaid. "For what it's worth," he whispered. "I'm glad you feel the same."

He left then, pulling his coat from the rack and putting it on as he strode across the veranda. He cleared the yard in a few long strides and went into the stables. The frigid air soon took care of the arousal issue.

The horses were quiet, and the cow was standing at the back of the pen. Albie's heart quickly sank, certain he'd find the newborn calf lying lifeless.

But then a little white face peered out from behind his mother, and Albie grinned, flooded with relief.

"Ay, little one," he said.

Then Des came through the doors. "How'd he fare? Any good, or no?"

Albie was sure his smile was answer enough. "Come take a look."

Des walked in, his leg stiff as it often was first thing in the mornings. And he smiled too when he saw the little calf. "Well, I'll be damned."

"A day or two in here should see him right," Albie said.

"Hopefully we'll have no more early arrivals. It's too bleedin' cold."

It sure was.

"I saw Percy's bed was empty again," Des said.

Albie played it cool. "Ah, yeah. The eggs are collected, the dogs are fed, and he's made a start on breakfast."

He made a face. "Guess the snoring's pretty bad, huh?"

Albie gave him a tight smile and decided to just put it out there. "Yeah. About that. I told him he could sleep in the main house tonight."

Des's gaze shot to Albie's, so Albie quickly explained. "He said he'll start sleeping in the loft," Albie said, pointing up to the mezzanine for dry hay. "I can't have any of my men bunking in with the animals in the barn, Des." Then he shrugged. "And I was thinking maybe it was time I moved into my father's room. That'll give Percy my room. No hard feelings, I hope. It's just that he hasn't slept more than a few winks in a week, and he's trying to work hard to prove himself, doing too many things. He's gonna cause himself an injury if he's not thinkin' right."

Des nodded. "I get it. 'S okay. You don't need to explain any decision you make, Albie. You're the boss now."

Albie almost smiled. "That may be so, but you deserve the respect to hear it from me."

And that made him realise something else.

"And speaking of that," Albie said quietly. "I wasn't going to say anything because it's not something I want known, but Percy's also helping me with my reading. I never spared the time for it as a kid, and to have the likes of McAllister handing me letters and John Bailey writing receipts, I need to be better prepared. I don't trust any of 'em." He shook his head. "I thought I had time to learn better before I had to worry about that kinda stuff, ya know? Remember all those times my father told me to open a book and I ran off on a horse instead, didn't come home till sundown." Albie smiled then. "I should have listened."

Des chuckled. "You woulda been too busy kicking and screamin' to learn anything."

Albie snorted. "True."

Bandit came over to the gate, so Des gave him a scratch on the forehead. "Percy's got himself a good horse. We'll get him in and around the cattle this week, see how he holds up."

"Good idea."

"Robert said Percy did well taking the cattle to town. Being on Minnie woulda helped, but he held his own."

"He did."

Des sighed. "I'm glad you got someone around here your own age, Albie," he said. "Be good for ya for a change. Sure, you gotta be the boss but you can live a little too. It's good to see ya smile."

If only he knew . . .

Albie willed himself not to blush or give himself away.

Thankfully Des seemed oblivious. "And Robert

tells me Percy stood beside you when folks around town decided to try it on ya."

"He did. First time was before I even hired him."

"Good." Des nodded slowly. "And Robert also tells me he's terrible at cards."

Albie laughed. "He's about as good as me."

"So, terrible."

"Exactly."

"Makes a bloody good damper though."

Albie had to agree. "Should we go in and see how breakfast is looking?"

Des gave a nod and they walked back to the house, and they soon got their answer.

He made porridge like he played cards.

It was a grey, gloopy gruel. Lumpy too. When Percy sat down, all four of them looked at their plates in silence.

Des was the bravest, taking a mouthful first. His look of curious horror made Albie laugh, and Robert grinned . . . until he tasted it.

"Tell me," Albie said. "Have you ever made porridge before?"

Percy shook his head. "Uh, no."

He looked a little embarrassed, so Albie knocked his knee to his under the table. He gave him a reassuring smile before taking his first spoonful.

It was . . . not good. But to everyone's credit, or perhaps more of a testament to their hunger, they ate it, washing it down with a lot of tea.

"So," Robert said. "If I can make a suggestion. While I appreciate any food the good Lord puts on this here table, I'd appreciate it a whole lot more if maybe Albie cooked breakfast and Percy cooked dinner."

Des laughed, and even Albie chuckled. He knocked his knee to Percy's again, and when Percy looked up at him, he relented a smile. "It was pretty bad, wasn't it?"

"It was fine," Albie said.

If fine was terrible, that is.

"So," Des said, changing the subject. "Robert and I will go bring in the yearlings, then this afternoon, we can put Bandit in with them, see how he goes. Start getting him used to cattle." He looked right at Percy. "How does that sound?"

Percy glanced at Albie as if seeking permission. "Uh, sure! That sounds great."

Albie gave a nod. "That'll give me and Percy time to clean up here and change bedrooms."

Percy shot Albie a wild look as if he would dare say that in front of Des and Robert. Albie looked at Robert and explained, "I've decided I should take my father's bedroom. There's more room and a desk for me, now I'll be doing the books. Then Percy will take my old room so he can actually manage to get some sleep."

Percy was back to being horrified. "Oh, it's just that . . . I don't mind, it's no problem. I didn't mean to—"

"Percy, it's fine," Des said. "I know Robert's snoring is bad."

Robert gasped and turned to Des. "You're the one who snores the worst!"

Albie snorted, giving Percy's knee another knock under the table.

"Actually, you're both as bad as each other," Percy said, grimacing. "It's like having competing logging teams at opposite ends of the room." He grimaced again. "For eight solid hours."

Albie laughed, and both Des and Robert quit arguing, admonished even. But eventually, Des fought a smile. "Well, we better get started. We'll be heading to the western range," he told Albie. "Shouldn't be longer than two o'clock."

"Okay," Albie said. "I'll have lunch waiting."

Des and Robert left and Percy began clearing away breakfast. Albie helped and came to stand beside him at the counter. "I told Des about you taking my room," Albie said quietly. "Like I told him about you helping me with reading. It didn't feel right keeping that from him, should he wonder why we might spend time together. I don't know if he'll tell Robert. I suspect not. I've known Des most of my life, and he's a good man."

"Will you tell him about—" Percy turned to look at the pantry. "—about other things."

"About us?" Albie almost laughed. "Oh, heavens no. Just as I assumed my father never told any staff about his personal doings, I don't expect private matters made into public discussion." He shrugged. "Reasons for your spending time in here helping me and not out there doing chores is a matter for Des to know. What we do when it's just us, that's no one's concern but ours."

Percy gave a nod, still not really meeting Albie's gaze.

"Can I ask you something?" Albie's stomach was suddenly soured, and it had nothing to do with the terrible porridge.

Percy stilled. "Yes. Of course."

"Are you comfortable with me?"

Percy's eyes shot to his then. "Yes, why would you ask that?"

"I mean, comfortable with taking my room. Comfortable with me kissing you. You need to tell me if I overstepped. I don't want you to feel you have to oblige me in such things to keep your job. That's not how this works. If you'd rather take a step back, I will understand."

He'd be devastated, but he'd understand.

"Your job remains. The offer of my old room remains," Albie added. "No pressure for anything more."

Percy opened his mouth to say something but decided on a shy smile instead. "I'm not adept at talking about such things. Don't take my inexperience as reluctance, Albie. What I lack in confidence . . ." He shook his head. "I've never been shy about anything in my whole life. Until you. You look at me a certain way and I . . ." He met Albie's eyes then. "I lose the ability to speak, to think."

"So that's a yes, then," Albie hedged. "To being comfortable with me."

Percy scoffed out a laugh, his cheeks dark pink. "Do you not remember before?" Then he whispered, "I kissed you, remember? I mean, you shoved me against the shelf and all, and my insides near caught fire, but I distinctly recall me being the one who . . ."

Albie hummed. "Kissed me?"

Percy huffed, flustered. "Why must you do that?"

"Do what? You can talk about kissing but I cannot?"

"But when you talk about it, I . . ." He waved his hand. "I lose all sense and reason. And now Des and Robert think I can't make porridge, but I'll have you know, it has nothing to do with skill and everything to do with how you . . . what you . . ." He groaned and looked away again.

Albie chuckled and went over to him, trailing his palm across Percy's back, his shoulder. "How our bodies touched," he whispered. "Where no one has touched me before."

Percy sucked back a breath, whining on the exhale, his hands wringing the cloth he was holding. "You need to go do something else, go be somewhere else, while I clean up this mess. I can't . . . function properly or think clearly, and when you talk like that . . ." He turned around and looked up at Albie. Was he mad? He looked a little mad. "Talking of such things right now isn't helping. You're coercing me to think of things I should *not* be thinking about." He pushed Albie out of the kitchen. "Go. Leave me to finish this in peace."

Albie laughed, but he went willingly enough. "Fine. I'll go. Just know that I'll be thinking those things wherever I am."

Percy groaned and went back into the kitchen. Albie heard the clatter of pots and plates, so he did what Percy had asked, and left him to it.

He stood at the door to his father's room. It'd been closed since Marcy had been kind enough to strip and wash the bedding when they'd got the news of his passing. She'd said it helped with the cleansing and goodbyes, and Albie hadn't given it much thought back then, but he sure appreciated it now.

He wasn't sure he could have done that.

With his hand on the door handle, he took a moment to close his eyes, to prepare himself, and he opened the door.

The room was cold, the air stale. He shouldn't have kept the door closed, but for the life of him, he couldn't bear to see the room empty.

He wasn't sure what he expected to find. The ghost of his father, perhaps, telling him to get on with living, not to waste a minute.

That was madness, and Albie knew it. He didn't even believe in ghosts.

But boy, it sure would be nice to hear his voice just once more . . .

The curtains were drawn, the bed was made. A pair of shoes neatly pointing to the wall by the dresser drawers, his dinner coat hung behind the door.

And silence.

So much silence.

There was a gentle rap on the door. Albie turned to find Percy watching him. "Are you . . . is everything good?"

Albie let out a sigh. "Yeah."

Percy stepped into the room, and it felt like a breakthrough over the threshold. The silence was gone; it wasn't so cold.

"First time back in here?" he asked.

Albie paused for a moment. "I had to pick out his burial clothes, and Marcy washed the bedding, but it's been closed since."

Percy came and stood beside him, and he slipped his hand into Albie's. A lifeline if Albie had ever had one.

"Did he die here?" Percy asked.

Albie shook his head. "No. He was helping old man Wilcox fell some trees. Wilcox had helped my father a time or two, so he was returning the favour. Most folks around here help out when they can, so it wasn't unusual. There was an accident when a log came down . . . They rode him into town, but it was too late."

"I'm really sorry," Percy whispered.

"Me too." Then he sighed. "I can talk about him now without feeling like the log hit me instead of him." He put his hand to his chest and rubbed the ache that burned. "Still isn't easy, though. But it helps."

"I'll listen, anytime you want to talk."

Albie gave him a smile. "Thank you." Then he held up their still-joined hands. "This is another first for me."

Percy made a face. "It's not for me, sorry."

Albie gasped. "Was it the girl you were supposed to marry?"

He gave a nod. "Though I can tell you this is the first time it felt good. The first time it gave me a thrill, and not a lump of dread."

Albie laughed. "That poor girl."

"Poor her? What about poor me?"

He turned to face Percy. Still holding his hand, he lifted it to his lips and kissed his knuckles. "Poor you," he murmured.

Percy's eyes seemed to darken and he licked his bottom lip. "You shouldn't look at me like that," he whispered.

Albie grinned and kissed Percy's knuckles again, smiling this time. "And how am I looking at you?"

"Like you want me."

"I do. In ways I don't even know."

"Oh," he squeaked. "You shouldn't say such things, Albie."

Albie couldn't hardly believe he was saying these things. "Sorry," he said, lowering their hands but not letting go. "I look at you and my manners disappear."

"I can tell," Percy said. There was no bite in his tone though. He looked around the room. "Did you want to pack things away? Or leave them as they are?"

Albie sighed. "Most of it will get packed away, I would think. I'll keep anything personal or practical. Not that my father kept many personal things. He had some decent coats and woollen socks. Some gloves."

Percy squeezed Albie's hand. "Want me to help, or would you rather some alone time?"

Albie met him with a smile. "Company, I think. To keep me moving. So I don't dwell on every single piece."

He let go of Albie's hand and rubbed his arm. "Then let's start."

They sorted clothes first, setting aside anything worth keeping. Some were barely fit for rags, or as an undershirt perhaps, or even—

"Robert and Des might appreciate a look at these," Percy said, adding a pair of long johns to the pile.

"I was just thinking that," Albie agreed. "They're too big for you, but I might have some clothes I no longer fit into."

"I'm not *that* much smaller than you," he said, though he did smirk. Because he was indeed that much smaller. "But I do appreciate the offer."

"You didn't bring much with you," Albie noted.

"I was lucky to leave with my horse," he replied.

Albie put the shirt he was folding onto the pile and touched Percy's arm. "I'm so very sorry."

"As am I." He tried to smile but it didn't hold. "I'm grateful to have found a place here. To have met you."

"Remember what I said," Albie added with a squeeze of Percy's shoulder. "No pressure for anything other than the job you're hired to do. If you'd rather keep a professional distance, I would understand."

Percy gave him an irritated, hard stare. "Are you doubting me already? We had this conversation not one hour ago."

Albie smiled at his attempt to be stern. "You might change your mind at some point, and that's fine."

Percy narrowed his eyes at him. "Then perhaps I should kiss you again so you understand. Though if you keep doubting me and making me say these things out loud, perhaps I should say no until you learn."

Albie laughed. "Okay, teacher. Deny me and we shall see who breaks first."

Percy groaned. "I can be stubborn."

"I don't doubt that."

"I promise you'll break first."

Albie took Percy's shoulder and pushed him against the desk, pressing hard up against him, their bodies flush. Percy gasped, his eyes wide, mouth open, his hands quickly fisting Albie's shirt, looking up at him, melting into him, ready to be kissed. Licking his lips . . .

Just begging to be kissed.

Albie smiled victoriously. "That's a wager I'm prepared to take."

Like Percy knew he'd already lost, he shoved Albie away. "You're the devil."

Albie laughed and put his hands up in surrender. "I'm sorry. That wasn't fair."

Percy pointed to the rest of the clothes. "Keep working, or I'll go find something that needs doing in the barn. Like making myself somewhere to sleep tonight."

Albie chuckled, but he did what he was told, going back to sorting and folding the few remaining clothes.

Until Percy grabbed him by the shoulder, spun him around, and pushed him to sit on the bed. He took a rough grasp on Albie's chin between his thumb and forefinger and planted a hard kiss on his lips.

"How's that for a wager?" Percy asked, shoving him with a grin. "Believe me now?"

Albie was stunned and incredibly aroused. His heart was hammering, his body singing. "Now who's the devil?" he breathed.

Percy grinned. "I'm going to grab my few things from the bunkhouse." And with that, he turned and walked out.

Albie's head swam, his heart thumping painfully, and he could feel it thundering under his palm. But something ached even more, and he slid his hand down, palming his arousal through his trousers.

Percy was indeed the devil, sent to test him, he was sure of it.

He willed his body to calm down, taking in a few deep breaths. Then he remembered where he sat. In his father's room, on his father's bed.

It wasn't appropriate to behave so indecently.

It's no longer your father's room, nor is it his bed. It's yours, Albie. You're free to behave however you want in your own room . . .

He shook his head to clear it, ridding himself of ghosts and doubts.

And he finished clearing out his father's things.

CHAPTER TEN

PERCY PUT HIS FEW BELONGINGS ON THE BED IN Albie's room.

Albie's *old* room.

Percy's new room.

Albie had transferred his things to the room that had been his father's, leaving Percy a small chest of drawers and his very own room.

He didn't even have his own room back in his parents' house. Granted, their house was nicer. No, not nicer. It was built with more money, that's all.

Albie's house was a home.

Something his parents' house could never quite manage. It certainly wasn't a home when he was told to leave . . .

But now he had his very own room.

And Albie across the hall. Something he tried not

to think about. How they'd be sleeping in the same house with no one else around.

He couldn't even believe that he and Albie were the same. That neither of them had an eye for women. He never dreamed he'd ever meet another man like him, let alone one who looked at him in that way.

Who kissed him.

Who pressed him up against the shelf or the desk, allowing him to feel the hardness of his manhood.

Percy had almost expired on the spot.

He'd always known he was attracted to men, even when he was a young boy, but he didn't know it could feel like that.

He didn't know it would set his blood on fire and make his brain shut down.

All he knew was that he wanted more.

More of what, he wasn't sure. That feeling. The rush, the thrill. The pleasure.

He understood now why men lost all reasoning when it came to the pleasure of the flesh. He understood now what might make a man risk everything for one chance . . .

He understood now.

Granted, his desire was for men, but he assumed it to be no different.

To want, to crave, to desire.

The need that made Percy push Albie to sit on the bed and crush his mouth to his. To kiss him. To want more but making himself stop.

"Everything all right?"

Albie's voice startled him. Percy jumped, his hand to his heart. "Oh, yes, I'm fine. Just thinking . . ."

"Of?"

He smiled with a rush of breath and dared to meet Albie's gaze. "Just how grateful I am."

Albie rubbed his arm. "We should leave this, finish our chores outside before Des and Robert come back. They'll be cold and hungry, so I'll need to make a start on lunch."

Percy nodded. Yes, work. Work seemed like a very good idea.

They had everything done by the time Des and Robert brought the small herd into the front holding yard.

While they ate a hearty lunch, Percy got Bandit ready for his trial with the cattle. He saddled him but walked him across the yard and in through the gates.

He knew all eyes were on him, so he just prayed he didn't make a fool of himself. He knew Bandit would be okay with some time. He was used to sheep, after all. And he rode okay around the bullock teams in town.

But still, he didn't appreciate the audience.

He took Bandit's reins and led him closer to the herd. They were yearlings, so while there were no big horns, they were skittish, but Bandit did okay.

He only shied away a time or two, but Percy didn't want to push his luck. He tied his reins to the railing allowing him to simply get used to the cattle. He wasn't

about to ride him into a skittish herd of young cows and
bull calves.

He didn't fancy getting bucked off and trampled.

Des came over, limping across the yard to lean on
the railing. The morning ride must've given his leg a
workout. "You did good," he said.

Percy felt a rush of pride. Praise coming from Des
was a merit. "I don't want to rush him too soon. If he
gets bumped or startled, I'll never get him near them
again."

Des gave a nod. "That's right."

"How long will they be in this yard for?"

"Coupla days. We'll separate 'em and put the bull
calves out in the southern paddock."

Ah, right.

For breeding stock or for slaughter. It made sense.

Percy gave Bandit a scratch behind the ear. "Then
he'll have a few days to get used to them."

Des gave a nod. "Go walk to the back of this lot and
bring the cattle in. I'll hold Bandit."

Percy did that, and for a good while, they worked
the cattle in and around Bandit. Though Percy got the
feeling Des was giving him a lesson more than his
horse, conditioning him to be around the livestock, but
he loved it all the same.

They laughed a lot, despite the cold, and by the
end of it, Percy felt a part of the team. As if he
belonged here.

Robert came over, a little sheepish. "Hey, Percy,"

he hedged. "How about I take Bandit for ya and you go and save dinner? Albie mentioned getting started on it and, uh, jeez . . . you'd be doin' us all a great favour if you did the cooking. If you know what I mean. No disrespect to Albie at all—I'm grateful for any food, lemme tell ya. But there's bein' grateful, and then there's bein' *grateful*. If you know what I mean."

Percy laughed and handed the reins over. "Be my guest. I like my damper chewable as much as the next man."

"I will tell on both of you," Des said with a laugh.

"You told me yourself that Percy's cookin' was ten times better than Albie's," Robert whisper-shouted at Des. "Don't you back out on me now."

Des hissed at him to shut up, but Percy laughed as he put his hands up. "I sure as hell ain't gonna tell him. Your secret's safe with me." He took a few paces toward the house and stopped, turning back to them. "Don't think I've forgotten what you said about my porridge this morning."

Robert patted his belly. "You know, I wasn't even hungry by lunch time, so maybe it wasn't so bad."

Percy was still smiling when he headed inside. He hung his coat up and went into the washroom to scrub his hands. He found Albie in the kitchen, holding the butter as if he was entirely unsure what to do with it.

"You put some in the flour, yes?"

Percy laughed and took it from him. "Let me."

Albie gave him a smile, studying him for a long moment. "You had a good afternoon."

"I did. Great, even. Never would have guessed Des has a sense of humour."

Albie chuckled and his smile lingered a few seconds before fading. "I miss being out there. I understand things need to be done in the home, and I went over more of my father's ledgers. Not sure I'm any the wiser for it, but seeing how he did things helps."

"You'll get on top of it," Percy said as he folded the dough. "In no time flat. You're smarter than you think."

Albie's smile was rueful, a little sad even. He gave a pointed nod to the pot on the stove. "Probably only a day left in the stew. Will have to start one from scratch tomorrow. We haven't hung a beast in a while, so I'm not sure what I'll make it from." He sighed. "I guess we'll find an old cow, one that won't make us much at market. Should keep us fed for a while."

Percy perked up at that. "Ever had rabbit stew?"

Albie shook his head. "Not for years."

He grinned. "Then tomorrow we'll set some traps. We can take down some pigeons too. Or galahs."

Albie screwed his nose up at that. "Galahs? I think I'd rather not."

"Or a wallaby," Percy suggested. "Wallaby stew's pretty good eating. Plenty of options. We'll make do, Albie. We'll get by just fine."

Albie gave him a soft smile, his eyes warm and kind.

It was a personal and private expression that made Percy stop what he was doing.

"Thank you," Albie murmured.

"What are you thanking me for?"

"You're a light to my dark," he said softly. "Where I see doom and gloom, you're looking for a break in the clouds. You brighten me."

"Oh."

He wasn't sure what else he could say. He'd never heard such beautiful words.

"You speak like a poet," Percy mumbled, going back to his dough. He was embarrassed now. "You say things out loud that I've only read about in books."

Albie chuckled. "A poet, huh? You know, just the other day, I likened this—" He ran his thumb across Percy's jaw. "—the blush on your cheeks, your blue eyes and pink lips, as something a poet or painter could only dream of."

Percy gasped, swatting Albie's hand away. "All the heavens above, Albie," he hissed at him. "Robert or Des could see us, or worse, hear you. You can't say things like that to me."

He was sure his skin burned from his toes to his scalp; he could feel the heat in his face.

And what did Albie do?

He laughed. "Hold still," he said, taking a wet cloth and gently wiping Percy's cheek. "You have flour. I think it's endearing, but the others may not."

"*I* do not," Percy said, wiping the back of his hand

across his cheek, probably making it worse. "If you want this damper ready for supper, you'll do well to leave me be. Go on, go make yourself useful somewhere else."

Albie snorted, surprised, a little shocked. Perhaps Percy had overstepped. He was just about to apologise when Albie laughed, "Fine. Yes, I'll go make myself useful somewhere else."

Percy felt bad, but Albie gave him a smirk over his shoulder as he left, as if he was enjoying this bickering and game of push and pull a little too much.

He's such a devil, Percy thought. Though he smiled as he worked.

Dinner was quiet as they ate, though the soft sighs of appreciation as they tasted the damper were worth all the effort.

"Didn't, by chance, make any of that Cocky's Joy again, did ya?" Robert asked. Des and Albie both waited for a reply, and Percy couldn't help but grin.

"I did. As thanks for helping me and Bandit with the cattle today."

Des looked surprised. "Oh, you don't need to—"

Robert elbowed him. "Yes, he does. And you need to help him do something every day, so we get sweets."

Percy laughed. "I'll make it whenever I can. No need for special favours."

When they each had their first mouthful of the syrupy bread, they sighed and closed their eyes, and that right there was enough reason for Percy to make it for them.

This was a hard life. They worked hard, and they gave their all to help Albie, so a little sweet treat in return was a small gesture by any means.

It made Percy happy to do what he could.

When they were done and when Robert and Des got the door for the coats, Des gave Percy a nod. "Hope you manage some shut-eye tonight."

Percy almost dropped the plate he was holding, and he pretended his cheeks didn't burn hot.

What did he know?

That he and Albie were maybe going to . . .

"Yep, enjoy the quiet," Robert said. "Sorry Des snores so bad you gotta sleep elsewhere."

Des shoved him out the door and they bickered across the yard until Percy couldn't hear them anymore.

Albie cleared his throat. "That was quite the reaction, Percy."

"I wasn't . . . I didn't . . ."

"You were thinking something."

Percy continued to stack the plates. "I was thinking you and your innuendos are a burr in my boot, that's what I was thinking. Now, go and get your books while I clean this up. Reading or ledgers, you choose."

Albie sighed. "You're very bossy. Are you sure you're not the one in charge around here?"

Percy put the pile of plates in the kitchen and sighed. "Sorry, I . . . I forget my place."

Albie was suddenly behind him, and he pressed a soft kiss to the back of Percy's neck.

It made his knees weak.

"Don't be sorry. I like it. I find it endearing. You're like a baby fox. You think you're fierce but . . ." He kissed the same spot again and Percy shivered. "You're really just a small, innocent—"

Percy turned around and met him with a hard glare. "I'm not small."

Albie smiled, his eyes on Percy's lips. So close, their bodies almost touching. "You're small and fierce."

Percy shoved his shoulder, putting some distance between them. "You're enjoying this. You tease me on purpose, for no other reason than to make me mad."

"I like it when your attention is on me," he said.

Percy glowered at him. "Go clear the table and you'll have my attention. Fetch the boiling water from the stove and you'll have my attention. Go and get your books and you'll have my attention. Leave me to finish my work and you'll—"

"Okay, okay," Albie said, putting his hands up in surrender. But he smiled as if he still found him amusing.

"A baby fox," he mumbled to himself. "I am not a baby fox. Of all the insulting things."

"What was that, sorry?" Albie stood by the door, holding a tray of tableware.

"Nothing," Percy said sharply.

Albie slid the tray onto the counter, then without warning, he ran his hand along Percy's jaw, lifted his face, and kissed him. "And now you look like a baby rabbit, with your big eyes, all wide and scared."

Percy gave him another shove.

Albie simply grinned as if this was the most fun he'd had in a long time. "And there's the baby fox again."

Percy wasn't even going to dignify that with a response. He simply turned around to fetch the pot of boiling water from the stove. Only when he went to lift it, a splash of water caught his hand and he yelped.

Albie was right there, alarmed, frantic even, pulling him from the stove and holding his arm, inspecting his hand, his wrist. "Are you hurt? Where did it get you?"

It took a second for Percy's heart to stop hammering for him to realise there was no pain, no burn mark. "No, it just startled me. I'm fine."

Albie let out a sigh of relief and Percy liked that Albie was so concerned that he came to his rescue. Despite the fox and bunny comments just a moment before.

"I'm sorry," Albie said. "This is my fault. I was caught up in playing this silly game of prodding you for a reaction. I'm sorry, Percy. You could have been seriously hurt, and I know better."

Percy rubbed his wrist. It was just a few small spots, nothing at all, really. "Well, I'm glad you learned your lesson. Now, go get your books set up at the table, and start reading. I'll be out when I'm done."

Albie relented a nod and left him this time, without a snide remark. He finished cleaning up, and by the time he was done, he was much calmer and even feeling a little remorseful.

While he didn't appreciate the name-calling, he did appreciate his concern.

And his affection.

With his big hands and soft kisses to the back of Percy's neck.

Who would have ever guessed a kiss to that spot on the back of his neck would near buckle his knees? Of all the places Percy dreamed of being kissed, that wasn't one of them.

Until now.

It might very well go to the top of the list.

When he finished cleaning up, he took the lantern from the kitchen and found Albie at the table, reading out loud. Quiet and slow. He wore a look of concentration and frustration, but he was reading, nonetheless.

Percy pulled his seat out beside him, and Albie closed the book and pushed it away. "I'm done with that. Shall we try some numbers in the ledger?"

Percy gave him an encouraging nod. "Sure."

So that's what they did. Percy covered the total column and had Albie try and work out the sums to see if he could get the same answer his father had.

Albie was frustrated and embarrassed. "This is a

waste of time," he grumbled on the second attempt at one in particular.

"No, it's not," Percy offered gently. "You're doing really well."

"I have to count on my fingers," he griped. "Like a child."

"Now. You have to do that now. If you want to get better, you need to practice."

Albie sulked, frowning at the ledger.

"Is it no different to me learning how to drove cattle?" Percy asked. "Do I not need to make allowances? I've never done that before, so you made me take Minnie. You made me listen and watch. How is that different?"

Albie's eyes met his, and Percy could see Albie knew he was right.

"It's no different to me and Des getting Bandit familiar with the cattle before we use him to muster, is it not?"

Albie sighed. "Right, fine. I get it."

Percy patted Albie on the back. "So, use your fingers now if you have to. And let's keep practising so eventually you won't need to."

Albie kept going with the sums, writing his working-outs down in a separate notebook. Percy kept his hand around Albie's back, sitting a little side-on to him and their knees touching under the table.

Albie leaned in closer, and soon he wasn't paying any attention to the numbers on the page. His eyes drew up Percy's arm, slowly, to reach his eyes, his face closer than necessary. "I think I've had enough books for tonight," he murmured.

The low rumble of his voice, the dark desire in his eyes made Percy's blood run hot and his belly tightened.

He pulled back. "Right, yes. Well then." He straightened the books. "We should call it a night."

Albie's hand on his leg stopped him, burning through his trousers. Percy knew what he wanted, and for some reason he couldn't name, it frightened him.

Percy wanted it, yes.

But was he ready?

He wasn't sure how such things between men would work, and he was scared to find out. No matter how much he yearned for Albie's touch, his kiss.

Oh, how he wanted him.

But there was a voice in his mind that told him to wait.

"I should leave you to finish up," Percy said quietly, and he stood. "Thank you for this evening. Are you making breakfast? I think Robert and Des would appreciate me not on porridge duty. Perhaps I can get up early and set some rabbit traps." That was a good idea. He could do that before sunrise. With a new plan in his mind, Percy nodded again. "Good night, Albie."

Before he could get too far, Albie stood up. "Percy, wait."

He stopped, too scared to turn around.

"I won't force you to do anything you don't want to do," he said. "I can see you're reluctant, scared, perhaps. I need you to know it's fine. I will wait for your permission."

Percy's heart hammered painfully against his ribs. He couldn't speak, not even if he knew what to say. So instead, he gave another nod and somehow got his feet to move. He went into his room and closed the door, leaning against it, breathing as if he'd run a hundred-yard dash.

His mouth was so dry, his palms were sweating, and he listened for Albie's approaching footsteps.

He heard nothing.

He stripped to his undergarments and climbed into his bed. Albie's old bed. It smelled of him, and the silence was blissful, though he swore the sound of his own heartbeat filled the room.

And he waited for his door to crack open.

He waited for Albie to perhaps knock or to speak through the door. He waited for shadows under the door to appear, for Albie to want to explore this newfound temptation.

He never did.

So instead of the sound of Des and Robert snoring, this night Percy fell asleep to the sound of disappointment and regret warring with longing and desire in his mind, in his heart.

The next morning, he overslept. He couldn't believe he'd slept so late. He rushed out, pulling his boots on, to find Albie stirring a pot of porridge.

"Morning," Albie said.

"I was going to do things this morning," Percy said. "I'd intended to be gone and back by now. I can't believe the time."

"Yes, good morning to you too, Albie. Thanks so much for asking."

Percy stopped. "Oh. Sorry. Yes, good morning. Sorry, I, uh . . ."

"You must have needed the sleep," Albie said, smiling at the oats he was stirring. "I take it you slept well."

"Eventually, yes."

Albie's eyes met his. "Eventually?"

Darn it.

He winced. "Uh, yes, it must have been the silence. Took some getting used to."

Albie smiled, stirring the porridge. "If you wanted to make some bread, I'm sure it will go over well with the men."

Yes. Work, Percy. Work.

"Of course. Should I go check on the calf in the barn? The horses? I haven't collected the eggs yet. I was going to have set rabbit traps by now. I'm behind already and the sun's not even up yet."

"Percy, it's fine," Albie said. "You and I can go set

some rabbit traps after breakfast. Maybe shoot a wallaby or something."

"Okay." He nodded. He wanted to say something . . . to mention last night. To apologise.

Albie gave him a smile. "Damper?"

"Right. Yes." He rushed to get it started and they stood next to each other, moved around each other in the small kitchen, but Albie never once touched him. Never pressed him against the shelf or lifted his chin to kiss him. Never even looked to consider it.

And Percy had never wanted it more.

He ached for it. His skin remembered how it felt to be caressed. His lips recalled the press of Albie's mouth, his hands, his arousal . . .

Even when they sat at the table. Albie's knee never once bumped his. And when they set off with rabbit traps and a rifle, and later that night at supper time and when they did more reading, sitting close and almost touching.

Albie never did.

He never mentioned it, and he never instigated it.

And the next day.

And the day after that.

And the days that followed.

Percy thought he might catch fire if Albie didn't touch him soon, and he didn't have the bravery to touch him first.

I'll wait for your permission.

That's what Albie had said.

Which meant Percy was going to have to say something. Do something.

And even though he often felt the heat of Albie's gaze lingering, it wasn't the same.

It wasn't enough.

Percy needed more.

For almost a week, he burned for it, until he couldn't stand it a moment longer.

It was before supper, and he and Albie were getting dinner ready while Des and Robert finished up with the horses. *It's now or never*, Percy thought.

Say something.

Say it now.

"Albie," he whispered, his mouth suddenly too dry to speak.

Albie looked at him, waiting. "Yes?"

His breath left him in a rush, and his heart was squeezing painfully. He felt lightheaded, and for the life of him, he didn't know how Albie had said all those forthright things to him without dying.

Albie was concerned now. He put the tray down. "What is it?"

Percy felt the need to laugh, which was bordering on hysteria, surely. "Uh. Before," he said, breathless. "You said you wouldn't pursue anything with me without my permission, so if you still want that, this is me saying you have it. My permission, that is. I don't know what this feeling means, but it's been seven days since you touched me and I feel I might go mad if you don't soon."

Albie's smile was slow spreading. "Your permission, huh?"

Percy nodded. "Yes. If you want it. You have it. Not that you ever really needed it. You always had it. But I was scared, and truthfully, I still am, but the alternative is a fate worse than death. I kept waiting for you to knock on my door in the middle of the night, and I would fall asleep disappointed when you didn't, and—"

Albie did that thing where he put a fingertip to Percy's chin and lifted his face. That very thing that made Percy's heart stop and his knees weak.

"Do I have permission to come to your room tonight?"

Percy thought he might die on the spot. He nodded quickly, though all memory of how to breathe was long gone, and he leaned in, desperate for Albie's kiss . . .

Until the sound of Robert running along the veranda with a loud knock on the door made them jump apart. "Albie," he yelled. "We got company."

Company?

They rushed to the door and sure enough, there was a wagon coming down toward the house. A single horse wagon, two people sitting up front.

Not just any people. Two women.

Was that . . .

Elsie?

Des was walking out to meet them as Percy followed Albie out onto the veranda.

It was indeed Elsie and Clara with a shawl pulled up over her hair, her head down.

Was she unwell?

Albie raced down the steps, Percy with him. And Robert too. Des met Elsie at the side of the wagon and helped her down, and Albie rushed to meet her.

"Elsie?" Albie asked. "What brings you here? Did something happen?"

"You said we'd be welcome should we need it," she said. She glanced up to Clara who looked up then, and . . .

Oh no.

She had a fresh black eye and a swollen lip.

"Of course, yes, always," Albie said, helping Elsie get Clara down from the wagon.

Elsie pulled Clara into her side, her arm protectively around her shoulder.

Albie fussed over Clara, not sure where or if he should touch her, helping her toward the house. "Des, Robert, please take care of the horse and wagon, and bring their things in. Percy, set two more seats at the table."

Percy nodded and dashed up to hold the door for them. "I'll make some fresh tea."

Albie sat Clara by the fire, his eyes meeting Elsie. "Who's responsible for this?"

"Williams," she replied.

"That no-good bastard," Albie seethed. Then he seemed to remember his temper.

"He tried to . . ." Elsie winced. Then she sat beside Clara and brushed her hair from her forehead, ever so gently. Tenderly, full of love. "He tore her dress and he almost had his way with her, but she fought him hard. That's my girl," she said quietly. Then she looked up at Albie. "We left first thing this morning."

"Good," Albie said.

Percy came back with a cup of hot tea for Clara, and she took it with a sad smile. Percy quickly produced another cup for Elsie, but when he brought over a basin of clean water, Elsie put her tea down and took the basin and washcloth. "Thank you, Percy."

He stood back, next to Albie, unsure of what to do next. The way Elsie tended to Clara seemed personal, as if he was invading a private moment. He felt the need to look away.

It didn't help that Clara looked so desperately sad and bruised and sore. She'd always been shy and quiet, from the time Percy had spent in town at the hotel and saloon, but she was always kind to him.

It was then Percy noticed her torn dress and Albie seemed to notice at the same time because he growled. "Someone needs to teach that Williams a lesson," he hissed.

Percy grabbed Albie's arm at the same time Elsie said, "Not today, he doesn't. And not from you. He'll get what's coming, but not today."

Albie grumbled under his breath, and Elsie looked up at him and smiled. Percy dropped Albie's arm but not before Elsie saw. "He'll get what he's owed, don't you worry," she said. "The likes of men such as him always do."

"Not often enough," Albie said. Then he looked again at Clara and sighed. "Sorry."

"I should set the table," Percy said, remembering.

Elsie put her hand up to stop him. "If it's not too much trouble, I'd rather we didn't eat with company tonight. I don't mean to offend, and your generosity is already too much, but perhaps Clara could have something to eat away from the scrutiny. Some privacy, if that suits you, Albie. I don't know what you have in way of accommodations. We'll take whatever you can spare."

"My room," Percy volunteered.

"No," Elsie said quickly. "We couldn't do that."

"I insist," Percy said. "Let me clear you some room for your things."

He didn't want to move back into the bunkhouse, but he certainly didn't expect Elsie and Clara to share with Des and Robert. As he shoved his few things into his rucksack, he reminded himself of worse places he'd slept.

And Clara needed this more than he did, so it was only right.

Albie was soon beside him, helping him pack his

things, and when the drawer was empty, he took Percy's rucksack and walked it into his bedroom.

"What are you doing?" Percy whispered, following him in.

Albie spun to face him and there was a different look in his eyes now. Something Percy hadn't seen before. A determination, but also a fierceness and an authority that made Percy's belly tighten.

"If I cannot come to your room tonight, then you shall come to mine."

"But the others—"

"I don't care. Des and Robert don't need to know, and I'm certain Elsie and Clara are to each other as you are to me."

Percy's belly swooped. "Oh. Really?"

He had noticed that they were close, affectionate even, but he never realised . . . he never thought . . . "Oh. And what am I to you, Albie?" he whispered.

Percy didn't know what possessed him to ask that, to be so bold to ask such a thing.

Albie softly tapped his finger to Percy's chin, briefly, perfectly.

"You are everything to me."

A quiet knock on the front door made them both turn, and Albie darted out of the room, Percy following.

It was Des and Robert, bringing in the items from the cart. "Sorry to interrupt," Des said. "Thought you might like your belongings."

Clara turned toward the fire, hiding her face, and Elsie gave her a squeeze before standing up. "Thank you so much. I do appreciate it."

She picked up one sack, weighing a few pounds at least, and handed it to Albie. "I have little money, but hopefully this will help."

Albie looked inside, then he looked at her. "What is this?" He put the sack on the table and pulled out smaller paper envelopes. Many of them. He opened the fold on one and inspected its contents, giving it a shake. "Seeds?"

She gave a nod. "All kinds. Mostly vegetables, some fruit trees, I believe. The names are written on them. Enough to plant an orchard, I'd reckon."

He rifled through the sack, his eyes wide, before smiling at her. "How did you get these?"

She shrugged. "The saloon acquires payment in all kinds. I considered it compensation in lieu of wages. Old man Doyle owed me more than this, and I told him I was taking it. He weren't game to argue."

Albie snorted, and Percy smiled. He really did like Elsie. She had more fortitude than half the men he knew.

"There's some oats and sugar too," she added. "Now, those he didn't know about, but they'll be eaten before he realises. If he realises at all." She looked at Albie, serious now. "We come with little else, but I promise we'll earn our keep. We'll cook and clean, and tend the vegetable garden, and keep the house. We'll be no bother at all, and you won't hear a peep of trouble, I swear it."

Albie put his hand on her arm. "I told you before, you're welcome here. You'll be safe here; you have my word. Now let's take your things to your room."

Percy carried the old port case to the bedroom and sat it at the foot of the bed.

"There's only a single bed," Albie noted. "I trust that's suitable?"

Elsie's eyes met his and she gave a nod.

It was an admission, an understanding, and it made Percy's belly tighten, and for some reason his cheeks felt warm.

I'm certain Elsie and Clara are to each other as you are to me.

That's what Albie had said, and Percy was sure Albie was right.

Then Albie cleared his throat, and he glanced to the door across the hall, to his bedroom. He straightened his back and kept his eyes down. "My room," he said. "Which Percy will share with me."

Percy's eyes almost popped out of his head and he gasped, horrified. Oh my word, Albie . . . "Des and Robert snore too bad," he said quickly. "I couldn't catch a wink of sleep, so I took this room but now it's yours and I—"

Elsie clapped him on the side of his arm. "No need to explain."

But there was.

There had to be.

He couldn't believe Albie would admit to such a thing. Regardless if Elsie and Clara were involved, Albie had no right . . .

"Excuse me," Percy said, dashing out of the room.

He went to the kitchen and finished pummelling the damper dough. He was mad now, livid, and betrayed. A moment later, Albie came into the kitchen and stood there, watching, waiting . . .

Percy pummelled the dough some more, glaring at him. "How could you say such a thing?"

"She's going to know," he murmured. "They'll be across the hall. They will know we share a room."

"Perhaps I should go back to the bunkhouse. You know what? Maybe I will." Percy threw some flour into the cast-iron pot, then threw the dough in on top of it.

Albie gave him a smirk and stepped in behind him, far too close. He hummed and pressed his lips to the back of Percy's neck, to that one spot that made Percy weak.

"My little fox," he said.

Percy spun to face him, anger flaring in his blood. "I am not."

Albie's smirk became a grin, and he stepped in and pushed Percy against the shelf, their fronts pressed together. He could feel Albie's hardness and it stole his breath, made his knees buckle.

"You won't go to the bunkhouse. You will share my

bed tonight," Albie whispered. "And every night after this."

Then he stepped back and walked out, the front door closing behind him. Percy had to put his hands on his knees; trying to breathe at all was a chore. His head was spinning, and he had a certain ache in his groin he found difficult to ignore.

Part of Percy wanted to move back into the bunkhouse to prove a point. To tell Albie he was not in charge of him like that.

But a bigger part of him wanted to find himself in Albie's bed, in his arms. And that bigger part was always going to win. His body wouldn't allow himself to be denied. He ached at the mere thought of it.

So yes, tonight he would share Albie's bed.

And come tomorrow, he'd be a changed man. He'd be taken and had in every unimaginable way, and heaven help him . . . he couldn't wait.

He had to somehow get through dinner first. And with company, no less. Des and Robert ate in silence, the two women were in their room, and their absence was notable.

Des looked back to the hall every so often. Eventually, he spoke, voice quiet. "Is . . . is she okay?"

"She will be," Albie said. "They'll stay in the house," he added. No explanation, no justification. He said it like the boss, and it was taken as such. Though Percy shovelled in his food so he didn't feel obliged to bring up the subject of room sharing. Albie, thankfully, didn't either.

"The wagon's in good order," Des said. "Their horse is poor, though. She'll do well with some proper feed."

"And Elsie said they'll cook," Robert added, excited. Then he winced. "Not that I don't appreciate your cooking, Albie."

Albie laughed. "For a man that's never cooked a meal in his life, you have such strong opinions on my food. Did you want to cook one night and see how you fare?"

Robert made a face and ducked his head. "Ah, no. I don't think that'd be fair on anyone, least of all the rabbit that gave its life for the meal."

Albie was still smiling. "But I do agree. Not having to worry about cooking means I can spend more time working the farm, and hope to bring in more money."

With two more mouths to feed, he'd need to, Percy thought. Though he didn't say it out loud. It seemed he didn't have to. Everyone nodded and went back to eating.

But then dinner was done and cleared away. Des and Robert had gone back to their quarters, and Elsie had declared goodnight and promised to be up to cook breakfast first thing.

Then it was just Percy and Albie, and only the fire and one lantern for light. Percy could have sworn the house felt smaller, hotter, and the air seemed thicker. He knew they'd be heading to bed soon and what that meant.

His nerves were strung tight; anticipation and a mix of fear were pooling deep in his belly. He wanted it so badly, yet he also wanted to delay it. Put it off, maybe.

Was he ready for this?

Albie fixed the fire and with a knot in his belly, Percy took his books and set them on the table, first ledger open. "Ready when you are," he said.

Albie looked at the books, then at Percy. His eyes were dark and dangerous, full of desire. "I'm ready," he murmured. He strode to the table and closed the book. He collected the lantern and then took Percy's hand and led him to their room.

Percy's feet felt heavy, his legs trembled, and he wasn't sure they'd carry him. His heart thumped so erratically, painfully almost, so nervous he felt a little ill.

Albie set the lantern on the dresser, closed the door, and turned the key with a quiet snick. The sound made Percy gasp and Albie smiled. He came over to him, gently running the back of his finger down Percy's cheek.

"You look scared, little fox," he murmured.

Why did being called that now feel so different to before?

Why did he not care? Why did he like it?

"I am," Percy admitted.

"Do you want this?" Albie asked.

Percy nodded.

And Albie's smile in the dark room was a lifeline. Safe harbour and protection, and Percy's fear ebbed away.

"We've not done this before," Albie said. "So I can only go by what feels right."

Percy nodded again.

Albie cupped Percy's face with one hand, bringing him in for a kiss. Open mouths and hot breaths, their bodies almost touching, and when Percy slid his arms around Albie's lower back and pulled him closer, their bodies pressed tight, hardness against hardness, and Albie groaned into Percy's mouth.

Percy almost withered to the floor, but Albie held him strong and walked him backwards to the bed. He slid Percy's suspenders from his shoulders, then unbuttoned Percy's shirt and let it fall away before he pulled his undershirt over his head. Percy wanted to help Albie with his own shirt, but his fingers trembled too much. Albie made short work of it, tossing the fabric to the floor. Then he studied Percy's naked torso, skimming his hand over his chest, up to his neck, before he took his face in both hands and crashed their mouths together.

Open lips, tongues entwined, and Percy's skin felt

as if he was too close to a fire. Burning hot and yet not hot enough.

Albie pushed him back and laid him down on the bed, kissing him as he did, and finally—finally— pressing their bodies together.

The weight of him was divine, taking Albie's tongue in his mouth, and the press of Albie's arousal against his own made Percy ravenous for more. He raked his hands down his back, feeling his lean, muscular body.

All man.

Albie was bigger than him, stronger, and Percy loved it. Having Albie in control of him was a need Percy didn't even know he had.

He'd never wanted anything more.

His cock was hard, it felt so good, and he writhed for more. He was desperate for more. More contact, more pressure, more touch.

He needed *more*.

And then, as if Albie could read his mind, or perhaps he felt the same, he began to rock his hips, rubbing and grinding. And Percy followed his rhythm, in a dance they'd had no lessons for but their bodies seemed to know the moves.

It was passion and desire. Percy's body ached and pleasure pooled low in his belly, and oh . . .

Oh, heaven help him, the pleasure was climbing, building, his cock now so hard, the pain was exquisite. Percy spread his legs wider, lifted them higher, and

Albie's cockhead pressed something lower and pleasure exploded inside him.

Percy gripped Albie's backside and his back arched as his release hit him.

He'd never known a pleasure like it.

Albie shuddered and stiffened, his body jerking as he succumbed to it.

Percy swore he felt Albie's cock pulsing, and it made him gasp.

He was boneless, panting, and clinging to Albie. He wanted to laugh and weep, and when he shivered, Albie rolled them onto their sides, and he wrapped his arms tight around him.

"Are you . . . are you cold?"

Percy shook his head, unable to stop the giggle. "Far from it. I think I may catch fire."

Albie pulled back then so he could look into Percy's eyes. He pressed his palm to his cheek. "I never imagined this," he whispered. "Not in my wildest dreams."

Percy smiled at him, sleepy now. He waited for regret to creep in or the echo of his childhood priest's sermons on sin . . .

But it never came.

As he lay there in Albie's arms, feeling safe and loved, he couldn't imagine how this was ever wrong.

When nothing in Percy's life had ever felt so right.

"In my dreams," Percy murmured, barely able to

keep his eyes open, "this is where I belong. Promise me something, Albie."

Albie pulled the blankets over them, tightened his arms around him, and kissed the side of his head. "Anything."

"If I'm dreaming," Percy mumbled, "don't ever wake me."

Chapter Eleven

Taking Percy to bed was the most amazing experience of Albie's life. He'd endured hardships and heartbreak and the bleakest grief. And now he'd experienced the purest joy, exquisite pleasure, and dare he say it—dare he think it, even—he felt love.

He was in love with Percy Collins.

The small but feisty, funny, smart man that had walked into his life in the darkest time as if he were a ray of light.

He'd saved him.

Not just from a fight in the saloon, or with his ability to read McAllister's letter and his wise reply.

But Percy had saved Albie from himself, Albie had no doubt of that.

His pride would have been his downfall, but Percy had given him reason to pause, a reason to focus.

And as he lay there in the early morning with a

sleeping Percy still in his arms, with his head on Albie's chest, with the barest of sunlight touching the room, Albie was sure he knew.

This is what poets and painters dedicated their lives to, and now he understood why.

He wanted to tell everyone he knew, he wanted to sing it for the whole world to hear.

He was in love.

But of course, he couldn't declare it for anyone else.

He told himself keeping it private made it more special. It was their secret and no one in the world knew but them.

And that would have to do.

Albie gave the sleeping man a squeeze and another kiss to the top of his head. He wished he could stay in bed with him forever, but they couldn't risk being seen like this.

Not that he expected anyone to barge in, even with the door locked.

He needed to get up.

He pulled on his shirts and realised their underwear might fare better if they removed it next time. He scrubbed at the dried evidence of their night together, pulled on his pants, and unlocked the door.

Elsie and Clara's door was still closed, so he pulled his door closed behind him and tiptoed out. He fixed the fire first, then made his way into the kitchen.

That's when Elsie came in, in her full skirts and fixing her hair. "Oh, morning, Albie," she said. "I wasn't expecting you. Didn't I say we'd do the cooking?"

He smiled at her. "I thought you might need a slow start today, given yesterday's events. Did you sleep well?"

"Better than I have in years," she said.

"And what about you, Albie? You sleep well?" She gave him a wink.

Albie couldn't stop the smile or the heat in his cheeks. "I, uh, don't know what you're talking about."

She smirked, as if her suspicions were confirmed, then made no fuss of it. She turned to the stove and opened the door. "Where's the . . . ?" she said, looking beside the stove, finding the kindling there. She threw some in and blew on it. There were usually some embers in the morning, so it caught without too much effort. "Good," she said, closing the door. "Now where's the . . . ?" she said, looking on the shelf and finding the pot she was after. "Good."

She busied herself, getting familiar with everything in the kitchen as the stove heated. "Clara is better at this than I ever could be," she said. "But I'd like to give her another day's rest, if that suits you."

"Of course," Albie said. "As long as she needs. I'll get some chores done if you don't need me in here."

She shooed him out, and truth be told, Albie was happy and relieved he was no longer expected to cook. It gave him more time to get work done and more time to daydream about the man still asleep in his bed.

Memories invaded his thoughts, of how Percy looked underneath him, how he'd felt. To kiss him like that, to hold him like that. To feel his erection, to watch him as he succumbed to his pleasure.

The look on his face as he did, how his body reacted and arched, and how Albie had followed him directly after.

Albie never imagined life could be like this.

He also had to imagine other things and busy his mind, lest he wanted tented trousers all day.

Until they were in bed again.

He would dare to touch Percy in sacred places tonight. He would hold him in his hand and stroke his release out of him, both of them naked, lying together, no sliver of skin untouched.

Tented trousers would be the least of his worries at this rate. Maybe he and Percy could take the horses and spend the day together far from home, where no one could see them, because night was far too far away.

"Morning," a quiet voice said from the doorway to the barn.

Albie turned to find Percy standing there, uncertain, shy.

"Oh," Albie breathed, the sight of him sending his heart into a rush. "Are you . . . uh . . ." He looked around unsure if anyone else was about. He'd been so lost in his thoughts. In fact, he only just realised he was still standing there with a bucket in his hand. Percy walked up and took it from him. "Did you sleep well?"

Percy smiled, his cheeks a pretty pink. "Very. And you?"

"I didn't want to get out of bed," he whispered. "But I thought it was best if I did."

Percy gave a nod, his blush now crawling down his neck. "I don't think we should talk so openly," he whispered. "I've not seen Des or Robert yet, but I doubt they'll be far away, and I don't want us to get complacent."

Albie understood. "Fair enough."

Percy held the bucket to his chest. "I'll milk the cow. You turn the horses out. And the eggs need collecting, and water from the well."

Albie chuckled. "Yes, boss."

Percy shot him an amused glare, all fire, no heat. But then he got to work and Albie did the same.

As per usual, Percy was right.

There would be time for personal matters later. Even though Albie could barely think of anything else, he did manage to get the morning chores done, and by the time they all sat at the table for breakfast, Albie had worked up an appetite.

And Elsie's porridge was a far cry better than Albie's. He'd expected Robert to make a comment, but he was too busy shovelling it down. Elsie had also made proper bread, not a damper, and they toasted it over the fire with butter and eggs, and even the tea tasted better.

It was the best thing Albie could remember eating.

It made for four happy men, that was for certain.

They set off to get their work done with full bellies and smiles, and the best part was that Albie didn't have to clean up. Elsie shooed him away when he'd offered, and he didn't need telling twice.

"Percy and I will go check the rabbit traps," Albie announced. Given the weather looked clear, Des and Robert were heading to bring the pregnant cows up the paddock closer to the homestead for spring, and they could handle that easily enough.

They set off on foot, not needing their horses, heading to check their traps, walking in silence. Though Albie couldn't help stealing a few glances at Percy as they made their way from the house.

"I was thinking," Albie said. "About last night. In fact, I've not been able to think of much else. I fear I may never want to do anything other than take you to bed."

Percy shot him a bewildered look, his face red, then he looked around as if someone might overhear, his hand to his forehead. "Albie! You can't say such things."

He laughed, looking back at the homestead. "There's no one around. Tell me you've thought of anything but what we did last night."

Percy grabbed his arm, trying to put a hand over Albie's mouth. "I will beg you to not say such things out loud."

Albie dodged his hand but didn't miss the opportunity to sling his arm across Percy's shoulder. Percy quickly shoved him away, then stopped walking. "That's it. I'm going back to catch up with Des and Robert."

Albie burst out laughing, but he took Percy's arm and dragged him forward. "No, please spend the day with me. I promise only my best behaviour from now onward."

Percy glared at him again. "No more talk of . . . that."

"I promise. Until tonight, when we are in bed again. I will be talking of these things and doing so much more."

Percy stopped walking again, this time letting his head fall back with a groan. "Now I'll be thinking of that all day long. How am I supposed to get any work done?"

Albie laughed, and this time hooked his arm around Percy's neck, not letting go as they continued to walk. It felt good to joke and laugh, to be free to act in such a way.

They took their three snared rabbits back to the homestead to a grateful Elsie. Clara was out of her room, sitting by the table and looking a little brighter. She was churning butter, trying to be useful, Elsie had explained with a roll of her eyes and a fond smile.

Percy and Albie turned the hay in the loft and then spent a few hours hunting kangaroo, shooting a decent-sized one that would do for meat, fur, and the remaining carcass for the dogs.

When they came back, carrying the beast between them, they found Elsie tilling soil in the vegetable garden with a long-handled hoe. She stopped, stretched her back, and wiped her brow with the back of her hand. "A good shot, I see," she said with a smile.

Percy laughed. "He missed the first three. But four bullets isn't a bad price for a week's meat."

They dumped the beast on the back veranda, and Albie nodded to the hoe she was holding. She'd been at it a while by the looks of it. "You don't need to do this. One of us men—"

Elsie stomped the hoe into the dirt. "I ain't useless, Albie. And I ain't afraid of a bit of hard work. Did all kinds of jobs at the hotel." She looked skyward. "Plus, it's a nice day for winter. A bit of sun'll do me good."

Albie wasn't sure he was game to argue.

"Well, if you're sure," he said. "If you need anything done, just be sure to say."

"I'll have this garden up to scratch in no time," she said, going back to tilling the soil, tossing weeds to the chickens. "Already got a pile ready for pickling." And sure enough, there was indeed a pile of carrots and turnips.

Albie hadn't realised there were any in need of harvesting. He really wasn't an expert in these things—though he made a note in his mind that he should learn—but he felt so much better now that Elsie was here to right any of his wrongs.

Percy gave Albie a nudge, then he nodded to the kangaroo. "Let's get it strung up."

"Good idea."

They got it strung up in the tree, leaving it for Robert to gut and bleed it, when he got home. He was skilled with a knife, knew how to cut the skin and carve the meat. Albie was never a fan of watching that, truth be told, but it was something he'd now have to learn.

Now that he was the boss.

Something he still had to remind himself of every now and then.

"What's the frown for?" Percy asked, pointing to his own forehead. "You got a line right here."

Albie sighed and took his gloves off, stuffing them into his pocket. "Nothing, really. I just . . ."

"You just what?"

He took a deep breath in and let it out, feeling foolish for admitting this out loud. But if he could share this with anyone, it was Percy. "I'm realising something about myself," he began.

Percy gave his undivided attention. "Oh?"

"About my position here and my ability to do my father's job."

Percy put a hand on Albie's arm. He didn't say anything, but he was waiting patiently for Albie to continue. Silent support that was everything Albie needed from him.

"It occurred to me just now," Albie said quietly, "that I'm both cursed and blessed, in a way."

"Cursed? How so?"

"My inexperience. My lack of know-how. I'd have let those vegetables rot in the ground, probably. I mean, I'd pulled some for us to eat, but it didn't occur to me to pickle them for later. And the meat." He looked at the dead kangaroo. "I had the thought just now that I should have Robert teach me how to butcher it now that I'm the boss. And I should have Elsie show me how she knows what to do with the vegetable garden. And you, helping me with reading." Albie sighed. "I'm cursed by my lack of years to know such things, yet I'm blessed, in a way, that I have people here to teach me."

Percy smiled at him, soft and kind. "You are blessed. And everyone here will happily teach you."

"Do you not think they'll consider it odd to be teaching their boss? Does it not prove the point that I'm too young for this?"

"Not at all," Percy said quickly, seriously. "Where is this self-doubt coming from, Albie? Because the man I see knows how to do more than he gives himself credit for. You seeing just now that you can learn from these good people means you're better than half the men I know. Do you think the likes of McAllister would ever admit that he can learn from a woman?" Percy snorted. "He'd see himself starve before it came to that."

Albie took Percy's words as the comfort they were intended to be and the kindness in his eyes, in his tone. "There you go again, speaking reason and wisdom. I cannot imagine doing this without you, Percy," he whispered. "You've been here for no more than a few weeks and now I struggle to recall a time without you."

Percy blushed a deep red. "There you go, saying things out loud again."

Albie laughed. "Shall I tell you again when we're alone later tonight?"

"Argh," Percy said. "Albie, stop it."

He turned just as two figures came up from down past the homestead. Albie and Percy walked to the stable to meet them, and Des and Robert rode up and dismounted. Percy took their horses into the stable.

"How did you go?" Albie asked.

Des groaned at his leg, giving it a bit of a rub. "All good. They're all in, safe and sound."

"Good, good. Thank you."

"Been busy, I see?" Robert asked, nodding to the kangaroo.

"Thought I'd leave it for you to butcher, actually," Albie said to him. "Might get you to teach me how it's done."

Robert seemed pleased by this. "Sure thing."

"But Albie," Des said. "Gotta tell ya what we saw." Robert nodded, and Albie was immediately intrigued.

"What was it?"

"Mob of wild horses. Down through the valley toward the creek."

"The creek?" That was a fair distance . . . then he realised what that likely meant. "Is there a fence down?"

"Not that we could see," Des answered. "Lord knows where though. Lotta land to cover, lotta fences, Albie. Maybe a tree fell down and took out a run of fencing, I dunno."

"And in the far bottom lot, you said?" Percy asked.

Des gave a nod.

"Shoot." The wind picked up, cold and damp, cutting through them, and Albie shivered with the bite to it. And Des and Robert had been out in it all day. "Come on, this kangaroo can wait. Let's get you both a cup of tea by the fire."

Chapter Twelve

The news of the brumbies was talk around the dinner table. Apparently wild brumbies weren't uncommon in the high country. Over the years, horses got turned out or escaped, and they now ran free in sizeable herds through the mountains.

Albie said his father had spoken of them often, of the damage they did to crops and fences, and how they disrupted cattle and sheep, and other horses, of course.

Not all of Albie's land was fenced. It was too big, too many cliffs, mountains, and rocky outcrops to bother. So where the horses were was on the bottom flats, all open, and for now, Albie wasn't concerned.

"The mob will move on," he'd said. "They probably drink at the river, but it's not likely they're coming up the sheer mountainside anytime soon."

"I remember you mentioning the river before," Percy mused.

Albie nodded. "Echo Creek. This property was named after it. But it's more a river now though it dries up a bit without rain. They must have named it in a dry spell," he said with a wry smile. "It runs through the southwestern part of the property. There are sheer mountain cliffs that cut this place in half. Not much good for farming and probably the reason my father got it for the price he paid. McAllister's land flattens out some, so he can get better crops down, farm more cattle. We've got cliffs with a sheer three-hundred-yard drop, and the access to the flats down below is rugged."

Percy had nodded, not thinking much more of it.

He helped Albie with reading after dinner was cleared away, and they waited until Elsie had bid them goodnight before they turned in.

Percy wasn't so nervous this night. Nerves still tingled along his bones but there was a good dose of anticipation and excitement too.

He had a better idea of what to expect, and he knew now how good it could feel.

And how sleeping in Albie's bed, in his arms, was his favourite part.

Well, almost his favourite.

What Albie did to him was clearly his favourite everything in all the world, ever. He'd made good on his promise to do it better this time, to save them soiling their underwear.

Albie had Percy on his back, kissing him slowly and touching his chest, his stomach, before slipping his hand inside his pants and gripping him.

Percy thought he might die right then.

But then Albie began to stroke him, and he made the shortest work of unravelling Percy. Percy's climax hit him hard and fast. He almost made too much noise, but Albie kissed him, drinking in the sound.

He didn't know if Elsie and Clara heard, nor in that moment did he care.

Albie's touch was heaven.

When his senses returned, when he could finally think again, he offered to do the same for Albie.

So Albie lay on his back, legs spread, and pulled down his pants.

Percy got to see him so clearly, even in the darkened room. He could see the magnificence, the completely arousing sight of another man's manhood. Hard and inviting.

The smell of him was intoxicating, and Percy wrapped his hand around him and began to stroke. Albie gripped the bedding, his hips flexing as he fought for control.

The power Percy held over him in that moment was heady. The way Percy controlled him and watched every flinch of muscle, heard every gasp and groan.

He couldn't begin to say what made him do it. What on earth had possessed him, but Percy leaned in and licked the tip, salt bursting on his tongue.

Albie fisted the bedding, his back arched, and he groaned as he spilled his seed over his belly and down Percy's hand.

Percy had never seen anything like it.

He'd never experienced anything so hedonistic, so absolutely beautiful.

I made him do that. I made him climax like that.

Albie slumped back down, breathing hard, his eyes heavy-lidded, smiling. "Ohhh," he whispered. "What did you do to me?"

Percy wasn't sure what to say. He thought it'd been obvious. "Well, I . . . I don't know why I did that."

Albie laughed, and he sounded drunk. "I think we'll be doing more of that."

Rather happy with himself, Percy cleaned himself up, then Albie, and Albie quickly pulled him into the bed. His arms tight around him, their bodies entwined. Wearing nothing but their long underwear.

Albie's naked chest was so warm against his, and Percy sank down into the mattress, into Albie's embrace. Albie kissed the side of Percy's head. "Goodnight, my love," he murmured.

Percy's heart thumped hard in his chest, and he smiled against Percy's warm skin.

My love.

Albie had called him his love.

Percy's heart felt as if it might burst. He couldn't bring himself to say it back. He could barely speak at all.

"Goodnight."

THE NEXT FEW days passed much the same way. Work during the day, reading and ledgers of an evening, and exploring each other's bodies in bed long after the last lantern had been blown out.

Albie had returned the favour the following night, licking and tasting Percy's length, and he understood why Albie had reacted the way he had.

The second night they licked a little more, sucking a little, and making each other lose their minds in record time.

The more nights that passed, they tried again and ventured a little deeper in unknown territory. Using hands, mouths, writhing bodies, always kissing, always clinging tight to the other as they fell asleep.

And so the week went on.

Clara was feeling much better, looking much better, and happy to be productive. She was even smiling and chatty now, though it was clear she was most comfortable in Elsie's company.

Something Des and Robert didn't need explanation of, apparently. They gave her a polite nod and smile but kept a distance, giving her space as she needed it, and by the end of the week, she was smiling with them too.

Percy knew Albie worried that taking in Elsie and

Clara might be an overstep in the ability to feed and pay everyone, but having them both was a blessing.

Clara took over most of the cooking, while Elsie tended the house, the gardens, chickens, pigs. She'd carry water or hay—no job a man could do that she couldn't, Percy was sure.

But they brought something else with them too. Order and structure and an easiness Percy hadn't expected. Instead of Albie and Percy stopping work and then scrambling to get meals done, they got more work done which made Robert and Des's lives easier too.

And the cooking was so much better. Though Percy's damper and Cocky's Joy had been welcome, even he could admit it paled in comparison to Clara's cooking.

Albie was happy, which made Percy happy, and life at Echo Creek was good. There was no bickering, only laughter, no power struggles, just everyone doing their jobs the best they could.

Though Percy did notice one thing.

When he was helping Albie with his reading—his reading was improving just fine. He was so much better already—but the ledgers . . .

Albie's father's records of income and taxes, and what Albie could add to that in the weeks since his father's passing were lean. Too lean, probably.

They needed money.

Self-sufficiency would only get them so far. If Albie wanted his farm to be successful, if he wanted to prove to those naysayers that he was capable, that he was man enough, something needed to change.

"It doesn't look good, does it?" Albie asked.

He was looking at the same numbers Percy was studying, and he was no fool.

"We'll do better at the next sale," Percy said.

Not wanting to think about how Mr Bailey at the saleyards had duped Albie last time, swindling him out of a fair deal.

Clearly that was where Albie's mind had gone too. "Hmm. Doubtful when the likes of John Bailey is in McAllister's purse."

Percy hated that he was right.

"What about the horses?" Percy hedged. "The wild horses Des and Robert saw."

Albie's gaze shot to his. "The brumbies?"

He nodded. "We could round them up. Take them to the sales. They'd have to be worth a few decent pounds. Keep some for breeding, even."

Albie's eyes danced, first with possibilities, then hardened with reality. "We'd never get them up the mountain."

"So we don't bring them back this way. We can take them around and back into town. Or further south to a saleyard in the next town, and not in Alpine Falls," Percy said, liking the idea of it more and more. "McAllister can't have his hand in pockets in every town, surely."

"I wouldn't put it past him," Albie mumbled. He frowned at the books for a few long seconds, then his eyes met Percy's. "It's not a bad idea. We should think on it and ask Des and Robert." Then he frowned. "Well, I think I know what Des will say. There'll be some name-calling, I'd reckon."

Percy couldn't help but chuckle. "I'd reckon you're right. But there's one thing he'll never be able to call you, Albie, and that's a quitter."

"He might question the size of my brain. And my sanity."

Percy laughed and gave Albie's knee a squeeze. "He'll come around."

Albie smiled but it soon faded. He was serious then, his brow knitted. "You know, I reckon I'd get more for them if they were broken in. I could make good stock horses out of some of them, I'm certain of it." Then he made a face and sighed. "But that'd mean getting them back up the mountains."

Percy closed the books. "We can think on it. It's time for bed."

Albie was quick to stand up. "My favourite part of the day," he whispered.

Percy gave him a playful shove. "Mind your manners."

"I'd rather mind yours," he murmured with a wicked gleam to his eye. "If you know what I mean."

Percy pointed his finger up at him, aiming for stern but unable to stop from smiling. "I know exactly what you mean," he whispered.

Albie grinned at him, part devil. Percy was sure of it. He picked up the lantern from the table. "To bed with you, my love."

Percy gasped. "Shh or someone will hear."

Albie simply laughed, took Percy's hand and led him to their room.

———

PERCY WOKE EARLY, his body urging him awake.

As if he didn't have enough last night, with Albie's hands and his mouth. But now he found himself on his side, with Albie pressed in close behind him, his arms around him . . . and his arousal pressed against Percy's behind.

It shouldn't feel so good.

Should it?

Why did he feel the urge to rock back, to feel more, to roll his hips? Why did he want Albie to grind against him, to slide his erection against his bottom? Percy had never imagined such a thing, but now . . . to feel him so close, so hard . . .

Why did he want to feel Albie inside him?

He ached with the need for it. He burned, desire deep in his core, his balls drew down, his erection filled.

He wriggled back a little, not meaning to. His body moved on its own, desperate.

And he felt the moment Albie woke. He froze, his hand going to Percy's hip, holding him still.

"Morning," Albie said, his voice rough.

"Mm." Percy hummed. "Morning."

"Been awake long?"

Percy, desperate and shameless, took Albie's hand from his hip and brought it down to his crotch. "This long."

Albie groaned out a laugh, but he rolled his hips, grinding against Percy's buttocks as he stroked Percy's length. "You seduce me," he murmured, his lips now at the back of Percy's ear.

Percy backed up, rubbing his behind against Albie's arousal as Albie fisted Percy's. "Albie, I need . . ." He wasn't sure what he needed. He just needed more.

Albie's hand was slick with Percy's arousal, his slide over his erection now wet, and it felt so, so good. And when Albie's thrust against his bottom got harder and faster, with a kiss to the back of Percy's neck, fireworks exploded behind Percy's eyelids, his body rigid as his pleasure spilled out of him.

Albie's hand was on his hip then, holding him still while he ground his erection, hard and hot against the cleft of Percy's buttocks, and then he stilled, groaning as hot seed spilled onto his back.

Percy had never been so aroused.

He'd never known desire so consuming, so blinding.

They lay there breathless, the silence far too loud.

"You can wake me like that any day," Albie murmured. "Wowzers."

But as reality dawned and light filled the room with the sunrise, Percy was filled with something he didn't like. It took him a moment to put a name to it, but once he realised what it was, there was no going back.

Shame.

He tried to move forward, needing some space.

Albie pulled away first. "Let me get you cleaned up. Stay there."

Percy wasn't sure he could move anyway. He felt leaden with the weight of what they'd just done.

What he'd instigated.

What he'd begged for.

Albie came back with the rag and wiped Percy's back clean, then his front. Then he took a clean cloth, and wetting it in the basin in their room, he wiped him down.

Albie studied Percy's face for a moment before putting his finger to his chin and raising his face. Percy pulled away, unable to meet his eyes.

Albie went to his knees in front of him, in nothing but his long johns, hands on Percy's legs, looking up into his face. "What is it? Did I hurt you?"

Percy shook his head. "No."

"Then what? Please tell me. I thought you wanted that. I thought—"

"I *did* want that," Percy said. "Exactly that, and at the same time, not even that. I wanted more. I wanted such things that . . . dirty things, wrong things. I wanted . . ." He trailed off with a shake of his head. "Albie, I'm sorry."

Albie put his hand to Percy's cheek. "Don't ever apologise. You've nothing to be sorry for. This is new to both of us, and we're finding our way. If we do something you don't like, we don't do it again."

"But I did like it. Too much. I wanted you to . . ."

He couldn't even bring himself to say it out loud.

Albie held Percy's face and brought him in for an embrace, holding him. "Whatever troubles you, my love, you can tell me."

My love.

Oh, how Albie called him that warmed him through, every time. And perhaps hiding his face in Albie's neck made it easier to admit.

"I wanted you to have me as you would a woman," he whispered, his eyes squinted shut. Albie froze, and when he tried to pull back, Percy clung to him tighter. "Please don't look at me."

So Albie rubbed his back instead and let out a shaky breath. "I'm no expert in the anatomy of the female body," he said. "But I don't . . ." He froze again. "Oh."

Now it was Percy who tried to pull away and it was

Albie who refused to let go. "See?" Percy said. "I told you it was wrong."

Then Albie gripped his shoulders, pulled him back, and met his gaze. Percy had expected to see disgust or blame in Albie's eyes, but no. What he saw was anger.

"Percy Collins, you listen to me," he said sternly. "Nothing we do is wrong. Not one thing. You cannot sit there and tell me, after all that we've shared, after all that we've found in each other, that any part of us is wrong."

Percy blinked in surprise. He hadn't expected such words or the honesty in which he'd said them. "I wanted you to sodomise me," he whispered. "Albie, I wanted it so much I burned with the need of it. How is that right?"

Albie was surprised, clearly, but it was quickly replaced with that stubborn determination Percy had grown to love. "Percy, listen to me. I'm not a religious man, and neither was my father. He swore that any god that would take his wife and unborn daughter was no god worth praying to. And here I am now, saying to you that any god who would tell us our love is wrong is no god I believe in."

Oh, how Percy wished he could believe that.

"Now, I don't know if"—Albie continued, his cheeks now pink—"me taking you as I would a woman is something we'll even do. To be frank, Percy, I hadn't given it a thought. Everything we've done so far is more than I ever dared dream I'd have. If it's all we ever do, I'll die a happy man."

"Die?"

"Fifty years from now," Albie said with a smile. "Old and grey, here in this very house, with you."

Percy could have cried at that. He almost did. His eyes watered and his nose burned. He could barely nod.

Albie cupped his face and searched his eyes. "All I want is you. And if you do want me to take you that way, I will."

Percy gasped. "Albie!"

"What? You mentioned it, and now I'm not entirely sure I can think about anything else."

Percy buried his face in his hands, mortified. But still grateful that Albie could make light of it. "I'm so embarrassed."

Albie laughed and got to his feet. "You'll be a whole lot more embarrassed should Elsie come in here looking for us. Come on, let's get dressed." He picked up his trousers and tossed Percy's to him. "As much as I like the view of you in your underpants," he said with a smirk. "I don't think the others would agree."

Percy was embarrassed, yes. But as he dressed, he reassessed how he was feeling now and realised he no longer felt shame.

Albie had comforted him, and reassured him, and now even made him feel better by offering a joke.

As Percy fixed his shirt and buttoned his

suspenders onto his waistband, Albie slid the strap over his shoulder, and it was such a caring, such an intimate thing to do.

Percy looked up in Albie's face, seeing Albie's eyes so soft for him it made his heart flutter. "I don't know how I ever got so lucky," Percy admitted in a whisper. "To find you."

Albie smirked and tapped his finger lightly to Percy's chin. "I was just thinking the same thing."

With a sweet kiss, Albie went out first, and as Percy pulled his woollen cap on, he heard Albie laugh with Elsie and Clara in the kitchen. He didn't feel facing them was appropriate—as if they knew all too well what he and Albie had done this morning to make them this late—Percy snuck out the front door, taking his coat with him as he went.

He went straight to the barn to tend to the horses, giving them fresh feed and water. Ox nipped at his knitted cap, pulling it off his head and tossing it, neighing with delight.

"Oh, you devil," Percy said, scampering to go pick it up, just as Des laughed from the doorway.

"He's a cheeky one," Des said, walking in.

Percy picked up the cap, dusting the hay off it, grateful it had only landed in hay. "I think he was aiming for the dung pile."

Des laughed even more, but then he nodded to the way he'd come. "I think the sow's about ready to birth any day. We should get working on the new pen."

"Excellent," Percy said. Then he figured now was a good time to bring this up. "So, I was thinking . . ."

Des cut him a look. "No sentence ever ends well when it begins with that."

Percy chuckled. "About those wild brumbies."

"What about them?" he asked, roughly the same time he assumed the answer. "No. No, don't even go thinking it. And don't go putting crazy ideas into Albie's head."

"Too late."

Des groaned. "It's too risky. Too dangerous."

"We need the money."

"Then we work harder. Chasing brumbies through these mountains will get you nothing but killed."

"I suggested we take 'em further south, out of the mountains and away from McAllister's grubby hands at the saleyards," Percy tried. "But then Albie thought maybe if we brought them back here, we could break 'em in and get more for them. Good money."

Des cast his gaze out across the misty morning, at the clouds clinging to the mountains like a winter cloak, and sighed. "I promised his dad I'd look after him," he said quietly. There was a sadness in his eyes as he recalled a memory only he could see, until he shook it away and refocused on Percy. "If we need more money, we work harder."

Percy wasn't sure what to say. He wasn't even sure he could speak around the lump in his throat, the ache in his chest.

Des loved Albie like a son; Percy could see that now.

He wished he hadn't brought it up, not with Des right now, and not with Albie last night.

He gave a nod and let it go.

———

THEY DID WORK HARDER. Not that Des made any mention of it, he just pushed the men for more. He squeezed out every minute of daylight he could, and Percy did everything he could do to help.

Three days later, they had the new pig pen built. Post and rails, hand-sawed, holes dug, and a shelter with a scrap-tin roof. Another calf was born early and abandoned by the cow, so it was now in the stables with the dairy cow, and there were two new chicks in the coop, and some of Elsie's seedlings near ready to sprout in pots of soil in the mudroom.

Life was busy.

Percy never mentioned the brumbies again, though he did still help Albie with his reading and with the sums in the ledger. Albie was getting so good at it, Percy doubted he'd need his help much longer but he was reluctant to say that.

He enjoyed their time at the table, knees and shoulders pressed together over the books.

Percy had been reluctant the last few nights in bed too. Too afraid to start something that might end up with what he'd wished for. So he'd opted for cuddling and falling asleep in Albie's strong arms instead.

Well, he hadn't been so reluctant when Albie had an erection problem that morning when he'd woken up. He sat on the edge of the bed, as if he didn't want to trouble Percy, and Percy was all too happy to kneel between his feet and take his *problem* into his mouth.

And for the first time, he hadn't pulled back when Albie spilled his seed.

Percy drank it instead.

Hot and salty, but oh-so rewarding.

Albie had fallen back onto the bed, groaning out a laugh. But given it was already sunup, he made the promise to return the favour that night.

Percy had to sit through breakfast with tented trousers as he couldn't seem to think of anything else. It didn't help that Albie was smiling as he ate his porridge, and he swore he caught Des looking between them.

When they'd barely finished their cups of tea, the dogs began to bark and Robert got to the door first. He opened it to show two men riding toward the house at a gallop.

Something was wrong.

The four men rushed outside to greet them. Elsie stayed inside by the door, hidden from view, and Clara was nowhere to be found. Percy didn't blame her.

Because the two men who rode up to the veranda, not even getting off their horses, were Williams and

McAllister's foreman, Bill Kelly. They pulled hard on their horses, turning in a tight circle.

It was Kelly who spoke, his Irish accent strong. "McAllister's youngest, little Christopher, is missing. Was not in his bed this morning. We searched the barn, the stables, the pens. He's nowhere. Don't know how long he's been gone. Early morning, we suspect."

Albie pointed to the stables. "Robert, saddle the horses." In a flash, Robert turned and raced to toward the stables.

"He's a wild one," Kelly added. "Three years old, not an ounce of fear in him."

"Did you check the well?" Des asked.

The two men stared at him, Percy felt ill at the thought, and it was Williams who nodded. "Yes. Thank the Lord above, it was covered. But we checked it all the same."

Albie was already pulling on his coat. "We'll head adjacent to your boundary."

Kelly gave a tip of his hat. "Much obliged."

"Fire a shot in the air if you find him," Williams said.

Now, Percy had no time for Williams, and he knew no one here missed him now he was gone. He was also responsible for trying to force himself upon Clara, so Percy could only imagine the restraint it took Elsie not to come outside swinging for his head.

But there was a child missing.

McAllister's child, no less. And no one here was

overly fond of McAllister either. But in times such as these, differences were put aside and people banded together to help.

Percy, Albie, Robert, and Des rode out, southward, as Albie had said they would. It was likely that the kid walked out the back of his house and kept on walking, so that was the direction they went.

Albie and Percy went left, closer to McAllister's property line, while Robert and Des veered slightly right.

"Christopher!" Albie called out, top of his lungs.

Then Percy did too, and after a few seconds, they heard Robert, some distance away, yell the same.

"How far can a three-year-old walk?" Percy wondered out loud. "In this scrub, no less."

It was rough terrain. Granite boulders, trees and shrubs, small valleys, tall grasses.

"I spent days on end in these parts," Albie said. "As a small child, not much older than three. Sunup till sundown. I could play and hide all day. I could get some distance. Some days I was lucky my horse knew which way was home."

Percy gave a bit of a nod. "We lived on flatter, low ground. But my days were mostly spent at school. On weekends I helped out on the farm, never really venturing too far." Then he shrugged. "Until I ventured here."

Albie gave him a smile. "I'm grateful for that."

Percy felt himself blush, but he blamed it on the

bitter cold. He pulled his collar up against the bite of wind and sleet . , . until he remembered there was a small child out in this weather. No doubt ill-dressed for it.

And with a sense of urgency, he pushed Bandit a little harder and called out the boy's name.

CHAPTER THIRTEEN

THE WEATHER TURNED BAD. THE LOW CLOUDS made it impossible to tell the difference between sleet and snow. Percy had veered off a little, yelling for the boy, though Albie kept an eye on him. The last thing he needed was for him to get lost too.

Albie pushed closer to where his property met McAllister's. He had spent his childhood in these mountains. Clearing his mind in the tall trees and long grasses for days at a time. Not so much in this poor weather though.

And he didn't like the idea of a small child being lost out here at all.

The thick tree cover afforded a break in the wind at least, though the cold seemed to come from the ground up. Once it got in your bones, it was hard to warm up.

He thought he heard other men call out the boy's name, though he couldn't be sure if the mountains

were playing tricks on his ears, the way these mountains and the wind sometimes would. Bearings and
thoughts could get all turned around, and when it was
this cold and wet, your mind couldn't see reason.

Even Albie wasn't sure how far they'd gone now.
Too far, perhaps. He knew there was a drop-off coming
up soon, the ridgeline, but surely a small child couldn't
have come this far on foot. He wondered if they should
double back and spread out some more when he heard
Percy yell. "Albie!"

There was an urgency in his tone that put Albie on
alert. He spun Minnie to the sound and she fought her
way through ferns and trees, through a gully, and up on
the other side and through the thicket, he saw Bandit
by the cliff edge . . . minus Percy. Albie raced over,
sliding off his horse before she'd even stopped, and he
rushed to the edge. "Percy!"

"Down here," he yelled.

And when he peered over, he saw Percy on a ledge
holding a small boy with a muddy and tear-streaked
face. He'd taken his own coat off, wrapped the boy up,
though Albie could see his muddy, scratched and
bleeding bare feet.

Barefoot. Out here.

Then he noticed a line of blood running down
Percy's face.

"I'll get you up," Albie said.

The ledge wasn't that far down, maybe eight feet,

nine at best. And even though they couldn't see anything over the edge for the misty clouds, Albie knew the drop-off wasn't the longest in these parts, not by a long shot. But it'd mean death if a man were to fall off it, much less a child. And while it wasn't a sheer rock face, the earth was now slippery mud, and Albie could see the slide marks that Percy had made on his descent.

Albie took the rope from his saddle and rushed back, tying one end to Minnie and dropping the other end over the edge to Percy. "Hold on. We'll pull you up."

Percy clung onto the boy with his left arm and with his right, he wound the rope around his wrist, gripping tight. "Ready."

Albie urged Minnie forward, nice and steady, and slowly, inch by torturous inch, they pulled Percy and Christopher up.

Albie helped him up the last part, desperately checking both their faces, ensuring himself that they were okay. "You're bleeding," Albie said to Percy, wiping at the blood on the side of his face.

"I'm fine," Percy said quickly. He was pale, scared, his hands shaking, teeth chattering. He was without his coat now, it was still wrapped around the boy, and Christopher still clung to his neck. Albie wasn't game to separate them.

"Take Minnie," Albie said. "She knows her way back." He helped him up into the saddle, handing him the reins. "Go. I'll be right behind you." He gave Minnie a tap on the rump to get her moving.

He wound up his rope and ran over to Bandit, urging him to follow. Then he remembered . . .

Fire your rifle if you find him.

He took out the rifle, aimed it at the grey sky, and pulled the trigger. The sound was deafening in the silence, echoing through the valley. Birds took the skies, crying as they went, and Bandit skittered but Albie managed to hold him.

He knew that would send all the men homeward, and he needed to be one of them. He dug Bandit in the flanks and headed back as fast as the terrain would allow.

Bandit was a good horse, but Minnie was mountain-bred. She'd get Percy back unassisted, able to jump rocks and gullies like a billy goat. All Albie could hope for was that Bandit got them home uninjured. He was careful not to push him too hard, but the urgency he felt—that panic in behind his sternum—found it hard to ease up.

He caught a glimpse of Percy's white shirt through the trees every now and then, and he was mad that he'd not thought to bring a blanket or an extra coat.

He'd been too focused on finding the boy alive. He hadn't given much thought about what would happen if or when they did. They'd be lucky if Percy didn't catch his death out here, let alone that small boy wearing only pyjamas and no shoes . . .

Albie tried not to think about that.

They'd found the boy. That was all that mattered.

Albie gained some ground and wasn't so far behind Percy now, but as they got closer, he realised they weren't heading for home. They were heading for McAllister's.

Smart.

Whereas Albie's first thought was to head for his house, Percy knew Christopher's parents must be about beside themselves.

As the trees cleared into grazing land, Percy was still at a gallop, up ahead now, and before Albie came out of the tree line, some of McAllister's men were racing home too. They fell in behind Percy, and Albie followed them. Bandit was faster on flat ground, and he'd almost caught up to them by the time they reached the house.

Mrs McAllister and some staff were on the back veranda, Mrs McAllister crying as she saw her boy.

Percy slid off Minnie, rushing the boy to his mother, and they were ushered inside. Ignoring the looks from McAllister's men, Albie was quick to follow through the door where Percy had gone.

The house was large and worth more than Albie could ever dream of. He followed the sound of voices to the extravagant living room where Mrs McAllister knelt by the fire, holding Christopher. The boy was crying, covered in mud and scratches.

"Quickly, prepare a bath," she ordered, and one of the maids dutifully dashed out of the room.

Albie's gaze fell on Percy, who stood there, unsure of what to do. He was also covered in mud, wet from the sleet, but his wrist was red raw from the rope, Albie realised. The skin on his neck, face, and arms was flushed dark pink from the cold.

Albie picked up Percy's coat and put it around his shoulders, and Percy blinked up at him, almost surprised to see him. "You're frozen to the bone," he said.

Mrs McAllister looked up then. "Yes, please, sit by the fire. Get these men some tea, quickly," she said to another maid who disappeared. Then she pulled on Percy's coat. "Please, come sit by the fire." Then she took a better look at Percy. "Oh, you have blood . . . Does your head hurt?"

Percy smeared the blood with the back of his hand. "No, I'm fine. Just a scratch."

She nodded and turned her attention back to her boy. Her face was gaunt, her eyes puffy, cheeks blotched. Albie had only met her a handful of times, never looking anything less than impeccable. She'd clearly had a harrowing day, thinking the very worst.

"Where was he? Where did you find him?" she asked. "I'm forever in your debt—"

The front door swung open and McAllister stormed inside, stopping when he saw his child safe in his wife's arms. He stopped again when he saw Albie and Percy but then rushed to his wife's side. He cradled the boy's head before he looked at Albie, then at the state of Percy, and he quickly deduced who'd found his boy.

"Where was he?"

Albie got to his feet, his manners not letting him stay seated. But just then, the maid rushed in with two cups of hot tea. Percy's hands were still shaking, and he was reluctant to take it. "My hands are too dirty," he said.

"Nonsense," Mrs McAllister said kindly. "Drink up, dear. You need it."

Albie sipped the tea, the warmth spreading through his belly. Then he nodded to Percy for him to do the same before he answered McAllister. "The first ridgeline on my land from yours. Over the ledge, eight feet down."

Mrs McAllister put her hand to her mouth, instant tears welled in her eyes. "Oh my word."

McAllister paled. "He made it that far?"

Two maids carried a small bathtub of water out to the fire, and it was then Albie realised Marcy was one of them. She met his gaze briefly before lowering her head and rushing back to the kitchen. She came back out a moment later with a kettle of steaming water and added it to the tub.

Mrs McAllister stripped Christopher down, and both Albie and Percy turned their attention to McAllister. He looked a man wrung tight, and Albie even felt a bit sorry for him.

"It was you who went down to get him?" McAllister said to Percy.

He gave a nod. "Yes, sir."

"Mighty brave of you, son."

Percy kept his eyes down and shook his head. "I didn't think on it, sir. I called out his name and heard him crying. I saw him down there and just slid down to get him, not thinking of myself, sir. I just had to get to him." He shrugged. "I couldn't see over the edge for the clouds. It was probably just as well. Albie had his horse pull us up."

McAllister nodded, then barked an order at Marcy. "Get this boy cleaned up. Clean that wound on his wrist and the blood on his face."

Albie wanted to bristle at the word *boy*, but he knew now was not the time.

"I'm okay, sir," Percy said quietly, pulling at the sleeve of his shirt to hide his wrist. "Just glad your boy's safe."

Christopher was now sitting in the bathtub, washed and clean, eating a lump of bread. Marcy came back with a basin of warm water and a clean cloth, setting it down by Percy's feet. She began gently washing his hands, and Albie wished it was him doing that.

But then Evalyn was there with a fancy China

plate of bread, butter, and jam, offering it to them. "Albie," she said quietly.

He took the plate but directly offered it to Percy. He was still looking a little too pale for Albie's liking. He took a piece of the bread and managed a bite, but then he held onto it instead of eating some more. His tea looked barely touched.

It was then Albie noticed it wasn't a scratch on his head where the blood had come from, but a sizeable bump. Had he banged it on the way down to the ledge?

"I think we should get him home," Albie said, taking the cup and bread from him. He handed them off to a waiting maid and pinched Percy's chin to get a better look at the bump above his temple. It wasn't bleeding now, thankfully, but there was quite a large egg on his head.

"The doctor's been called for," another maid said.

McAllister, now seeing the bump on Percy's head, looked at Albie. "I'll send the doctor over when he's done here."

He wanted to say it wasn't necessary, but this was for Percy . . .

Bill Kelly walked in then. "I've taken the liberty to tend to your horses," he said, looking right at Albie.

"Thank you," Albie said. And he meant it. Kelly was a good man. "But we'll be going now." He gave McAllister a nod, then offered a parting smile to Mrs McAllister. "I hope young Christopher will be fine."

"Thank you," she said, looking between them both. "Thank you."

Albie took Percy's arm and helped him to his feet. "Are you well enough?"

Percy, pale and dazed, met his gaze and gave a nod. "I'm fine."

Albie didn't believe that. And he wanted nothing more than to get Percy home, cleaned up, and tucked into bed.

McAllister took a money clip from his inside coat pocket and counted out some notes. "I promised thirty pounds to anyone who found him," he said. "I'm a man of my word."

Albie wanted to tell him to keep it. Actually, he wanted to tell him to eat it. But McAllister handed the money to Percy.

Rightfully so, given he *was* the one who found him.

Part of Albie wished Percy would decline the offer, but it wasn't Albie's call to make. Percy took the money with a nod. "I'd have done it for nothing," he said quietly. "But this is appreciated, sir. Thank you."

Albie gave McAllister a tight nod and ushered Percy out the front door.

"Bring their horses," McAllister hollered, and before they got to the edge of the veranda, one of his men led Minnie and Bandit toward them.

Albie noticed Williams and Fitzgerald standing by, watching them, with a look of distaste on their faces. Were they mad that they'd not found the boy and scored the money? Or mad that it was Percy and Albie who had?

McAllister was on the veranda then, pointing at Williams and Fitzgerald. "What are you standing there for? I told you already to make a start on those fences!"

Albie helped Percy onto Bandit, then swung himself up onto Minnie. He tipped his hat at McAllister, then gave Williams and Fitzgerald a smug nod as they scurried like rats across the yard to one of the work sheds.

And as much as he'd have liked to bask in that moment, his main concern was getting Percy home. It wasn't an overly long ride but the weather was setting in, low and bitterly cold, and Percy seemed to be fading fast.

They rode into their farm, Des and Robert rushing out to meet them. "I was worried about ya both," Des said to Albie. Until he saw Percy and helped him off his horse. "Jeez, kid, what happened?"

"He was the one who found the boy," Albie explained, climbing down off Minnie. He was quick to grab Percy. "He's in a state. Cold, shock, I'm not sure. He has a large bump on his head."

"I'll take these two," Robert said, leading the horses toward the barn.

Des went ahead, limping on his bad leg, to the front door where Elsie met him. "We'll need some hot water, some tea, maybe some soup." He held the door for them, and Albie helped Percy inside. He considered putting him by the fire but thought bed might be a better option.

He helped him sit down on the bed, Elsie helping untie his boots, and Des stood in the doorway.

Did he see their clothes by the hamper? Did he see the bed rumpled for two?

Albie would have to worry about that later.

"I'll get a wash basin," Elsie said, ducking out of the room.

Albie shucked out of his coat and threw it toward the dresser, then put his hand to Percy's face. "I need to take your shirt off. It's wet."

Percy gave a nod. "Sorry. Just a bit . . . tired," he said, slow-blinking.

Albie pulled Percy's suspenders off with a familiar ease, followed by his shirt. Then he urged him gently to lay down. "Take it easy," Albie said quietly. "Gonna get you cleaned up."

He undid Percy's pants and pulled them off him. Realising Des was still at the door, Albie pulled the blankets up to cover him. Elsie came back with the wash basin, and Albie took it from her. "I need more blankets," he said. "He's cold to the bone."

She gave a nod and disappeared again, and Albie took the washcloth and wrung the warm water from it. He sat on the edge of the bed and taking in Percy's beautiful sleeping face, he ever so gently wiped at the bump on the side of Percy's head.

"What happened?" Des asked. "Percy found the boy?"

Albie nodded. "Yes. He was over the edge of the first cliff. Percy went down to get him. Must have hit his head on the way down. Lucky he didn't fall off."

Albie couldn't bear the thought . . .

"We heard the gunshot," Des said, still at the doorway. "We came back, and when you didn't follow, we were worried. Robert was about to go back looking for ya's."

"Sorry," Albie said. "I had Minnie pull Percy and Christopher up. Then I put them on her because she'd know her way back. Percy had the sense to ride straight to McAllister's. Mrs McAllister was about beside herself with worry."

Elsie came in with a blanket from her bed and draped it over Percy. "I'll go see how his tea's going."

"Might just keep it warm for him," Albie said. "He wasn't up for eating or drinking at McAllister's. I think he needs some rest. I'll just get him cleaned up first, then I'll join you."

Elsie gave Albie's shoulder a squeeze. "Call out if you need."

She collected Percy's wet and dirty clothes from the floor, ushered Des away from the doorway, and she closed the door behind them. And then in the dimly lit bedroom, Albie wiped Percy's forehead, his cheek, his jaw, taking in the lines of his face. He swiped his thumb across Percy's cheekbone, cradling him gently. "Oh, my love."

Percy's eyes opened slowly, took a second to focus, and then he smiled. "You."

"I'm here." Albie nodded, cupping his face and planting a soft kiss on his lips. "You gave me quite a scare. Rest easy, now. We'll get you some tea and soup later if you're up for it."

"Head hurts," he mumbled, his eyes drifting closed again.

"Go to sleep," Albie whispered. "I'll be right here."

When Percy's breaths evened out and deepened, Albie pulled the blankets down and, with the warm washcloth, began giving him a bath.

First, his face and neck, his chest, then his hands, to properly wash away the mud and dirt. Then he gently patted the rope marks on his wrist.

He loved this man. This body, this face. And seeing him lie so still now made him miss his smile so much. The way his eyes would shine when he laughed, the way his blond hair would shine in the sunlight.

Percy just needed to sleep, Albie reminded himself. He'd be right as rain tomorrow.

With that in mind, he pulled the blankets back up and tucked him in safe and sound. He kissed his forehead, took the washbasin of dirty water, and went back into the living room.

Robert was there now too, and all eyes landed on Albie.

"How is he?" Elsie asked as she took the washbasin from him.

"He's sleeping," Albie said, wiping his hands on his trouser pants. "He took a knock to the head, it seems. McAllister said he'd send the doctor over, but we'll see."

Albie would believe it when he saw it.

"What did McAllister say?" Des asked.

"He was grateful." Albie shrugged. "Though I don't doubt it hurt his pride some that it was me and Percy who brought the boy back."

He considered telling them that McAllister paid Percy thirty pounds, but that wasn't his story to tell.

"Mrs McAllister was very relieved and upset," Albie said. "Understandably so."

Clara put some plates on the table. "Please come eat," she said quietly. "You all must be cold and hungry."

Albie gave her a nod and a smile. "Thank you."

They sat, and after a few bites, Robert asked, "Was the boy okay?"

Albie chewed and swallowed his mouthful. "He appeared to be. Wearing pyjamas and no shoes. He had scratches all over him, but he was eating bread in the bath when we left."

"Kids are resilient," Des said. "I remember you being not much older than that, going out into the scrub on your own. Never went barefoot though, right?"

Albie smiled at him. "Not in winter."

"And he went over the edge of the first ridgeline you said?" Des clarified.

Albie nodded, and Robert shook his head in amazement. "Damned lucky."

"Very." Albie took a sip of tea. "McAllister was yelling at Fitzgerald and Williams to start making fences as I was leaving. Got a good deal of satisfaction out of seeing them scurry off like rats."

Des and Robert chuckled. "Fences, huh?" Des asked.

Albie shrugged. "Yeah. I dunno if it'll keep his kid in, but if he wants to run a fence line along the length of my land, I won't stop him."

Des smirked at that, but then it faded. "As long as he doesn't claim land that ain't his."

Albie hadn't thought of that. He sighed. Another worry for another day.

He had enough to worry about right now.

AFTER DINNER when Albie was helping Elsie and Clara clear away the table, he heard Percy cough, followed by a retching sound.

He raced for the room and found Percy trying to sit up, covering his mouth. Thankfully Elsie followed Albie in with the washbowl for Percy to be sick in.

He'd hardly eaten all day so there wasn't much to expel, but he was cold and clammy, pale.

Albie gave him some fresh water to sip, and he sagged back onto the bed with a groan. Albie wiped a clean washcloth over his face while Elsie replaced the washbasin, Clara watched from the doorway.

"What can we do?" she asked.

"I'll sit up with him tonight," Albie said. "And watch over him."

Clara frowned but nodded. "I wish I could do more."

Same, Albie thought. *Same.*

And that's what Albie did. He sat by the bed and watched Percy sleep. He had no more bouts of vomiting and he did seem to rest more peaceful in the early hours, and sometime around three o'clock in the morning, Albie must have nodded off and almost fell off the chair. He climbed into the other side of the bed, just to rest his eyes for a moment . . .

And woke up when daylight was peeking through the blinds and there were pots and pans clanging from the kitchen. And Percy was tucked into his side, his head on his shoulder.

Albie rubbed Percy's arm, his back, and kissed the top of his head. He was still asleep, but he had moved during the night, to curl into Albie's side, and he took that as a good sign.

He was loath to wake him up but he needed to pull his arm free.

"Morning," Percy mumbled.

Albie's heart sang, his whole body flooded with relief. "Oh, good morning. How are you feeling?"

"Head hurts a bit, but I think I'm hungry."

Albie gave him a squeeze, kissing his head once more with smiling lips. "I'll get you something."

Percy rolled onto his back. "Why am I undressed?"

"Do you not remember?"

He was quiet a second. "No." Albie got out of bed and Percy looked at him. "Why are you fully dressed?"

"Because I spent most of the night in the chair beside you, fearing you'd be sick again in your sleep."

His eyes narrowed in confusion and he tried to sit up, but he sagged back down, his hand to his head. "Ow."

"Okay, stay right there," Albie said. "I'll bring you breakfast."

He rushed out to where Clara and Elsie were in the kitchen, standing a little too close together. Elsie was fixing a whisp of Clara's hair and Albie cleared his throat, smiling. "Sorry to interrupt."

Clara ducked away, hiding behind Elsie, but Elsie simply smiled right back at him. "You don't look too sorry, Albie."

He chuckled. "Percy's awake, and he's hungry. I was hoping to fetch him some porridge and tea."

"Ah, a good sign," Elsie said. "Yes, I'll bring it in for him if you like?"

"I can take it," Albie said. "He's still not dressed, so

he might be embarrassed, that's all. And his head still hurts. He can't sit up just yet."

Elsie smirked as she dished up some oats. "Then you best spoon-feed him, given he's near naked, huh?"

Clara's eyes went wide and she nudged Elsie. "Elsie, shush with that."

Albie smiled despite the heat in his cheeks. "Well yes, I best feed him." He cleared his throat, his mouth dry. "The man needs his strength."

Elsie put the plate of porridge on a tray and set a teacup beside it. Then she gave Albie a wink. "I bet he does."

Clara gasped and swatted Elsie with her kitchen towel, and Albie's face burned red. But this was an acknowledgement out loud of what they'd both assumed before now.

That Elsie could take a private moment to fix Clara's hair any time she wanted, and yes, Albie would look after, feed, and sleep next to a near-naked Percy.

With a smile and a nod to Elsie, Albie took the tray into his room. Percy was dozing again but he woke at the sound of the door snicking closed. Albie set the tray on the foot of the bed and helped Percy sit up, slowly and gently, with a pillow at his back.

"How do you feel now?" Albie asked. "Do you need a moment for your head to feel right?"

Percy sighed and blinked slowly. "I'm fine."

Albie wasn't so sure of that. He pulled the tray

closer, scooped up a spoonful of porridge from the side of the plate, and lifted to Percy's mouth.

"I can feed myself," Percy mumbled.

"I know. But let me look after you," Albie said gently. "I looked after you all night. I don't intend on stopping now." He met Percy's eyes. "Or ever. I will always look after you."

Percy smiled shyly, and took the mouthful of porridge. Then he closed his eyes, letting his head rest on the headboard. Albie could see the bump at his temple was less swollen, but it now had more colour.

"You took a knock to the head," Albie said. "Must have been when you went down the ledge."

Percy opened his eyes, focused on Albie. "I don't remember much. Just parts."

Albie traced his fingers over Percy's wrist where the rope burns still showed. Percy looked at them as if he was seeing them for the first time. "Oh."

"Do they hurt?"

"No."

Albie offered him more porridge, and he ate half the bowl before refusing anymore. He sipped his tea but he'd had enough, and Albie didn't want to push him.

Percy settled back down in the bed. "Tired. But I feel better, thank you."

"Clara washed your clothes," Albie said. "And dried them by the fire. I'll bring them in. But you can rest all day. Sleep as you need to."

Percy looked too tired to argue.

Albie left him to sleep, doing some morning chores before he sat down to breakfast with the others. He told them Percy had eaten a little, but he was still tired and their concern for him was a comfort Albie wasn't sure he even knew he needed.

Before their plates were even cleared away, the barking dogs alerted them to another visitor. Albie went out onto the veranda to see the doctor riding in.

"Mr McAllister asked me to do a house call," he declared before getting off his horse. Then he slid down and took off his gloves. "I only arrived up here after dark last night. I'd have come sooner but for the late hour."

Albie greeted him with a shake of his hand. "Thank you for coming now. Have you had breakfast?"

He smiled warmly at Albie. "I have. Mrs McAllister insisted. But thank you, young Albie. You've grown two feet since I saw you last. Very sorry to hear about your father."

The reminder hit Albie hard and unexpected, the way grief often did. "Thank you," he managed. Then he gestured to the front door. "The patient is this way."

The doctor grabbed his bag and followed Albie inside.

"He was sleeping when I left him this morning," Albie explained, standing at the closed bedroom door. "He did manage to eat something this morning, though he took ill last night, vomiting, and he was confused and sleepy."

The doctor gave a serious nod. "Very well. Let us see him."

Percy was asleep, though he woke when they walked in. He seemed startled, pulling the blankets up as if he'd been caught in a bed he shouldn't have been in.

"Percy," Albie said gently, "This is Doctor Dawson. He's here to check on you." Then Albie turned to the doctor. "I put him in this room to keep an eye on him, if you were wondering."

That was more for Percy's peace of mind, but the doctor didn't seem to even notice. "Right then, give us a few minutes privacy please, Albie?"

Albie left them, closing the door quietly and he found Elsie and Clara in the kitchen. "He's checking him over," Albie said.

Elsie put a comforting hand on his arm. "Percy'll be fine. He's a tough one."

But then a few minutes became a few minutes more, and Albie couldn't stand it. "I'll be outside, doing . . . something. Anything."

He checked on the new pig pen and gave the new piglets fresh hay in their bed stall, and when he was on his way back to the stable, he saw Elsie walk the doctor out. He rushed over, and Elsie quickly went back inside.

"How is he?" Albie asked.

Doctor Dawson met his gaze, but he smiled. And smiling had to be a good sign, right?

"He's taken a knock to the temple." He pointed to the spot on his own head. "It might seem a small injury but it's not insignificant, Albie. The sleepiness, the confusion, that's about right for a concussion."

"Is he . . . will he be . . . what does that mean?"

"I think he'll be just fine," Doctor Dawson said. "Give him a day or two rest. Keep the room dark to save the headache. You said he's eating, so that's a good sign. And he has his faculties, which tells me there's no lasting damage."

"Damage?"

"The human brain is a fickle beast, Albie. He's lucky. He doesn't remember hitting his head, but he also doesn't remember how he got down onto that ledge. Was the ledge in question a long drop? Rocky, perhaps?"

"Both."

"Well, there's your answer." He began pulling his gloves on. "Keep him rested, fed, and watered, and he'll be back to work in no time."

Funnily enough, Albie didn't care about work right then.

"Just as long as he's okay," he managed.

Des brought the doctor's horse over. "Ah, Desmond Blackwell. How's the leg?"

Des tapped the side of his knee. "Still got it," he replied. "Best barometer around."

The doctor laughed, but then he saw Robert and he did a double take. "Robert Fuller, I'll be damned. Best I've seen you look in ten years, man."

Robert was clearly embarrassed, but he tipped his hat. "Doc."

Doctor Dawson gave Albie a brilliant smile. "Whatever you're doing up here, boy, you're doing it right. Keep it up."

For some reason, having the doctor call Albie a boy didn't rankle him. He was an older man, and Albie could only guess anyone younger than him copped that name. "Thank you."

Elsie came back out with a small parcel and waited for the doctor to mount his horse. She handed the parcel up to him. "For your trip back home."

"Ah, you spoil me," he said, tipping his hat and riding up toward the gate.

Des and Robert watched him leave but Albie headed straight back inside, Elsie quickly following. She grabbed his arm. "I hope you didn't mind the bread I gave him," she said.

"Not at all. I'm glad you offered it to him."

She was relieved, clearly. "He, uh, he tended to Clara's eye after Williams hit her. He was surprised to see us here, but I asked him to not tell anyone . . ." She shrugged. "He said he wouldn't."

Albie now gave her arm a squeeze. "I'm sure he's a man of his word."

"Thank you, Albie," she whispered. "Now, go check on your boy."

"What is it with people calling us boys today?" he grumbled, and Elsie smiled at him. He didn't mind the term of affection coming from her either, probably because it wasn't meant to insult him. Or that she implied Percy was *his*.

Albie rather liked that.

He gave a quiet knock on the bedroom door and cracked it open. "Can I come in?"

"Mmm," Percy said, his voice croaking. "Since when do you need permission to enter your own room?"

He grinned as he walked in. The room was still dark, curtains drawn closed, but he could see Percy's sleepy smile. "You're feeling better," he noted.

"My head hurts," he said. "And I'm so tired. I don't know why. Seems the more I sleep, the tireder I am."

"The doctor said you'll need to rest," Albie said quietly.

Percy slow-blinked, half smiling. "He gave me a bitter tonic for my head."

"Good."

He made a face. "It was not good. I'd prefer the cool washcloth if I'm being honest." Then he lifted his arm, showing the redness was still there. "And he put a balm on my wrist."

Albie sat on the edge of the bed and cupped Percy's face. "I'm just glad you're okay. He said it might take a few days before you're well enough to work. But don't worry about any of that. We'll all chip in and get everything done. I just need you to rest."

Percy closed his eyes, leaning into Albie's touch, and when he didn't open his eyes again, Albie realised he'd fallen asleep. He pulled the blankets up, gently kissed Percy's forehead, and let him be.

Albie worked around the house for the rest of the day. He knew Elsie would holler for him if needed, so he didn't want to venture too far.

He fed Percy some dinner, one slow forkful at a time. "I can do this by myself," Percy had said.

"I know, but I like looking after you," Albie had replied, and Percy smiled as he opened his mouth for another bite.

He put a cold compress to Percy's forehead afterward, then practised his reading on his own, finally slipping into bed beside Percy when the day was done.

Percy was quick to find Albie's arms, sighing when he drew peaceful patterns on his back. But he wasn't up for anything more, and that was fine.

If holding Percy was the only thing Albie ever got to do with him again, he'd be fine with that.

The night after that though, Percy's hand had begun to wander downward, lower, lower, until Albie stopped him. "Uh, you need to rest. Doctor's orders."

Percy whined. "I'm bored and I miss you, and my body misses you."

Oh, heavens above.

Albie bit back a groan. "You're not helping, Percy," he said. "Testing my patience like this."

"But—"

"No buts. You're not well enough." It was true. He'd tried for sunlight with open curtains in the bedroom today and it had done his head no favours at all.

Percy let out a sigh of frustration, a sound Albie was becoming familiar with. But he also knew Albie was right. "I'll be fine tomorrow. You'll see. And when I offer myself to you tomorrow night, you won't deny me."

Albie tightened his hold on him. His feisty little fox was back. So clearly he was feeling better, but not well enough. "No, I won't deny you."

Percy froze. "Oh?"

"Tomorrow," Albie clarified.

Percy sagged. "Oh."

Albie chuckled, rubbing Percy's back some more. "Goodnight, my love."

Percy sighed one last time. "You think you can call me that and any misgivings are done away with."

Albie laughed again, his smile not even fading in sleep.

———

IT WAS early afternoon when Albie and Robert rode back into the yard. They hadn't gone too far, but Albie had wanted to check the progress of McAllister's fence to see if it was encroaching on his land.

There'd been no progress yet, but it was something he'd keep an eye on.

Even after Percy had found Christopher and McAllister had sent the doctor over, Albie still didn't trust McAllister. His father had been of the same opinion. Civility for civility's sake, but never to be underestimated.

And never turn your back on him.

But when they rode into the yard, who should Albie see on the veranda waiting?

Percy.

Up and dressed and out of the house. He'd been up yesterday, in the living room only though. Then today he'd even managed breakfast at the table. He was feeling much better, and his smile was proof of that.

"How are you feeling?" Albie asked, riding over to him instead of heading to the stable. He noted Percy was wearing a knitted cap and not his wide brimmed hat, probably because of where it sat along the bruise at his temple.

"Feeling better. Can't stay in the house another minute, Albie. Going mad with boredom."

"How are your eyes? Not too bright out here?" It was overcast but there was glare.

"Not so bad."

Albie grinned at him and slid off Minnie. He

handed the reins to Percy. "Good. Can you take care of her for me?"

Percy grinned at him. "I sure can. Thank you, Albie."

Albie watched him take Minnie across to the stable, then sat his backside against the veranda and waited. He didn't want to just walk away and leave Percy, but he didn't want to shadow him either.

"Percy's up and about, huh?" Des asked him.

Albie nodded. "Not too soon, I hope. He's sick of being cooped up. I'm surprised he lasted as long as he did, to be honest."

Des snorted. "Same. He must've been pretty crook. Good to see him on his feet again. Just make sure he doesn't overdo it. He'll be too keen to catch up on missed work and see himself straight back in bed."

Albie nodded slowly, keeping his eyes on the stable. "That's what I told him."

A short while later, Percy came back out, still wearing that grin. But Albie didn't miss the way he squinted at the glare. Hm, maybe work out of the sun might be better for him.

"Oh," Percy said, still grinning and looking at Albie. "You got time to sit around, huh? No chores need doing?"

Des laughed. "Yeah, he's fine."

Albie got up and started walking over, pointing to the stables. "Comments like that will get you mucking out the stalls," he said.

Percy's grin only seemed to widen as he followed him back into the stables.

Albie helped him muck the stalls out, of course. Mostly to keep an eye on Percy, making sure he didn't overdo it or have a dizzy spell.

He did seem to tire a little, more than he would have normally, but he hadn't stopped smiling yet. Even when Ox nipped his knitted cap and flung it across the stall.

He was even still smiling at dinner, though he was clearly tired. He didn't even suggest reading afterward, and when he could barely keep his eyes open, Albie quietly told him to go to bed. Percy didn't argue.

When Albie climbed into bed beside him, Percy still wore his shirt and socks and his long underwear and was sound asleep. He barely stirred as Albie pulled him close, only to fold himself into the crook of Albie's arm, making himself small, his face a picture of peace and perfection.

Albie would never tire of it, of this. At the wonder of having this when he never thought it possible. He didn't even care that Percy's demand for intimacy tonight was dashed. He didn't care if they never shared that again, because this, this right here with Percy safe and asleep in his arms, was all he'd ever need.

UNTIL EARLY MORNING, that was, when Albie woke to find himself on his side, Percy's back pressed to his front, rubbing his backside against Albie's very awake cock.

"Good morning, my love," Albie murmured. "How are you feeling?"

He whined. "I'm sorry I fell asleep last night."

That wasn't an answer. He put his hand on Percy's hip to still him. "Feeling better?"

He tried to rock back, searching for Albie's hardness, but Albie held him firm. "You said you wouldn't deny me."

"Percy—"

Percy peeled Albie's hand from his hip and pulled it around to feel his arousal, rock hard and leaking at the tip. Albie instinctively wrapped his hand around him and drove his hips forward, making Percy's breath catch.

"Please, Albie. Please," he cried, his back arching.

Albie pulled the front of his long johns down and positioned his erection to slide between Percy's buttocks, sliding in behind his balls, his pre-come making the glide deliciously slick.

It was exquisite, hot and tight, and like this, he could imagine doing what Percy had asked of him before. To take him like this, to push inside him. He could imagine this was how it felt, only better.

So much better.

He slid back and forth and Percy rocked into it, his

cock swelling in Albie's hand, and a strangled cry escaped Percy's throat as he climaxed. The sight, the sounds, the feel sent Albie tumbling over the edge with him and he shot his seed still nestled into the crevice of Percy's buttocks.

Percy's eyes widened as he felt it, his mouth open and he gasped. "Yes, Albie. Oh yes."

Pleasure racked through Albie like he'd never felt, so intense, the aftershocks rattling him until his breaths were under control. His mind still spinning, he kissed the back of Percy's neck on the spot that made him shiver.

"Percy," he whispered. "My love."

Percy was heavy in his arms, and he groaned out a laugh. "I feel better now," he said. "To answer your question."

Albie chuckled too. "Same. You keep waking me like this."

"I'm not sorry. And so you know, I plan to keep waking you like this. I'll never not want to wake up like this."

Albie kissed Percy's shoulder. "I should get you cleaned up."

"Not yet," he replied quietly. "I want to feel your release for a moment longer yet."

"Oh my word, Percy!"

How could he say such a thing to him?

Percy laughed. "I'm not sorry for that either."

Albie gave his shoulder a gentle kiss. "It's not like you to say such things."

"Because I've been without it for too long." Percy rolled onto his stomach and stretched, wiggling his backside a little. "If you feel the need to do that again."

Albie felt his face flame. "Percy," he warned.

"I won't be falling asleep tonight until you do that again, I promise you that." He hummed and wiggled his backside. "I won't be thinking of anything else all day."

"Good heavens," Albie moaned. "Neither will I, now."

Percy laughed, pleased with himself, clearly. "You're welcome."

Albie heard the familiar clang of pots in the kitchen. "I should get up." He rolled out of bed and pulled on his pants. Percy made no attempt to move, his naked backside still on full display.

And so help him, it made Albie's cock twitch.

He could very much crawl back onto the bed and do exactly as Percy had asked . . . but he couldn't. Daylight was breaking; he had jobs to do.

He busied himself getting dressed, then took the wash towel, wringing the water from it in the basin. He knelt on the bed beside Percy and wiped it over the swell of Percy's backside. "To clean you up," he murmured. He couldn't help but feel embarrassed that he'd done this, covered Percy with his seed like this. But there was a flare of pride too, he couldn't deny it.

He liked it.

Percy widened his legs and raised his buttocks off the bed, giving Albie the access he needed to wipe him clean.

And heaven help him, the rush of desire that swept over him.

Of seeing this part of Percy painted with his seed, the pink pucker of his most sacred place.

The deep pang of desire, the raw longing to take him, to claim him, to do the very thing that Percy had wanted him to do.

It took every ounce of self-control he had not to do it right then. It was almost overwhelming, and the way that Percy spread his legs and rocked his hips, wanting.

Albie almost lost the fight, but he clambered back some control. He tossed the cloth toward the hamper, then leaned over Percy's back, growling in his ear.

"I will take you like this," he bit out. "I will have you as you want because seeing you like this has me losing my mind."

Albie shot up off the bed before he lost the fight to leave. The last thing he saw was the look of darkened surprise on Percy's face as Albie closed the door.

CHAPTER FOURTEEN

To say Percy was stunned at Albie's words would be an understatement.

To say he'd thought of anything else all day long would also be an understatement. He had to make himself busy, make himself keep his distance from Albie all day, lest he was tempted to drag him somewhere private to make him uphold that promise.

He'd felt no shame at all, lying on the bed, legs spread, as Albie cleaned him. In fact, he'd revelled under Albie's care, his gentleness as he tended to him.

Percy had never felt so loved.

But then Albie had growled in his ear, promising wicked things, and Percy had never felt a fire like it.

It ripped through him, burning white hot, with the embers keeping him warm all day.

He'd make sure he didn't fall asleep early tonight. Tiredness be damned. He was too worked up to feel tired. After dinner when they'd sat at the table to do his reading, Percy sat closer than was probably appropriate. He leaned into Albie, even resting his head on Albie's shoulder for a moment when Elsie and Clara were in the kitchen, but he couldn't bring himself to move.

He needed this.

He needed nothing else.

"You're being bold tonight," Albie murmured.

"Take me to bed, Albie," he whispered, meeting Albie's gaze. "Please. Please don't make me wait."

Albie shot to his feet, forgetting all about the books, took Percy's hand, led him to their room. He locked the door behind them, the click of the key making him jump.

Percy felt as if his blood was on fire.

He wasn't sure if Albie sensed his urgency or if he felt as desperate as him, but he was different tonight.

Still tender, still gentle, but serious and commanding.

Percy liked this side of him.

Loved it, even.

Loved it when Albie stripped him naked, laid him face down on the bed, and covered his body with his. His weight felt heavenly. The way he pressed him down, his erection filling that void beneath his buttocks, behind his balls. Sliding against where he so desperately wanted him, driving in over and over.

This is what heaven felt like.

A desire strung so taut Albie could have played him like a fiddle.

It wasn't exactly where he wanted him, but he was so, so close. And Percy lifted his hips, spread his legs a little wider, urging Albie to please, please press into him.

Albie raked his hands along Percy's arms, to his hands, linking their fingers and holding them to the mattress.

Oh, how good this felt.

Albie kept rocking, driving his hard cock against the place Percy so desperately wanted him. Until he pushed upward, his thick cockhead almost breaching him.

Almost.

So close. So desperate.

But so unsure.

Could Percy take him like that? Could he handle it? Could he endure the breach? Surely there'd be pain amidst the pleasure . . .

Albie drove upward again and he pushed in, hard. Almost inside him, almost pushing in . . .

But then he stilled and groaned, and Percy felt the warm rush of his seed spill into him, over him.

So close.

So very close.

"Oh, yes," Percy cried, bewildered at the pleasure it gave him, the pride he felt.

He wanted it for real now, more than anything.

That flicker of fear he'd felt before, wondering if he could endure the full breach of Albie faded away to nothing.

He was certain now.

"Oh, Albie, yes," he mumbled, rolling his hips, enjoying the slickness he felt. Enjoying the weight and press of Albie's now softening erection against his most sensitive flesh. "I need more. I need you inside me."

Albie grunted, his cock twitching, and Albie slid a hand between them, guiding, pushing, forcing. His cock wasn't rock hard but it was hard enough . . .

Percy raised his hips, willing, urging, and Albie pushed into him, breaching that sacred place and sliding in. Percy gasped, sucking back a breath and gritting his teeth. It was strange and wonderful and oh-so much to take.

But Albie grunted the most delicious sound, primal and pleading. He shuddered as he pushed in deeper and scraped his teeth at Percy's shoulder.

It was exquisite and different than what he'd imagined, but so much better. And this wasn't even Albie fully aroused, this was after he'd spent himself already.

Oh how he imagined it might feel to take him when he was rock hard, to take all of his seed . . .

He knew he would one day, and it sang to him. To that primal need he had to belong to Albie in every way. "Oh god," he gasped, surprised by the tears that sprang to his eyes.

Albie pulled out of him, quickly wrapping him up

in his arms. "Did I hurt you? Was it too much? Percy, I—"

Percy shook his head. "No, it was everything. It was everything and more. I need it, Albie. To be yours in that way."

Albie scanned his eyes in the dark, wiping Percy's tears away. "Oh, Percy. Are you sure?"

He nodded. "Please say it was good for you. Please tell me you're willing to do it again." He knew he was begging. He knew he sounded desperate, and Percy didn't care.

Albie barked out a quiet laugh, wrapping him up tight in his arms. "Oh, Percy. It was . . . better than good for me. It was . . . like nothing I'd ever imagined."

Percy pulled back so he could see Albie's face. "You mean it?"

Albie's eyes were full of wonder and he shook his head a little, as if disbelieving. "Percy, if Heaven was a place on Earth, I found it here tonight."

Percy put his hand to Albie's cheek and captured his lips with his own. "I love you, Albie Bramwell."

"And I love you, Percy Collins. All of you." He pulled Percy close, feeling his untouched arousal against his leg. "Oh," Albie said. "It seems I am remiss . . ."

"Oh, you don't have to worry," Percy said. "What you did to me was enough."

Albie's eyes flashed with a wicked gleam that matched his smile before he slid down under the blankets and that place Albie mentioned, Heaven on Earth? That place which Percy thought Albie was exaggerating about?

Albie took him there.

THE NEXT FEW days were blissful. Percy's head felt clearer every day, his tiredness subsided, and he was back to himself in no time.

It'd been scary, all in all, just how fast Percy's life changed in an instant. He had no idea that a simple knock to the head could be so worrisome. He didn't even remember hitting his head when he went down that ledge, but he realised that was the problem.

He remembered hearing the little boy cry. He remembered peering over the edge and seeing him. Then he remembered being on Minnie and heading back.

He remembered his head pounding, both dull and sharp pains, but his only concern was getting that frozen boy back to his parents.

He didn't remember taking McAllister's thirty pounds, and despite Albie's wishing he hadn't, Percy was glad he did.

He sat the money on the table with Albie's ledger, offering it to him.

"What are you doing with that?" Albie asked.

"I'm giving it to you."

"No, you're not," Albie argued. "It's yours."

"If it's mine," Percy countered, "then it's mine to do with as I see fit. And I'm giving it to you."

Albie glared at him, and Elsie and Clara took the pot of tea and backed out of the room, wide-eyed and very eager to take no part in this discussion.

"You might need new boots," Albie said, still refusing to accept the money.

"I have your old pair."

"With the soles almost out of them."

"Almost. Not out of them yet."

"Percy."

"Albie."

Albie growled. "I cannot accept this."

"You can and you will. Buy enough feed for the horses to see them fed for a year. Or buy some more stock, another bull and some cows."

Albie's eyes flinched, and Percy could see reason was warring with his pride, so Percy struck while the iron was hot.

"Use it to pay the farrier. Use it to—"

"It's not for me to use, Percy," he said, more gently this time.

No, not gentle.

Resigned.

Percy stepped in close so if Elsie and Clara were listening from the kitchen, they couldn't hear. "You took me in when you could barely afford it. You took those two women in when you could barely afford them either. You're a good man, Albie. And this thirty pounds is the least of what I would give you if I could." He searched his brown eyes. "Take the money and use it for the betterment of this farm. Being proud is one thing, Albie. Don't be foolish along with it."

Indignation flashed in his eyes. "I am not—"

Percy put his fingers to Albie's lips. "The money is yours, as is my heart," he murmured. "I would give you the world if I could, Albie. Don't deny me this."

Was that a low blow?

Probably.

But Percy knew Albie would never deny him when he put it like that.

Albie gave him a pointed look and he sighed, defeated. Percy grinned at him, then tapped the ledger book. "Okay, now we study. Sit down."

Albie growled at him and pulled the chair out with more force than was necessary, and he sat himself in it with much the same temper. Percy did his best not to smile, and when Elsie came out to collect the last teacups, she pressed her lips together to stop from smiling as well. Her eyes met Percy's and she grinned but turned and was gone before Albie saw.

Then they spent some time on the books. Albie did it petulantly, but he did it nonetheless.

When it was time for bed, Albie was still quiet. Percy closed the door and resisted sighing, barely. "Speak what's on your mind," he said, pulling his suspenders off his shoulders.

Albie's gaze cut to his before he looked away. "Nothing is on my mind."

Percy took Albie's chin between his thumb and forefinger and made him look at him. "You cannot lie to me. You raise your chin with indignation when you feel slighted."

He raised his chin. "I do not."

Percy smirked at him, then took the liberty of unbuttoning Albie's shirt. "You're mad at me."

"I wouldn't be if you didn't keep smiling as if you won some battle only you fought."

Percy snorted, kissing Albie's breastbone. "A battle only I fought? I don't think so. If it's about the money—"

Albie kept his hands by his sides, balled into fists. "It's not about the money. You emotionally blackmailed me into agreeing. You know damned well I'll give you everything you want, and you used it against me."

Percy used one featherlight finger to slide Albie's shirt off his shoulder. He kissed along his collarbone. "Like this?" he murmured, now kissing up Albie's neck. "Will you give me what I want?"

Albie growled and pushed Percy back onto the bed. Maybe a little too rough, maybe a little too hard, but the way he followed Percy onto the bed and pinned his hands above his head, Percy didn't mind one bit.

It made his heart thunder, his pulse quicken.

Percy's legs automatically widened and Albie fit so

perfectly between them. He drove his hips, his hardening arousal, against Percy's and it made him moan.

Their noses almost touching, Albie's eyes were alight with fire and warning. "The sounds you make are obscene."

Percy raised his hips, searching for more friction. Desperate for it. "Should you find something to gag me with?"

Albie's eyes widened with shock, and it made Percy grin. "I can't decide if I want you in my mouth or in my . . ." Percy wasn't sure he could say it out loud. He didn't have to because Albie knew.

He rolled his hips and grunted, fully erect now. Percy could feel the hardness, the urgency. There would be no time for much else tonight. He fought to get his hands free and quickly slid them between them, unbuttoning Albie's pants first, then his own. He fumbled with the material until he had both their cocks in his hand, sliding them against each other.

Albie's eyes rolled closed and he trembled above him. He had his hands by Percy's shoulders but soon went onto his elbows so he could thrust his hips better.

The glorious slide of their lengths, hard as iron and as soft as silk. Albie crushed his lips to Percy's, plunging his tongue into his mouth, devouring him, controlling him like a puppet on strings, beckoning his body, his bliss.

Albie came first, shuddering and groaning, and the

feel of his erection pulsing and spilling made Percy follow directly after.

Albie collapsed on his side, pulling Percy into a strong embrace. "You," he said, breathless. "I'm so weak for you."

Percy chuckled. "Weak?"

Albie kissed Percy's forehead. "Anything you want, whenever you want it, consider it yours."

Percy sighed, his eyelids heavy, the lull of Albie's warm body and deep breaths sending him to sleep. "I only want you. Nothing else."

Albie kissed the side of his head. "I'm already yours."

———

THE WEEK that followed was something close to the best Percy could remember. Their days were busy with farming, the nights were filled with pleasure and comfort.

It was warming up too, sunlight lasting a little longer. The wind still had some bite but spring was on the horizon. Newborn calves, baby chicks, and squealing piglets were a sure indicator.

Everyone's mood was lifted it seemed.

Life at the farm was good. They didn't have a lot right now, but with the seedlings almost big enough to go in the ground, soon they'd have an abundance of most things.

Elsie had plans for canning and pickling. Clara was always trying new ways to make meals go further, even though none of them could remember ever eating so well.

But the accounts ledger didn't lie. If they wanted to survive next winter, they'd need a decent income this spring and summer, that was for sure.

Percy wasn't even entirely sure how to bring it up or if he should.

"You and I will need to head down to Alpine Falls," Albie said.

Percy was so caught up in his head, it was a surprise to hear. "Oh? Yes, of course."

"We'll need more flour soon. I'll have Elsie and Clara make a list, and if the weather's good tomorrow, we can go early. Stay the night," he said, his gaze cutting to Percy's. "Just us."

Percy had to bite his bottom lip to stop from smiling so hard. "If you say so." But then he took a sleeve of paper from the ledger and pushed the pencil toward him. "You can write the list."

Albie rolled his eyes but he started to write. His handwriting wasn't perfect, and he had to sound a few words out, but he was miles better than he used to be. It all came down to practice and repetition, and he was doing great.

He asked Elsie and Clara what they needed. Then he went out to the bunkhouse and asked Des and

Robert. He came back in with quite a list, and so it was decided they'd head off in the morning.

Percy couldn't wait.

He barely slept, tossing and turning with too much on his mind, and was up before Albie had even stirred.

He had their horses saddled and ready when Albie came out looking for him. His hair was rumpled and he was still pulling his coat on as he came into the stables. "Percy, what are you doing?"

"You can ride Ox. Minnie's the pack horse. Sorry, sweetheart," he said, giving her neck a pat.

"I know I said early," Albie said, biting back a yawn. "But is this not too early?"

Percy was buzzing. "Is it ever too early? Let's get into town. See what's happening, see if there's any news."

"News about what?"

Percy did love being up here in the mountains away from it all, but they really were so far removed from the rest of the world. "News about anything. And I saw some boiled sweets in the store last time. They've got my name on them this time." He gave Albie's shoulder a clap. "Look alive, Albie."

Des startled them with a laugh. "Yeah. Look alive, Albie."

Percy was just glad he hadn't said anything meant for private ears.

Albie rolled his eyes and sighed. "Can we at least have breakfast first?"

Percy took a second to consider that. "I suppose."
He left the horses tied up outside the stable. "I'll go
check the chickens and the piglets."

"Just who's in charge here," Albie said.

"I don't think you want anyone to answer that,"
Des said, and when Percy turned around to laugh, he
saw Des pat Albie on the back with a huge smile on his
face.

Percy set about doing his chores, sat down for the
quickest breakfast ever, and was bringing the horses
over to the house when Albie was still giving Des and
Robert instructions.

Not that they needed them.

Percy mounted Bandit and stopped short on
clearing his throat to hurry Albie along.

He got the message though, because he saw Percy
already on his horse waiting and he rolled his eyes
again. "I should add patience to my list," Albie
muttered as he swung himself up into the saddle on
Ox. "We'll be back after lunch tomorrow. If I don't
throttle him first," he said, giving a nod toward Percy.

"You would never," Percy said with a laugh,
turning Bandit toward the gate. Albie would put his
hands on Percy in a number of ways, but never in
anger, and they both knew it. "Time's a wasting,
boss."

He gave Bandit a nudge and headed off in a trot,
tipping his hat at Des and Robert. Albie followed him,
and given he had Minnie tethered to Ox, Percy took

the liberty of opening the gate and closing it behind them when Albie went through.

"You're in a good mood today," he said as they began the ride down the road.

"Why wouldn't I be?" he replied. "I ain't ever been happier, Albie. I got a job. I got friends. I eat like a king, three meals a day. I got this view." He gestured to the misty trees, the mountains, the valley, then he looked over at Albie. "And I got you."

Albie shifted in his saddle. "Oh. Yes, well . . ."

"Yes, well, what?"

Albie's cheeks were a little pink and he smiled. "Do you really think the king eats wallaby stew?"

Percy laughed, incredulous. "That's what you took from that?"

"You said you eat like the king."

"I said *a* king. Not *the* king. And anyway, the King of England should be so lucky."

Albie laughed, and after a few moments of riding in silence, he said, "I'm happy I've got you too."

"Did you ever think it was possible?" Percy asked. He still couldn't believe it himself some days. "And that we're free to talk about such things when it's just you and me."

And it *was* just them. There was no one else around for miles.

Albie's cheeks were still pink. If it was from embarrassment or the cold, Percy wasn't sure. "I never thought it was possible, no. To be honest, I never thought of it at all. I never thought much past my next meal or the next chore my father gave me. I never thought much of my future. I just assumed it'd be me and my father on the farm forever. I thought we'd just get by, ya know?"

Percy nodded.

"But then that was cut away," Albie said. "And when everything seemed dark and pointless, I met this man, not much younger than me. He was smart and had fire in his blue eyes and a smile that knocked my heart around."

Percy smiled at him. "Me?"

Albie laughed. "Yes, you. Who else? Looking like something from a dream. One of my teenaged daydreams where I knew thinking of men wasn't right but imagining women felt more wrong. I just didn't know why."

"But now you know."

"Oh, yes. Very much."

Percy chuckled. "Same. I haven't ever felt so right than when I'm with you." He smiled as they rode, at the smell of eucalypt and pine fresh in the cold damp air, the birdsong in the trees around them. "I sure do hope the hotel only has one room available."

Albie laughed. "I don't much care if they do or don't," he said, shifting again in his saddle. "I'm only paying for one room whether they like it or not. The smaller the bed the better."

Percy groaned, his belly tightening at the thought.

"You keep talking about that and this saddle will do me no favours. We might have to find somewhere to tie the horses up along the way, away from the road, maybe a gully somewhere and you can make good on your promises."

Albie laughed at that, but he didn't say no.

Percy was almost disappointed when they eventually rode into Alpine Falls that they hadn't found themselves a private moment along the way. But he sure was looking forward to tonight.

Chapter Fifteen

They saw their horses to the saloon stables, made sure they were fed and watered, then went inside to do much the same for themselves.

Albie had been half tempted to spend the afternoon in their room upstairs, but he knew they had all night for that. There were other rooms available but he opted for only one. After all, it wasn't uncommon for men to share a room to cut the costs.

Those men probably didn't share a bed or share their bodies the way Albie and Percy did, but the woman behind the bar didn't ask for any such details, and Albie certainly wasn't offering them.

They ate a late lunch of beef and kidney pie, then went about the town. First to the store for their supply of flour, salt, sugar, tea, oats, and molasses, which he put on the counter. He spied the glass jars of boiled sweets that Percy had his eye on last time and added two jars to the tally.

"Two?" Percy asked.

"Robert has a sweet tooth," Albie said. "I'm sure he'll be grateful."

"I'm absolutely sure he will be. You might want to add some plums and oranges," Percy said, almost as a joke, but Albie thought it was a great idea.

Albie peeled a pound note from the fold and handed it over to Mr Collier, the man behind the counter. He gave Albie a smile. "Ah, young Mr Bramwell, good to see you in these parts again."

He was an older man, a little round in the middle, but he always offered a smile, which Albie returned. "Thank you, Mr Collier. What's news around town?"

"Here," Percy said, taking the heavier sacks. "I'll take these to the room and come back to help with these." Albie watched Percy leave, then turned back to Mr Collier.

The older man sighed. "Much the same in these parts. The old bullock pass road was cleared and reopened, so that's good. I heard the gold mine outside of Kiandra might be closing down soon. They haven't found anything there for a while now, so that's not surprising." Then he nodded to the door. "Say, that boy with you . . ."

Albie bristled at the word boy, but he knew Mr Collier meant no harm, so he let it go.

"What about him?"

"He's the one that found McAllister's boy, is he?"

Ah.

"Word travels fast."

"They said the doc was called, but he seems well enough now," Mr Collier added, prodding for details to gossip, no doubt.

"He's fine. Took a knock to the head but he's fine now."

"Good, good. And he scored himself the finder's fee. Good for him." Then he looked at the items on the counter and Albie could see it clicked when he realised that Albie had paid him with that money.

Albie took the folded receipt and looked at it, taking a second to do a tally of items—something he'd not have been able to do so quickly before Percy had made him study the books.

"Everything to your liking there?" Mr Collier asked.

Albie wasn't sure if he was affronted that Albie would check his calculations in front of him. "Perfect, thank you. I'm trying to get better at checking such things. Not something I had to worry about before my father passed."

Mr Collier gave him a sad smile. "I understand."

Percy came in, still smiling, and loaded up his arms full of their goods, so Albie did the same. Mr Collier helped him stack up the last few items and he walked them to the door, holding it open for him. "Albie," he said quietly, a hand on his arm. "If I may . . ."

Albie wasn't sure he wanted to hear this, but Mr Collins now seemed cautious, nervous. Albie was curious. "Of course."

"The money," he whispered. "However much it was, go put it in the bank. Folks in this town know he scored himself a windfall, and these are desperate times for some men."

Oh.

Albie hadn't expected that.

He also hadn't thought of that.

He gave Mr Collier a nod. "Thank you."

"You boys be safe now, you hear?"

He'd have shaken his hand if his arms weren't full but had to settle for a nod. "Thanks again, Mr Collier."

They walked back to the saloon, and maybe Albie was being paranoid now, but he swore he felt eyes on him.

He'd thought he'd imagined some strange looks when they'd eaten their lunch at the saloon but had disregarded them. Much like they'd looked at him the last two times he'd been to town, looks of pity and curiosity and even some anger, given he'd taken over his father's farm at such a young age.

But now he wondered if they were looking at Percy.

And Albie didn't like that one bit.

"What was that all about?" Percy asked him quietly as they crossed the street to the saloon. They had their arms full, and Albie felt unprepared should someone decide to confront them for money.

"I'll tell you when we're inside," he said, quickening his step.

Albie hurried up to their room, juggling his armful so he could unlock the door, then quickly locking it behind them once Percy was inside.

"Albie, what is it?"

"Mr Collier gave me a warning," he said, putting his wares on the floor with the others Percy had brought up earlier.

Percy did the same, then turned to Albie, his eyes narrowed. "What for? What did you ever do to—"

"Not for me," Albie cut him off. "More so for you and the money you got from McAllister. Word is that folks in town know you were paid handsomely, and here we are making purchases."

Percy was stunned momentarily. "Do you think . . . do you think it's a concern? I mean, the men in this town are a lot of talk, but . . . do you think they'd try to take it from us?"

Albie put his hands on Percy's shoulder, his gaze serious. "I won't risk any harm coming to you. We'll stay in our room all night like we did when Robert was with us."

Percy brightened. "Ooh, and now it's just us. However will we spend our time?"

Albie managed a smile, though he hardly felt cheerful. "Perhaps I should take it to the bank. At least if eyes are watching us, they'll see we no longer have any amount on our person."

Percy simply nodded. "If it would make you feel better."

Albie was torn. "My father never trusted banks, and I'm not sure I disagree with him. But if it takes a target off your back, then I'll take the risk."

"Albie, I'm sure it's not anything to be worried about."

He cupped Percy's cheek, studying the blue of his eyes. "I can't risk anything happening to you. If anyone tried to shake you for it, or if a group of men were to outnumber us . . . and hurt you to get you to hand it over." Albie couldn't even bear thinking about it. "I'd never forgive myself."

Percy clucked his tongue and sighed. "No, you'd fight them all and I'd have to pay the thirty pounds to bail you out of gaol. Then it'd be all for nothing."

Albie knew he was joking and he could appreciate that Percy was trying to make light of the situation.

Percy smiled up at him. "So, let's take it to the bank, then we can check on the horses before we come up here and lock the door and find a way to fill in some time. Because I have some ideas," he added with a twinkle in his eye.

Albie found himself smiling again, genuinely this time. "Some ideas, huh?"

Percy nodded brightly.

It made Albie smile. "I'd like to hear them."

"Well, we can read or practice some more accounting—"

Albie took his face in his hands and planted a kiss on his lips. "There'll be no reading tonight."

Percy laughed. "Thank heavens for that. Come on, let's go to the bank."

———

MY FATHER WAS RIGHT, Albie thought as soon as he'd walked in the door.

There were two men behind the counter: one banker, one clerk.

The banker was the younger of them. He wore an expensive suit and a greasy smile, with small round spectacles and his slicked-down hair. The older man beside him didn't seem to like him much either. He had a kind face and a quiet confidence. Albie liked him much better than the snake-oil man.

"Young Albert Bramwell," the older man said fondly. "I knew your father. He was a good man."

Albie got that a lot in this town. "I'm sorry, I don't remember you."

He smiled. "I wouldn't expect you to. You were just a boy last I saw you." Then he turned to Percy. "I don't believe you're from around here."

"Not originally, no sir," Percy replied cheerfully. "But I call it home now. The name's Percy Collins."

"Nice to meet you, Percy Collins. I'm Arthur Stanton. And this is Phillip Matthews, our new banking manager. He's from Melbourne."

Albie nodded, smiling courteously, all while thinking this was far too polite.

Then Arthur gave Albie an odd glance before he turned to face the banker. "Albie is the neighbour of Royce McAllister."

It wasn't just the way he said that, but *why* he'd said that, Albie realised.

Phillip Matthew's gaze cut to Albie's and his demeanour changed immediately.

Typical of men like him.

"That I am," Albie said, reading this play for what it was. "It was Mr McAllister's recommendation that I bring this in. No safer place for it, he said." He took the folded notes from his inside coat pocket and slid it on the service counter.

Mr Stanton gave a tight smile, pleased, and Albie knew he'd read the situation correctly. "Let me count that for you."

Mr Stanton counted the notes and handed Albie a receipt showing his total sum. He checked the numbers for the second time that day and was able to see that they were correct.

He wouldn't have been able to do that before Percy.

"Have yourself a good day, gentlemen," Mr Stanton said.

Albie tipped his hat at Matthews but gave Mr

Stanton a smile before they walked out. No sooner were they on the veranda, did Percy fix his coat. "What was that all about?" he asked quietly.

"Politics," Albie replied. "More or less." He felt some eyes on them. Some discreet, some not. Was it any more than last time he'd been here? Before they had any amount of money worth stealing? Albie couldn't be sure. Maybe he was being paranoid.

But when they went into the stables, the horses were fine, but the saddles on the railing had been moved and Albie's old gloves were on the stall floor. "What the . . . ?" Percy said, picking them up and seeing the saddlebag was open.

Not so paranoid after all.

"There was nothing in the saddles," Albie said. They'd made sure not to leave anything worth stealing behind.

"But they looked anyways," Percy said. He was mad and wary. Maybe a little scared.

"The horses are fine," Albie said. "Let's get upstairs."

There was quite the crowd in the saloon now. Men stood around drinking. The number of beers they'd had clearly indicated the volume in which they spoke, but a hush fell over them when they saw Albie and Percy.

He had to do something, say something.

Albie went to the bar, the older barman eyeing him cautiously. "Is Elsie not in?" Albie asked.

"She don't work here no more," the barman said brusquely.

"Oh." Albie acted surprised. "Shame." He took a few pence from his pocket and slid the coins onto the bar. "Can I order some bread for the room upstairs, please?"

"Rumour has it, you got more money than that, boy," a deep voice behind him said.

Boy.

Oh, how Albie hated that word.

He turned slowly and sure enough, it was none other than Peter Winnicott. The whole saloon was watching, waiting.

"Then the rumours are wrong," Albie said simply.

Winnicott snarled at him. "You got paid thirty quid for finding McAllister's kid."

There was no way he was correcting him on who exactly it was that got the money. "What we got paid," Albie said, "paid off debts and bought us enough food to last maybe a few weeks. Though I'm sure whoever ransacked our saddlebags can tell you there was no money in them. Because there isn't any." Albie looked at the men who were watching him before his eyes drew back to Winnicott. "The child was fine, by the way. I know that must have been your first concern, right?"

Winnicott's jaw ticked and he held Albie's gaze. Albie was not backing down. If Winnicott truly had a problem with Albie, it'd end here today either way.

"You sure got a mouth for a kid your age," Winnicott said.

Albie burred up at that, his hands became fists, and Percy quickly grabbed his arm. But it was Bill Kelly who stepped in between them. Albie wasn't even aware he was in town.

"It took a man bred from these mountains to find that boy," he said. "And a braver man to go off the edge of a cliff to retrieve him." He gave Albie and Percy a nod before he cut a scathing glare to Winnicott. "If respect is earned, he's got mine. And McAllister's. You'll do well to remember that."

Well, I'll be damned.

Albie couldn't believe it.

Kelly turned to Albie and Percy. "Mrs McAllister is most grateful."

Albie tipped his hat. "Just glad Christopher's okay."

Then Kelly looked at Percy. "She'll be happy to hear you're up and well."

Percy grinned at him and knocked his fist to his head. "Take more than a mountain to knock me about."

Kelly smiled. "And as for your horses," he said loud enough for the whole room to hear. "No one will touch them again as much as they'd dare touch mine. You have my word."

Albie locked eyes with the big man and gave a grateful nod. "Most appreciated." Then he looked around the room, Winnicott not even worth a glance. "Evening, gentlemen."

"Oh, Albie," Kelly said. "I hear the saleyard prices will be good next round."

Albie could have just about cried, though he surely wouldn't. "That's good to hear," he replied.

He and Percy left, taking the stairs to their room. It was still locked and just as they'd left it, though Albie made sure to lock it once they were inside.

"What in the blazes was that about?" Percy asked, wide-eyed. "Did you see Winnicott's face? He looked like he'd swallowed his tongue."

Albie laughed, scrubbing his hand over his face. "I still can't believe it. That Kelly would put me in McAllister's favour."

"None of those men would dare do you wrong now," Percy said.

"Or you."

Percy gave Albie's arm a squeeze, his smile as wide as his big blue eyes. "And you with the banker, and then at the bar. You said it was politics and you played it well."

Albie had almost forgotten about that.

"It's a game we all play to some degree," Albie said. "I wish it wasn't on the coattails of McAllister. My standing at the bank or with the men downstairs. They should respect me for who I am, for being my father's son, for having the right to stand amongst them as any other man in this town. It shouldn't depend on the respect they have for the likes of McAllister."

"But it does."

Albie nodded. "I don't like the game but I respect the rules. I'll take it though. Just to be treated with the respect my father's name deserves."

"That you deserve," Percy said quietly.

"And you," he whispered. "A man brave enough to go over the edge to retrieve the boy."

Percy's grin was blinding. "That sure shut them up."

Albie studied Percy's beautiful eyes and lifted his chin for a soft kiss. "Percy, I—"

A knock at the door made them jump apart. Percy went and knelt by the goods from the store as though he was checking something, and Albie took the key and unlocked it.

It was the man from behind the bar. He gave Albie a curt smile. He was holding a plate of bread and butter. "As you requested," he said. Then he noted Percy by the far wall first. "If you'd like a second room . . ."

"I'm fine with sleeping on the floor," Percy said, standing up. "Slept in worse places."

Albie took the plate. "Much obliged," he said and closed the door. He put the plate on the dresser, then took one side of the heavy wooden dresser. "Help me with this."

Percy did as he was asked, moving it to block the

door. "What are we doing this for? Do you not think what Bill Kelly said was enough?"

Albie smirked at him. "I do, but I want to be sure we're not interrupted. I don't think anyone should see what I plan on doing to you tonight."

Percy's pupils blew out and his cheeks flushed pink. "Oh."

Albie took the plate. "We'll save the bread for breakfast when we leave before first light," he said. "But the butter we'll use tonight."

Percy's eyes went to his, confused. "Butter?"

"It will help make things slide," he murmured. He licked his lips, liking the idea of it more and more. "If you know what I mean."

Percy's eyes narrowed at first but then Albie could see when the penny dropped. His eyebrows rose. "Oh." His cheeks flushed a deep scarlet that set Albie's blood on fire. "We're not eating the butter, are we?"

Albie shook his head slowly. "No."

Chapter Sixteen

Percy could admit to being clueless when it came to such things. How could he possibly know?

What on earth had given Albie the idea, Percy had no clue. But he was sure glad he did.

Percy liked that Albie seemed to think of bedding him almost as much as Percy did.

Almost.

Surely Albie didn't think of it as often Percy did. Heaven help him, it was all Percy could think about.

And since his accident, Albie had been so gentle with him. While he loved that Albie took care of him and felt the need to protect him, he'd almost gone a stretch too far.

He'd been so restrained in their bed. Was being too tender a problem? Was being too tentative, too careful a bad thing?

Goodness, no.

But Percy was feeling more than fine now.

And he had needs.

Needs that he'd never had before. Needs that Albie had awoken in him, needs that burned in his belly. And now he needed it all the time.

He never wanted to stop.

He felt wicked sometimes, the way his thoughts would take him down memory lane. He'd be sitting at the table with Des and Robert while he was remembering Albie's body, naked and hard in all the right places and doing ungodly things to him.

He thanked all the heavens that his thoughts were private.

And he thanked all the heavens that Albie's thoughts were aligned with his. To move the dresser against the door, to use the butter.

To have him face down on the bed, naked and willing, before the sun had barely set. The talk and laughter from the bar downstairs filtered up, disguising any noises Percy might make.

He always tried to be quiet. In bed, late at night or early in the morning, fearful that Clara and Elsie across the hall might hear him. He'd heard certain noises come from their room before, though he'd never dare to mention it.

But he was well versed in biting back groans and practising silence, though Albie had never sunk all the way inside him before. Not fully erect, not rock hard.

Percy was sure tonight would be the night he did.

And he wanted it more than he'd ever wanted anything.

As Albie smeared the butter over Percy's entrance, Percy grew impatient. He raised his hips and spread his thighs more, murmuring into the mattress. He even slid his hand underneath and gave his cock a few strokes to ease the desperate ache. "Albie, please."

Then Albie's chest pressed against Percy's back, and Percy could feel Albie's hand on his buttocks as he positioned himself, his cock to Percy's entrance.

"You'll regret your impatience," Albie grunted at the back of Percy's ear.

"You'll regret my impatience," Percy snapped.

But then Albie pushed into him. It took Percy's breath, took his ability to speak, to think. The breach was immense and too much, and Albie was too hard, too big . . .

Percy clawed at the mattress and the pillow, his head lifted from the bed, mouth open, and he was just about to object, to say no, to beg, when there was a push and a pop as Percy's body surrendered and took Albie in.

And Albie slid into him, slow and deep, his breath shuddering at Percy's ear. "Please tell me if I hurt you," he murmured, his voice strained. Then he pressed his forehead to Percy's shoulder and rolled his hips, pushing all the way in with a shuddering breath. "Oh sweet heavens, Percy, what are you doing to me?"

Percy couldn't explain how it felt.

An intrusion at first. Discomfort that soon became something else . . . a reward. He wanted Albie inside him. He wanted this, to take his cock inside him, to take his seed.

He wanted Albie to have him, to claim him. To finish inside him.

And the more Albie slid in and out, pushing in deeper, the more Percy wanted it.

He was gentle, yes. But he was also owning Percy with every thrust, with every grunt and quiet groan. "Oh, you feel like heaven, Percy," Albie whispered. "I can't . . . I can't hold back any longer."

"Then don't," Percy breathed. He rose his arse to meet Albie, and Albie drove into him, impaling him, so deep, so perfectly.

His pace quickened, giving Percy everything he wanted, everything he'd yearned for, craved. And when Albie drove up into him one final time before he grunted and groaned, he spilled inside him. Percy could feel the pulse, the release, and Albie held him tighter, kissing his shoulder and that sweet spot on the nape of his neck.

He collapsed on top of him, Albie's weight on Percy's back a comfort, and when he began to pull back, Percy was quick to stop him. "Stay there," he murmured. "Inside me, on top of me. Never leave me, Albie."

He hadn't meant it to sound like that, but once those words were out, he wasn't sorry.

He meant every word.

Albie slipped his arms underneath him, around him, and he held him. "Never," he breathed. "I will never leave you."

"Forever is a promise, Albie," Percy said. Not entirely sure why he was so emotional, so vulnerable.

Albie kissed the back of his neck again, nudging his nose into Percy's hair. "My promise to you. I love you, Percy Collins. Now, and forever."

Albie's words filled Percy with such warmth, with security and comfort he couldn't explain. "I love you too," he said, his voice catching and his eyes filling with tears.

Albie pulled out of him then, and Percy felt empty at the loss. Hollow, bereft.

But Albie flipped him over, scooping him up in his arms, cradling him. "Why the tears? Did I hurt you, Percy?"

Percy gave a teary laugh. "I can't explain my emotions," he said, sniffling. "You gave me everything I needed, Albie. Not just here tonight, but every day. And to hear you say you love me, for me to tell you I love you . . ." He shook his head, fresh tears welling in his eyes. "To find love when I was alone. To find you, Albie. I don't know what I ever did to be so lucky."

Albie swiped his thumb across Percy's temple, wiping away a tear that escaped, and searched his eyes. "I was alone too, until you came into my life. I can't say what the future will hold for us, and maybe it won't be easy, but as long as we have each other."

Percy's reply was soft and honest. "Always. I'll be at your side forever."

Albie smiled and kissed him softly. "Are you sure I didn't hurt you?"

Percy gave a teary laugh. "You can hurt me like that any time you have the need." He clenched his buttocks, feeling worn and wet. "The butter was a good idea."

Albie pulled him in close, holding him tight. "The butter was a great idea." He shuffled Percy closer, feeling Percy's erection, and he stilled. "You, uh . . . you didn't finish."

Percy chuckled. "No, but it's okay. If you feel up for a second round—" He wiggled his bottom. "—I'm ready."

Albie groaned. "A second round, and third, and more. How much can you take?"

Percy hummed, warming at the thought alone. "All of it."

They lay there for a moment, holding each other tight, relishing the closeness, the quiet, the privacy.

The love.

And Percy must have dozed off because he woke sometime later to Albie's mouth on him, taking in his cock, sucking and summoning his orgasm from just under the surface. Albie drank down Percy's release, and while his mind was still swimming in pools of bliss, Albie flipped him over and entered him once more.

Percy bit the pillow to muffle any sounds and he let Albie have his way with him again.

"You said you wanted all of it," Albie murmured between thrusts.

"Yes. Yes," Percy cried. "Please."

He felt bigger this time, harder too, and more determined, but somehow no less gentle. And he pushed down on Percy's back, rearing up as he spilled, and Percy could feel the rush of it inside him.

Heaven.

He collapsed on top of him again, breathing hard, his chest heaving. "Oh, Percy."

"Don't move," Percy murmured. "Sleep as we are."

He was spent and content and couldn't have moved if he wanted to. He closed his eyes and fell asleep, dreaming of weighted clouds of bliss and forever.

THEY WERE UP BEFORE first light and had the horses loaded with their store goods. Percy ached in all the right places, and he smiled at every twinge, reminded smartly of where Albie had been.

But it wasn't until he swung himself up into his saddle that the pain became a bite. "Ooh," he hissed, adjusting in his seat with more care this time.

"Are you sore?" Albie asked him, concerned.

Percy laughed. "Not terribly. Just reminded of last night."

"We have a half-day's ride. You must tell me if you need to rest."

"Don't concern yourself with my matters," Percy said.

Albie cocked an eyebrow at him. "Your matters? Am I not the cause of such things? Shouldn't we share—"

Percy met his gaze. "If I tell you it hurts, would you do it again?"

"Well, I . . . No, I probably wouldn't. I don't want to cause you any—"

"And that is why I won't tell you. Because you will be doing it again. Many times, between now and forever, I'll have you know."

Albie glared at him. "Percy."

"I won't hear any more of it, Albie. Though I will let you draw me a hot bath tonight, deal?"

He feared he'd need it.

"Fine," Albie said, somewhat mollified.

"And while I'm soaking away any aches and pains in the tub, you can steal some more butter from Clara's larder." Percy grinned at him. "If she catches you, it'll be your hide that needs soaking."

Albie finally smiled. "Maybe I should buy us a private stash of butter from the store before we leave."

Percy laughed. "I won't tell anyone if you don't."

ALBIE DIDN'T BUY any butter from the store, though he did call past the saleyard to double check when the next intake was. It was early, the yards mostly empty and not many people around, but Mr Bailey was there, and he most definitely was whistling a different tune in regards to Albie.

And yes, it was unfair that the saleyard, the bank, and the store all bowed to McAllister. They should have respected Albie before he found himself in McAllister's good graces. It clearly irked Albie, and rightly so, but Percy found it a little funny.

"Imagine living your life as a puppet like that," he said as they rode out of town. "McAllister's the puppeteer that makes all his little marionettes dance. They're fools to think he respects them. But you," he said, giving a pointed nod to Albie, "you he respects. Begrudgingly, perhaps. But respect, nonetheless."

Albie laughed. "I don't know about that."

"You didn't bow down to him when a weaker man would have," Percy added.

Albie wasn't sure what to say to that, so he settled for silence. It was an easy silence between them, comfortable even. They'd catch each other's gaze and smile, making Albie's heart thunder.

Percy whistled a tune for a bit, then he told of a story from his childhood when he'd been in trouble at school and caught the teacher's wrath.

Then his father's when he got home.

"Do you miss them?" Albie asked. It wasn't the first time, but he knew longing and sadness was something that came and went.

Percy scrunched his nose. "Sometimes. I think a part of me always will. But I'm not sorry I left. I'm sorry they told me to leave, and I'm sorry they felt me more of a burden than a son. I'm sorry for that. But I'm not sorry I left. Because if I hadn't gone out on my own, I'd have never met you. I've never been this happy, Albie. I'll take this life, this authentic life, over a lie any given day of the week."

Albie would never stop being amazed at this man.

"Do you think they knew?" Albie pressed. "That you were never inclined to bed a woman?"

Percy's smile turned rueful. "I think so, yes. Some part of my mother always knew, I think. My father lived in denial and would never think of such things. If I'd have told him the real reason I didn't want to marry Emily . . ." He shook his head. "He'd have flayed the skin from my bones and buried me with a Bible."

Albie sighed, his heart heavy.

"I wish it weren't so. And I'll never understand how people can clutch a Bible in one hand while they beat you with their other. It reeks of hypocrisy."

Percy was quiet for a few beats. "What about you? Do you think your father knew?"

Albie shook his head. "No. We were too isolated, too removed from the townsfolk for me to have any interest in courting anyone, much less a lady." He made a face. "Thankfully."

"Do you think Des and Robert know?"

"About us?"

Percy nodded.

"I would hope not." Albie dreaded the thought.

"I think Des might wonder."

Albie shot him a bewildered look. "What? How?"

Percy just laughed. "He misses nothing."

"He thinks it's good I have someone now who's closer to me in age," Albie justified. "I've never had that. He'd mistake us for nothing more."

"He knows we share a room."

"Yes, but that's . . . that's because there is little alternative. Unless you want to move back to the bunkhouse."

Percy threw his head back and laughed. "You're not getting me out of your bed that easy."

"Even after last night?" Albie asked boldly. He really wasn't one to say such things outright, but he'd noticed Percy shifting in his saddle more and more.

Percy rocked his hips forward and palmed his crotch. "Especially after last night."

THEY RODE into the farm around two in the afternoon. Tired, sore, and hungry, but oh-so happy to be home.

Elsie and Clara met them on the veranda, smiling

widely. "Good to have you back, Albie," Elsie said, immediately starting to unpack the food supplies.

"Everything well here?" he asked, sliding down off his horse and stretching his back.

"Oh, yes. Robert and Des went down to the west paddocks not too long ago. Said they'd be back by four. I kept a lunch aside for you both. Figured you'd be hungry," she said, lifting out the bag of sugar from the saddlebag. She hefted it as if it were nothing and handed it over to Clara who struggled with both arms.

"You should remember I'm not accustomed to moving kegs of beer," Clara said, giving her a cheeky scowl.

It was the first time Albie had seen any cheek from Clara, and it made him happy to see it now. It also made him happy to see Elsie grouse and fuss about it. She hefted the sack of flour up onto her shoulder and trudged up the steps, following Clara inside.

Then Albie noticed Percy walk around in front of Bandit. He limped and winced, giving Albie a sorry smile. "Remember how I said you should mind your own matters?" he whispered. "And how I'd let you run me a bath?"

Albie wanted to slide his hand along Percy's jaw and pull him in for a hug, to rub his back, to maybe even carry him inside. But he couldn't do that in case Robert or Des happened to come back and see.

"I shall draw you a bath. I'll have Clara heat some water," he said quietly.

Elsie came back out and saw Percy, making her frown. "What's wrong with you? You're being too quiet."

"He came off his horse," Albie said quickly.

Percy shot him a wild glare, because he'd probably rather tell her the truth than ever admit he fell off a horse. He huffed at Albie but softened at Elsie. "I'm fine, just a bit sore after the ride home."

"Can we prepare him a hot bath, please?" Albie asked.

She ushered Percy inside. "Ah, sore and sorry is never a good combination."

He stopped at the door. "Sore, yes. Never said I was sorry." He shot Albie a parting glance over his shoulder as he went inside.

Albie finished unpacking the horses, then he led them to the stables. When they were looked after, he went inside. Elsie was serving up his plate of stew while Clara poured more water into the washroom, to the tub where Percy was, no doubt.

"Has Percy eaten?" he asked, taking a seat at the table.

"Not yet," Elsie replied. She put the plate in front of him. "Fancy Percy coming off his horse. Never would have thought he's come off a horse in his whole life."

Albie didn't like the innuendo in her tone or the way she hovered over him. He didn't dare meet her eyes.

"And he landed right on his backside," she added, not even trying to hide her smile. Then she gave Albie's shoulder a gentle shove and lowered her voice. "And the day before he has to spend eight hours in a saddle, Albie."

He felt his face flame from his hairline down to his toes. "I don't know what you're talking about," he tried.

But he knew.

Just like she knew.

How she knew these things, Albie could never guess. Part of him didn't want to know.

"When you're done eating," she said, "you take his lunch into him and hand-feed him while he soaks before Robert and Des get back."

He almost said *yes, ma'am*. It was on the tip of his tongue, and he had to stop himself from saying the words out loud. Instead, he cleared his throat and shifted in his seat, still not meeting her gaze, his face burning hot.

"Fine," he managed. "Thank you."

Gee whiz.

For the boss of this place, he just got schooled.

She left him to eat in peace and he'd almost lost his appetite, but the smell of the fresh stew and hot bread was too good to ignore. He shovelled in a mouthful just as Elsie brought out a small plate of butter and slid it in front of him, and he almost choked.

"You all right there?" she asked, thumping him on the back.

He nodded, still trying to not die.

There is absolutely no way she could know about the butter. It was purely coincidental that she offered him some. Nothing more.

"Yes, yes," he said, then took a sip of water. "Fine, thank you."

He was just glad Percy wasn't there to witness his shame.

Chapter Seventeen

Percy lowered his sore and aching body into the hot water with a strained sigh. He grimaced at the twinge in his backside.

It really wasn't that bad.

Only that he'd had to spend the day in the saddle. If he'd just been doing chores around the house, he'd have been fine.

Or if he was more accustomed to it.

That's it. Just need more practice, he thought as he closed his eyes.

The hot water was now heavenly, ironing out his tired muscles and probably ridding him of the stink too.

He could have easily fallen asleep, but the door opening made him crack an eye. Albie stood there holding a tray. He seemed awkward at first, but then he rushed in and closed the door with his foot.

"I could have waited to eat," Percy said.

"Elsie insisted," he replied, pulling over the foot stool to the side of the tub and sitting on it. Then he whispered, "Did you say anything to her? About . . . not falling off a horse?"

"No. And I can't believe you said I came off a horse, by the way. Of all the ridiculous things to say."

"Hm," he frowned. "Maybe that's why she didn't believe it."

"What did she say?"

"She knows. What we did. I'm sure of it." His cheeks went a ruddy red. "She told me I had to come in here and feed you because of what I did to you."

"Oh my," Percy said. Then he couldn't help it—he laughed. "How did she know?"

"I don't know!" he whisper-shouted. "But she scares me."

Percy just laughed some more, at Albie's stricken misery than anything else. "Like she can talk. I've heard the noises coming out of their room."

"Oh god," Albie said, shrinking back. "Please don't ever say that to her. For the love of a merciful god."

Percy laughed so hard he snorted. Then he nodded to the plate and opened his mouth. "Some?"

Albie frowned. "You're going to make me spoon-feed you?"

"Want me to tell Elsie you refused?"

He growled at Percy, but then scooped up a

spoonful and fed it to him. "This may be my ship, but why do I feel like I'm not the captain? Heck, I'm not even second in command."

Percy laughed some more, then opened his mouth for more food. Albie, of course, complied.

"Do you feel better?" he asked quietly. "Does the bath help?"

"Much. Though I've decided we need to practice more so I become accustomed to it."

"Oh god," Albie mumbled, his cheeks reddening. "Elsie put butter on the table and I almost died. How could she know that?" He shook his head, still clearly mortified. "I'm so grateful you weren't there to see it."

Percy burst out laughing. "I'll ask for a double serving tonight."

"Please don't. Not in front of Des and Robert. I'll die on the spot."

Percy laughed some more, then opened his mouth for more stew.

THE BATH DID his body wonders and Percy was feeling almost back to normal by supper time. He'd managed some chores in the afternoon while Albie took a bath after him, and by the time Des and Robert got back, it was barely time for them to wash up a little and sit down for dinner.

Percy told them all about their time in town, at the store, the bank, and then at the saloon where Bill Kelly had intervened. Then this morning at the saleyard and how McAllister's respect held so much water in this town. Right or wrong, like it or not. It was proved today.

"Respect is one thing," Des said quietly. "Trust is another."

Robert nodded. "He'd sell his own mother if he thought it put him in front."

"I'm not sure I hold much of either for him," Albie said thoughtfully. "Respect, maybe. That he can run a business, make a profit. That takes grit out here. But trust him? No."

"He only makes a profit by undercutting anyone who comes close," Robert added. "People don't respect him. They fear him. And that's not a bed I'd wanna lie in."

"True," Percy allowed. "But those good-for-nothing men at the saloon now look at Albie a bit differently."

Des pointed his fork at Percy as he chewed and swallowed his food. "They respect Bill Kelly. That's true. He's tough as nails, but he's not always fair. He knows who pays his wages, so that's where his loyalty lies. But he's more honourable than McAllister, that's for sure."

Percy didn't entirely agree with that, but he could appreciate Des's perspective. When Percy thought of

Albie and how much he respected him, and how much Des and Robert respected him, he wasn't entirely sure it was because Albie paid their wages.

It was because he was an honourable man.

An honest man.

And that's what McAllister wasn't.

"Those men at the saloon can't think for themselves," Robert added. "I should know; I was one of them for a long time. They have a mob mentality, follow the herd, and do whatever will get them in favour for another beer. Don't go thinking too much of their opinions."

They were quiet for half a minute while they ate, and Des seemed to be thinking hard about something. "Speaking of a mob," he said quietly. "That mob of brumbies was back."

Percy and Albie both shot him a look. "When?" Percy asked.

"Just this afternoon," Des answered.

"Where?" Albie asked.

"On the flats, by the river," he replied.

"We saw 'em from the top of the ridgeline when we were moving the cattle."

Percy tried to keep his excitement in check but he was just about buzzing. He understood Des's reluctance over safety concerns but he was the one to bring it up just now, so he'd clearly had a change of heart.

"Oh, we should go take a look," Percy said. When

Albie's eyes met his, and when he didn't say no immediately, Percy saw his glimmer of opportunity. "We could go take a look tomorrow! Maybe even take a swag and camp out overnight."

Albie opened his mouth, clearly about to object, but Percy wasn't about to give up so easily.

"It's not that cold now," he added quickly. "And it'll be even less so when we're off the mountain, down on the flats."

"And what do we do with them?" Albie asked. "How do we corral them."

"Drive them back up the mountain," Percy said. He wasn't exactly sure how that would work but—

Albie shook his head. "Too risky."

"Impossible," Des added.

"Then we take them around," Percy tried. "Take them around the mountain to the bullock pass road. It's open now. Then directly into Alpine Falls, into the saleyards. We take the brood mares, yearlings, bring them back here. Sell the rest."

"Controlling a mob of wild horses isn't easy," Albie said.

"You only have to control the stallion," Percy said. "The mob will follow, right?"

Albie stared at him. "You'd have better luck controlling the weather."

Percy grinned at him. "We can try."

Albie scowled as he moved his dinner around with a fork, but Percy caught Robert smirking, and even Des found something funny. Albie looked up at them, seeing their reactions, then he shot Percy a hard glare before he sighed.

"If you get injured, I'll hear no complaints about it," he said flatly.

And Percy laughed, wiggling in his seat. "We'll leave at first light tomorrow." Albie wasn't smiling though, so Percy added, "We might not even see them, so don't worry just yet."

But he was so sure they would, and he couldn't wait.

THEY TOOK enough supplies to last them a full two days, should they need it. A swag, some bread and cheese, and fruit and water. Percy didn't particularly want to stay out overnight but part of him wanted to as well.

After all, camping out with Albie would be fun, right?

Even with Des and Robert. There would be no sleeping together, no romps by the campfire, but Percy didn't even mind.

Although Albie had jokingly threatened Percy with another arse so sore he wouldn't *want* to go searching for wild horses. But Percy had been all for it, so Albie's fake threat had fallen flat. And instead, they'd spent the night in each other's arms sleeping and doing nothing more.

Percy was all for that too.

At any rate, they were all saddling their horses before the sun had even cracked the horizon. Barely enough daylight to see properly, but Percy's grin was unmistakable.

Elsie and Clara had made an early breakfast, so when Des and Robert went in to eat, Albie quickly grabbed Percy's arm. "No foolishness today, please," he whispered.

"I would never," Percy said.

"I know," he murmured. "I just . . . I know you're excited, but if anything should happen to you . . . Percy, I'd never survive it. It was bad enough when you were ill from the knock to your head."

Percy looked up into his brown eyes with hints of gold and honey. "Same goes for you." Then he looked around to make sure they were alone. "I love you, Albert Bramwell. As the flowers love the sun."

Albie's cheeks flushed pink, and his shy smile became a grin, his eyes alight. "Poetry, huh?"

"Only for you."

He chuckled, then looked back toward the house. "We shouldn't be late. Lest we want the wrath of Elsie."

Percy started for the house. "No, we don't."

Breakfast was mostly quiet as they ate their porridge and stewed fruit. "We'll head down the property line," Des said.

The fact he was coming surprised Percy. His leg didn't allow long stints in the saddle, so Percy could only deduce his concern for Albie won out.

Or maybe he'd missed the thrill of the ride. He'd been a great horseman before his injury, Percy had heard. And he had to believe that Des's heart missed what his body would no longer allow.

Either way, Percy was glad Des was riding with them.

Albie pushed his empty plate away. "Our goal is to round up some horses, nothing more," he said. "If they get away from us, we leave them be. I'll not have anyone of us injured, or worse, for the sake of some wild brumbies."

He gave Percy a pointed look.

Percy sipped his tea, trying not to smile. "Yes, boss."

Albie huffed out a growl but then looked at Des and Robert. "Are we ready?"

They were both fighting a smile, but they gave a nod. "As we'll ever be," Des said.

Albie had a quick word with Elsie and Clara while Percy, Des, and Robert mounted their horses. Percy brought Minnie to the house for Albie, and Elsie walked him out.

"Don't you worry about us," she said. "I'll go ahead and strip beds and make some more preserves. We've got enough wood to last us a year and enough chores to keep us busy even longer."

Albie swung up into his saddle. "That's not my concern."

She grinned at him. "I've got a mean right hook and a shotgun should anyone turn up unannounced. Don't you worry about us."

Percy laughed, and Albie tipped his hat. "We'll be back soon enough."

"With a mob of horses," Percy added.

"I'll settle for in one piece," she said, then waved them off as they rode off.

They headed back behind the house and skirted abouts where Albie's property met McAllister's. There were now some fence posts intermittently placed, still not finished, but the beginnings of a very long and expensive job, Percy could guess.

"Is this your land or his?" Robert asked.

Albie looked around, his expression thoughtful. "Actually, looks about right. Hard to tell though. The big granite boulder I used to jump off, not far from where McAllister's boy was found, is on my land, so that'll be a good yardstick."

They soon came to the large boulder in question. The new fence line didn't run down this far yet, but there were some trees cleared to the left of it. As it looked now, if that's where the fence line would run, McAllister wasn't encroaching on Albie's land, but Percy couldn't help but wonder what it'd be like to be so untrustworthy.

No one trusted McAllister.

He couldn't even be trusted to run a fence line on his own land, and for all the "respect" and clout he had in town, no one trusted him to do the right thing.

And that was sad.

Percy would take Albie's righteousness and honesty over the likes of McAllister's ilk any day.

Before Percy knew it, they were at the edge of the ridgeline. The view down into the valley was spectacular. The morning sun painted everything clean and pastel. The air was fresh but not damp. It was a glorious sight.

"Why are you so quiet, Percy?" Albie asked. "Are you having regrets? Because this was your idea, I'll have you know."

The descent would be steep, yes. But not impossible. And they'd be taking it slow. It's not like they were racing off the edge . . .

"Regrets?" Percy asked. "I was just thinking that this is the best idea I've ever had."

"Best idea, as in the same as going over the ledge over there to save that kid while banging your head in the meantime?" Des said.

Percy looked over to the right, seeing the ledge in question. It looked a lot bigger now than what he'd remembered, especially now the mist was gone and he could see the sheer size of the drop. He shifted in his saddle. "Going over the ledge was fine," he said. "It was the landing that wasn't so great." He rubbed the side of his head for good measure.

Robert laughed. "Just keep your brains on the inside this time, all right?"

Percy grinned at him. "I'll do my best."

Albie looked at Des. "You good to keep going? Not one of us will think any different of you if you choose to stay. Actually, having one of us stay back might be a good idea."

Des gave Albie a hard look. "Then you go back; I'll take the lead," he said, taking his horse over the embankment first.

The four of them rode in single file, each allowing their horse sure footing and all the time they needed. It was a slow descent, snaking down the mountain side, through trees and long grasses, no path to speak of. Some parts were too steep and they had to hedge along sideways.

If Percy had entertained the idea at all of bringing horses back up this way, now he didn't.

Unless they took them further into McAllister's property, and that was never gonna happen. Not even with his permission, probably.

As it stood now, they were going further south and coming back around into Alpine Falls with the mob of horses, or without them. Coming back up this way was not an option.

Percy's heart was in his throat the whole way down. He let Bandit do all the work, trusting his horse more than his own abilities. Albie's horse, Minnie, made it look easy, though the way Albie handled her and rode with such ease, Percy had to wonder if Albie was part mountain goat too.

Des was more cautious, understandably. And Robert was sensible too. Percy was very happy to let them lead. He wasn't born and bred in these mountains like they were, and he wasn't fool enough to think he could pretend he was.

"Look," Des said, pointing out.

They were about halfway down with a clear view to the open land below, and there in all their glory was the mob of wild brumbies. A big bay stallion at the fore, his herd behind him, galloping free.

It was a sight Percy would never forget.

The sound of hooves thundering echoed up the valley and it made their horses a little skittish. It made Percy's heart hammer, his pulse quicken, his excitement grow.

This is what they were here for.

It made their descent to the bottom a little faster, more urgent now. And by the time they reached flatter, cleared ground, they began to trot, then canter. And when they spotted the mob cresting over the next rise, they took off at a gallop.

Their horses flew over the green grasses. The sun was warm and the wind on Percy's face as they raced made the thrill of it better.

Seeing Des ride flat strap was a sight to behold. Because right then, he wasn't a cripple or a man with just one good leg. He was a horseman, maybe the best Percy had ever seen.

Even Robert, as well. He was low in his saddle barely moving with the horse underneath him. He wasn't some good-for-nothing town drunkard. He was fast and a damn good horseman.

And then there was Albie.

His coat billowed out behind him, his hat pulled down, though Percy caught the grin he wore.

It made Percy laugh.

He could ride just fine. He'd grown up on a horse and could handle flat and open land as well as any man. But he wasn't as good as Albie. He'd never seen him ride like this, in full flight, and heaven help him, Percy had never seen a more handsome sight.

Whatever the outcome of this, whether they caught the mob or not, Percy wanted to do this, to ride alongside Albie like this, for the rest of his life.

But then the flat land became rises and gullies, undulating at first and then steeper. They rode them like waves, their horses sailing through, barely slowing with each crest.

The rise and fall made Percy's stomach plummet with each one, and his heart was racing.

The mob of brumbies were at a full gallop now, aware of their pursuit.

They had the advantage, being riderless and free, being familiar with this terrain. They could turn on a dime, swap and sway, and use the gullies and tall gum trees to their advantage.

Percy could have sworn the brumby stallion led them through the trees with low branches on purpose. He nearly copped a branch to the head but ducked just in time.

They followed them along the line of the gully, where they disappeared over the edge and out of view.

Des pulled his horse up just shy of the drop, and Robert pulled hard on his reins, stopping just before the edge. Albie and Percy got there not a second later, already slowing down.

Their horses were panting, snorting, breathing hard. The men were too. But they sat there and watched the mob meet the bottom and begin up the next rise.

"Too good for us," Des said.

Robert was still studying them. "I count thirty," he said.

Percy hadn't even tried to count them. He was too busy trying not to fall off his horse.

Albie looked at Percy. He was breathing hard, his nostrils flared. "You good?"

Percy grinned at him. "Are you kidding? That was the most fun I've ever had!"

Albie sighed.

"Did you see that first gully?" Percy asked, excited. "Bandit dropped out from under me so fast I almost lost my breakfast."

Robert laughed and Des snorted. "Fun, huh?" Robert asked.

Percy laughed, breathless. "Every second of it."

Des pulled his horse around. "Let's take them to the river. It's got decent flow this year. We now have the fun job of getting home."

Percy didn't mind one bit.

It was all fun to him.

Chapter Eighteen

Albie should have known that Percy would love it. The speed of it, the thrill. The danger, the rush.

They didn't even get close to rounding up the wild horses.

But part of Albie didn't even mind.

He hadn't been down this side of the cliff face since he was a young boy. As they rode down toward the river, he pulled Minnie up and pointed behind them. "Percy, look."

Percy stopped and looked up at the sheer rock face that jutted several hundred yards straight up. "What's up there?" Percy asked.

"Home," Albie replied.

Percy's eyes went wide. "All the way up there? Did we come down that far?"

He nodded to the far end of the cliff face. "Further that way. But now you can see how far you almost fell."

Percy paled a little. "Wowzers. That's quite a drop. I don't remember it being so high up. It was misty, I guess. Hard to see."

And because he'd knocked his brain about in his skull.

But suddenly the fact he'd *only* taken a knock to the head made it seem trivial. It could have been so much worse. Albie didn't need to say that because, from the look on Percy's face, he seemed to be thinking the same thing.

They rode on for a while, heading further downward, enjoying the warm sunshine, the birdsong, the crickets.

The flies, not so much.

"Ugh," Percy said, swishing his hand in front of his face. "I forgot about flies. The best thing about living up there," he gestured to the mountain behind them. "Is the lack of flies."

"Just wait for summer," Des said.

"Especially when you're mucking out the stables," Robert added.

Albie laughed at Percy's expression.

They reached the river, and each of them slid down from their horses. They let them drink and eat the green grass by the shade of the trees, and everyone pretended not to notice how Des limped on his leg, grimacing as he lowered himself down onto the grass.

Despite the obvious pain, he looked remarkably

happy to be riding like this again. And that made Albie smile.

Albie took a moment to appreciate it all. Not just the view, but how his men were working together as a team.

He wished his dad were here to see this.

"It's beautiful down here," Percy said. "How far is the road from here?"

"A fair way," Albie said. "Though I was just a boy the last time I came down here. Why?"

"Well, I just wondered if it's kinda close, why your house is up there and not down here?"

Des and Robert both stayed silent. Whether they were waiting on Albie's version of an answer or if they didn't know, he wasn't sure.

"The road past home was built first, probably. The bullock road this way came after," Albie answered. "And the only access to the road from here is through Crown land. I don't remember much of what my father said about it, only that he wouldn't pay the government one penny for access to his own land."

Des smiled at that. "Yeah, that about sums it up. From what he told me too."

"Makes sense," Robert said.

Percy frowned. "I thought Crown land had a right-of-passage clause." He pursed his lips. "Could be wrong. Maybe it's different here, but I remember my grandfather getting permission and it never cost him a single penny. My grandfather would have raised hell if it did." Then he shrugged. "Could be a different permission. It's not like I'm an expert in such things."

Albie stared at him, as did Robert and Des. "You know about these things?"

Percy made a face. "Only what I heard." He met Albie's gaze. "Could be worth asking your father's lawyer when we get into town."

"What would I do with the access anyway?" Albie wondered out loud.

"Build a second house," Percy answered simply. "Down here. Run a second farm. Lotta flat grasslands down here just doing nothing for cattle and sheep. Maybe even just in winter when it's too cold up on top of the mountain. Lambs'd be ready for the spring that way."

Albie stared at him in disbelief.

Could it be that simple?

No, of course not.

"You wouldn't even need a whole house," he added. "Just a hut, basically. You and me could come down here for the winter and run some sheep and horses while Des and Robert manage the main farm up there."

Des laughed, a long strand of grass sticking out of his lips. "Just full of ideas, aren't ya."

"Ain't had a bad one yet," Percy said with a grin.

Robert snorted. "This one hasn't exactly panned out too well."

"It's not finished yet."

Albie unpacked some lunch and they ate a quick bite in the shade by the river. The water was cold but refreshing, wide and shallow enough for them to cross over. Their boots barely got wet in the stirrups as they rode through, and guessing the wild horses were long gone, they headed southeast through the hills and woodlands to the valley that would eventually bring them out to the road.

The valley was walled by steep, rocky outcrops, and it was probably part of the river system at some point, Albie's father had once said. He couldn't decide if this part of his land now looked bigger or smaller now that he'd grown up.

When he'd been a boy, it'd all looked so big, but he never really appreciated the size of it until now.

Until it was his.

Could he utilise this parcel of land as Percy had suggested?

The river, or creek—whatever they wanted to call it —certainly made it valuable. But the sheer cliffs that divided his property in two had made it unfathomable, too difficult. But he'd never considered running it as a separate property to the land they farmed up on the mountains.

Maybe he could ask his lawyer when they were in town. Maybe he could re-read the papers he'd signed after his father's funeral.

Des snapped his fingers, and it caught their attention. He pointed then, and they all followed his line of sight to see what he was looking at . . .

And there through the woodlands, down on the next slope, was the mob of wild brumbies.

Des pointed to himself and Robert, then to the far west. "We'll go round," he whispered. Albie didn't think the horses would hear, but Des clearly wasn't taking any chances. Then he nodded to Percy and Albie. "Stay here. We'll flush them out, and you block them. We'll funnel them into the valley."

Percy's grin was contagious, and Albie nodded. "Be safe," Albie said.

Des gave him a serious nod. "Be patient. It's all about the timing. Rush them too soon and they'll scatter."

Albie and Percy watched in silence as Robert and Des back-tracked a little, then headed west as Des had said they would. They ambled slowly, as quietly as they could, and when they'd got around the herd, they broke into a gallop.

Robert cracked his whip, the sound biting the air and echoing off the cliffs. The mob startled, looked up, then turned as one and took off, heading straight toward Albie and Percy.

The sound of hooves thundered in time with Albie's pulse.

"Stay here," Albie said to Percy, taking Minnie out a little wider. Like their horses knew the chase was on again, both Minnie and Bandit stomped their hooves and pulled on their reins.

Albie's heart was in his throat, and he saw Percy shift in his saddle a few times, eager to go.

Robert cracked his whip again, the sound biting the air once more, and the mob of brumbies changed direction like a flock of birds.

"Now!" Albie yelled, and he and Percy set off at a gallop, heading straight toward the mob.

Albie took out his whip, gripped the handle, and swung it wide and high, cracking the tip. The sound rang out like a shot, and the wild horses turned again, heading straight toward their only free path.

The funnel of the valley.

Just as Des had said.

Albie rode out wider as the four of them chased the herd into the valley. Des was on the opposite side, Robert and Percy at the rear.

Albie spared a glance back at Percy, concerned and hoping he was keeping up.

Percy's grin told Albie all he needed to know.

And they continued to ride, herding them.

The stallion that led the brumbies tried to steer them off a time or two, but with a crack of a whip, they soon straightened up.

But Minnie was slowing up. She couldn't keep galloping forever. And Albie noticed some of the smaller yearlings in the mob were slowing.

Des seemed to notice too. He took out his rope and

rode high in his saddle, lassoing circles above his head. He went in close to the mob, their pace slowing a little, and he swung for the stallion.

The lasso slipped over its head and Des pulled them up to a stop. Albie went to the front, and with Robert and Percy at the rear, they boxed the horses in.

The stallion pulled on the rope, rearing up on his hind legs, braying and snorting. The other horses tried to scatter, but they kept them penned in.

But Des pulled harder, and Ox reared up too. He was bigger than the wild stallion, and with Des's expert touch in the saddle, the stallion eventually quietened.

They gave the horses a few moments to breathe, to calm down.

"Holy shit," Percy cried out. "Did we do it?"

Just then, one horse made a break for it and Robert edged it back to the herd. "We haven't done it yet."

Des, who was still holding the roped stallion tight, said, "Albie, rope him from your side. We're gonna ride him in like this."

Albie wasn't sure if that would work, but he trusted Des. He'd always known he was a great horseman, but he'd never seen him ride like he did today.

Albie took his rope and swung the lasso above his head, aiming for the stallion while trying to hold his line, lest the mob try and escape. He missed, startling the horse, causing him to rear up again, braying and snorting.

Des held his rope tight, and Ox pulled back,

keeping the lasso taut. Albie could see Robert and Percy moving, no doubt keeping the restless herd penned in.

He needed to get this.

No second chances.

He circled his lasso above his head, keeping Minnie steady with his left hand, and when the stallion threw his head down, Albie knew he was about to launch upward, rearing up to fight.

He swung his rope high and let it go, and it caught the stallion around the neck.

A perfect shot.

Except then the stallion fought twice as hard, rearing up and snorting, kicking and stomping. The other horses moved, and it took every ounce of strength Albie had to pull and hold him.

"Keep him steady," Des yelled as they restrained him. "That's it."

Albie didn't dare take his eyes off the stallion, not for a second, but he trusted Robert and Percy to hold the back of the herd.

"Now we're gonna walk him forward," Des yelled. "You ready to move 'em up from the rear?"

"Yes, sir," Robert yelled back.

Albie would revisit and probably laugh at the *sir* comment later, but for now, all his concentration was on the stallion.

He was a big bay-coloured stallion, at least fifteen hands. He was unkempt and feral, and there was wildness in his eyes. On high alert, ears up, watching every single thing, defiant and proud, even with two ropes around his neck.

Albie had to admire him.

He towered over Minnie. She was just a mountain pony by comparison. But he didn't have to steer or direct her at all. She knew what to do better than Albie did.

Once they got the stallion to walk without pulling or fighting them, they began to trot.

And, just as Percy said, the rest of the herd followed. Well, with Robert and Percy at the rear.

You only have to control the stallion, Percy had said.

And he'd been right.

It wasn't an easy ride. The valley had its obstacles: gullies and huge boulders to navigate and far too many trees.

But they barely slowed, keeping a steady pace the whole way. It made the mob more compliant, but their horses were getting tired.

Albie had no clue how long they'd have to ride or how they'd corral them if they had to stop for the night. It was getting on in the afternoon as it was, and he'd noticed Des wincing a time or two, clearly in pain. Albie was having doubts. Doubts that this had ever been a good idea. They should have made a holding yard first.

He should have taken the time and done it properly.

Like his father would have.

He was about to raise the question about stopping when Des wiped his brow and nodded up ahead. "Can you see what I see?"

Albie wasn't sure what he was supposed to be looking at.

Is that . . . ? Wait. Is that . . . ?

"Is that the road?"

Des grinned at him, opening his water cannister with one hand and taking a sip.

Albie looked behind him, at the tired horses, at the even tireder men. "Are you good to keep going?"

Robert gave some kind of salute while Percy just grinned.

It made Albie's heart squeeze, and his lips pulled at a returning smile. Then he caught Des wincing again. "What about you?"

"I'll be fine if I don't stop," he answered. "Best to keep 'em moving, yeah?"

Albie gave a nod. He thought so too. And now the ropes around the stallion weren't so taut, it was less strain on them all.

The leader of the mob was resigned to his fate.

For now, at least.

It really was best to keep them moving. They came up to the road and headed left, back toward the mountains.

Toward Alpine Falls.

The road made for easier riding, that was for sure, but the horses were slow now. Compliant and not an ounce of fight or flight left in them.

They rode and rode; it must have been close to sixteen miles to town. They encountered a few travellers coming in the opposite direction. Twice some men on horseback could get off the road easily enough. Once a wagon had to pull off to the side of the road and stop as they rode past.

It wasn't every day a team of horsemen brought thirty horses to town, especially with two ropes around the stallion at the front.

But the riders all tipped their hats, bidding them good day and good luck.

And the road got steeper, the ride uphill into the mountains. The mountain on one side, a steep drop-off on the other, and the mob of horses had no choice but to follow the road.

Albie was tired and sore, hungry as hell, and with night falling fast, the temperature along with it. But they passed a gate, then another, and soon more houses, the smell of woodfires on the cold air, and Albie knew they were getting close to town.

It was damn near too dark to ride by the time they rode into Alpine Falls.

"Clear the road!" someone yelled up ahead.

"Get out of their way!" yelled another.

And as they rode in through town, past the baker, the saloon, and the store, they had quite an audience.

People stood along the sides of the road, watching, smiling. Albie didn't focus on their faces. He was too tired and too focused on the stallion they still had roped at the front of the mob.

He got a bit flighty at the crowd, at the buildings, and the attention. But the streets made like a funnel, and they rode into the saleyard, someone already with the holding yard gate open.

And, just like that, they rode in to cheers and applause from the watching crowd.

Men in workwear, some in neat trousers and jackets, ladies in fine dresses, children with wide eyes and big smiles.

While they were covered in dust and sweat and looking rough and ragged.

But Albie had never been prouder than he had in that moment. He slid down from Minnie and knew the bigger test was upon him. He had to get his rope off the stallion while everyone watched.

He approached the wild stallion slowly, keeping his rope slack. He didn't want to pull too hard and frighten him. The horses were exhausted and thirsty, and Albie had to use that to his favour. Even as exhausted as it was, Albie could still see the wild fight in the stallion's eyes.

A hush fell over the crowd as he neared him, and

the horse dropped his head a few times, stomping the dirt.

"Easy, boy," Albie murmured, still inching closer. "Easy there."

His heart hammered, his mouth dry. Common sense told him he was crazy; his understanding of horses told him otherwise.

This stallion had had enough for one day.

He was run out, the last fight in him was gone.

Albie inched his hand closer, keeping his hands where the stallion could see them. No loud noises, no sudden movements, and he ever so slowly lifted the ropes from around his neck.

The stallion baulked a little, but Albie held his ground, as if the beast somehow knew Albie meant no harm. Albie looked him right in the eye, gave him a nod of respect, and backed away. He climbed the railing just in time to see Percy almost sag with relief.

He, Robert, and Des were off their horses now. Percy held Minnie's reins, and when Albie climbed down from the railing, Percy lifted both hands in the air. "We did it!" he crowed.

The audience all cheered and Albie couldn't help but laugh, and whether it was relief, exhaustion or pride, he could have almost wept. Until Des shifted his weight and his leg almost buckled and he grimaced in pain.

Albie and Robert quickly caught him. "Does

anyone have a cart?" Albie yelled out. Des was in no shape to walk to the saloon.

"No, I'll be fine," Des said. His face was etched in pain. "I can walk."

"Des—"

"I said I can walk," he snapped. There was no heat in it; Des was tired, most probably hungry, and most certainly in pain. "Just need to stretch it out some, 'tis all."

"Fine," Albie relented. "Robert, make sure he gets to the saloon. Order any food you want, and I'll speak to them about rooms when I get there. I just need to speak to Mr Bailey." The saleyard master had to be here somewhere. "Percy, see the horses watered, please?"

"Sure thing," he replied.

Des made it a few steps unassisted, but when they'd almost reached the line of onlookers, he stumbled again, and Robert was quick to throw Des's arm around his shoulder.

"Do you need a doctor?" someone in the crowd asked.

"Nah, he needs a drink," another replied.

"I'll take neither, thanks," Des replied, hanging on to Robert. "I'll be just fine without either."

Albie smiled after them, leaving the four horses in Percy's capable hands, and went in search of John Bailey.

ALBIE CAME out of the saleyard office to find the crowd gone. The mob of horses were settled, the water troughs gleaming in the cool moonlight.

And Percy, standing, waiting, smiling.

Their four horses were tied to the railing, but Albie couldn't take his eyes off Percy. His hat was in his hands, his blond hair flattened to his head. His face was smeared with dirt and sweat, but that smile . . . Albie had never seen such a welcoming sight.

"All good?" Percy asked.

Albie gave a nod and folded the receipts and shoved them in his inside coat pocket. "Yeah. Let's get these horses to the stable." He gave Minnie's forehead a scratch. "How's my girl?"

"She wants hot food and a bath," Percy replied.

Albie snorted and gave him a gentle shove. "Not you."

They climbed back into the saddles, leading the other two horses behind them. There was no rush in them now. They were sore and tired and in need of a very big feed of hay in the stables.

"We're almost done for the day, girl," Albie said, giving her neck a rub.

"I could say something about not quite being done for today," Percy replied quietly. "But I'm too tired."

Albie laughed. "I should think so."

As they got to the stables, they unsaddled their four

horses, fed and watered them, and as tired as he was, Albie still made the time to brush them down.

They'd surely earned that today.

"Do you think Des will be fine?" Percy asked.

Albie gave a nod. "He'll be sore, no doubt about it. But you know, I think he's missed this."

Percy's eyes got really big. "Did you see how good he was out there today?"

Albie laughed. "Oh, I saw."

"And you," Percy said softly. "I'm proud of you."

"I'm proud of you too," Albie murmured. "Of all of us. This town has called us a farm of misfits for the last time."

Percy beamed. "Come on, let's go eat. And see how Des fared."

And see if Robert was still sober, Albie thought.

He hated to doubt him. He hated that the drink was a demon Robert had to fight every time he came to town. But sometimes it was an unwinnable fight, and Albie wouldn't think any less of Robert if he lost that fight today.

But when they got into the bar, they found Des on a seat with his bad leg outstretched onto another chair and Robert telling the story of how Des had lassoed the stallion and never missed a beat to an enraptured audience.

"Here, good man," one fellow said, trying to hand Robert a mug of ale. "Have a drink. You've earned it today."

It was as if the world stopped turning. The room fell silent, all eyes on him. Robert swallowed hard, raised his hand, and for one moment, Albie thought he'd take the beer.

But he put his palm up. "Not for me, thank you. It does me no good."

Albie just about burst with pride.

"Des might need it though," Robert said.

Des waved him off. "Not for me either. Just another water," he said toward the barman.

"And four of the biggest plates of grub you've got," Albie added. "Whatever's hot and good."

Des shifted in his seat, Albie guessed to give the chair to either Albie or Percy. But he winced again and hissed. "Stay as you are," Albie said. "We can fetch another chair."

"Sorry," Des said. "Once I stopped, damn thing seized up on me."

"You'll be sore a day or two," Albie said. "If you want to see the doc before we leave tomorrow . . ."

Robert sat at the table. "If you need a shot or two of whiskey, don't deny yourself on my behalf. I'm good with it now."

Des shook his head. "I'll be all right."

"You loved being out there today," Percy said quietly. "The grin you wore the whole time was telling. And I can tell you, I ain't ever seen anyone ride as good as you rode today."

"You shoulda seen me before I got kicked in the

side of the knee," Des said. "I could have taken this whole mob by myself."

They all laughed, and two women slid plates of corned beef onto the table. "Thank you," Albie said to them, expecting them to leave. But they didn't.

But he realised, a little too late and a lot too awkwardly, that the two women only had eyes for Robert and Des. Percy was apparently much quicker on the uptake because he nudged his knee to Albie's under the table, and when Albie looked at him, he was shoving a forkful of food past his smiling lips.

They ate as quickly as they could while the two women skirted around their table with more water, more bread, gentle smiles, and flirty eyes.

Albie and Percy couldn't get out of there quick enough.

Albie had paid for two rooms—one for him and Percy, the other for Robert and Des. He probably should have got them separate rooms, but he didn't want to think about that.

When Albie closed and locked the door behind them, Percy put the lantern on the dresser, turned to Albie, and laughed.

"That was so awkward," Percy said. "I mean, I hope they have a good night and all. I just don't need to be there to see it."

"Agreed," Albie said, taking his coat off and hanging it on the hook. Then his overshirt, then his boots, and when he sat on the edge of the bed, he fell back, exhausted. "What a day."

Percy took his coat off and threw it over the corner of a chair, and Albie turned his head to watch as Percy slid his suspenders off his shoulders, letting them fall around his thighs. It was Albie's favourite part of their undressing ritual.

Oh, he quite liked the reveal of skin too. But there was something about when Percy let his braces down that sang to Albie.

"What are you looking at me like that for?" Percy said with a smirk. "We're too tired, and if you think I'm spending another day in the saddle like last time . . ." He shook his head. "It's all fun and games now, but by tomorrow night, I'll be back in a hot bath full of aches and regrets."

Albie chuckled. "I'm just admiring the view. Am I not allowed to look?"

"Looking is fine," Percy said with a knowing smile. "But looking usually leads to touching, and touching leads to fu—"

"Other things," Albie said quickly, cutting him off. "That mouth is too sweet for cussing."

Percy laughed. "Really? Could you really call what I've done to you with this mouth sweet?"

Albie groaned out a laugh. "The sweetest." Then he had to adjust himself. "Stop talking of these things. Certain parts of my body don't know I'm too exhausted."

Percy's eyebrow rose, full of cheek and hope. "Really?"

Albie threw a wash towel from the bed at him. "No, none of that. Go wash up. I'll go after you."

Percy grumbled as he walked out of the room, and Albie closed his eyes for just a second. Only to be woken by the face of an angel, with a light spray of freckles across his nose, bright blue eyes, and his blond hair washed and brushed down.

"Hey, sleepyhead," this angel said, looking down at him. "Go wash up. You smell like horse sweat."

Albie rolled off the bed, the angel smacked his backside as he got up, and he begrudgingly went down the hall to the washroom.

Much cleaner and desperate for sleep, Albie went back to their room. He'd hoped that maybe Percy had somehow stayed awake, but no, he was already in bed, sound asleep.

When Albie climbed in, Percy automatically snuggled into his side and Albie's arm went around his shoulder. He closed his eyes and didn't move a muscle till morning.

BOTH ROBERT and Des had sly smirks at breakfast, but Albie didn't want to know.

"Well, you two had a good night," Percy went and said outright.

They both ducked their heads, but Des cleared his throat, about to say something, when Albie put his hand up. "For the love of everything under the sun, I don't want to know."

Percy snorted his cup of tea, and they ate their breakfast in silence.

Smiling, eyes holding silent conversations, but thankfully, without another word.

Des's leg was still giving him grief. Despite the new skip in his step, his limp was worse, and he grimaced a time or two as they were seeing to their horses.

But Albie knew better than to mention it in front of anyone.

And they'd be home tonight, and then Des could rest easy for a day or two. They all could.

But first he had some business to attend to.

"I want you to come with me," Albie had said quietly.

Percy gave him a serious nod. "Of course."

THEY WALKED into Mr Flannigan's office as soon as the door opened for business. The lawyer was surprised to see Albie and even more so to see he'd brought someone with him.

Percy stuck out his hand and gave him a confident smile. "Percy Collins."

"Nice to meet you," he replied. "Albie, what can I

do for you? I hear you're quite the talk around town this morning."

Albie couldn't help but feel a rush of pride. "Yes, it's an unexpected visit, sorry for not giving any notice. We rode some wild horses in last night and decided to stay the night."

"Fair call. There was much chatter in the store this morning. And some interest in that herd. Hopefully that equals a nice profit for you."

"We can hope."

"So, what brings you in?" He looked again at Percy, then back to Albie, waiting for an answer.

"Well," Albie started. "What do you know about getting access through Crown land? Because I was thinking . . . what if I were to turn the bottom half of my land into a second farm?"

Mr Flannigan's smile was slow to spread, his eyes fond. "You got some smarts about you, Albie. You are your father's son. Easements through Crown land are one thing, but first, let's dig out your title deeds and read that small print."

Albie gave Percy a smile, hopeful this could actually be happening. Was it possible? Could he run sheep and cattle all year on the lowlands?

Albie wasn't sure, but it couldn't hurt to ask, right? To try?

"Thought you'd be in the mountains forever, Albie," Mr Flannigan said with a wink. "Now you're looking at coming down the mountain?"

"I'll always be a mountain man, sir. Echo Creek is in my blood," Albie said. "But Percy here is the brains behind it, and he's more familiar with farming lowlands."

"Oh?" Flannigan cocked his head, aiming a concerned look at Percy. "Are you doing this for Mr Bramwell, Mr Collins? Or are you doing this together?"

It was Albie who answered. "Together," he said confidently. "We're doing this together."

Flannigan turned his gaze back to Albie. "Am I adding his name to anything officially?"

Albie smiled at Percy, but Percy quickly shook his head, his eyes wide. "Oh no, I'm not a partner."

Not yet, he isn't, Albie thought.

There would be one way to have their names on a binding certificate.

"We'll talk about that," Albie said, trying not to smile. "But for now, no. It's just my name."

But it wouldn't be, not forever, Albie realised. They'd be joined, equal partners for life, one day. He was sure of it.

CHAPTER NINETEEN

LIFE ON THE FARM HAD BEEN PERFECT THESE LAST few months. Quiet, busy, prospering.

It wasn't always easy, and Percy never for one moment thought it would be.

But he loved every minute of it.

Sharing this life with Albie. Sharing his bed.

They'd brought eight broodmares and one young colt back with them from the mob of wild brumbies, and it was a good, solid start to securing yearly sales moving forward.

And the mountains in spring and summer?

The most beautiful part of the country Percy had ever seen.

Wildflowers, cool breezes on warm days, and the bluest sky you could ever imagine.

Elsie and Clara still worked hard, and they'd never been happier. Clara laughed more and more, her confidence growing every day, and Elsie now rode Minnie some days out to help round up cattle.

Des and Robert found themselves going back to town a time or two, but Percy wasn't sure if anything would come of it. He hoped it would, not that he was game to ask. It seemed an unspoken rule that Elsie and Clara were not a companionable option, as if they somehow knew they only had eyes for each other.

And if Des and Robert knew the same about Percy and Albie, they never let on about that either.

Percy was certain Des knew something, knew that they shared a bedroom at least. Maybe he thought it was innocent. Given the lack of bedrooms, there were few options of rooms . . . But there was a time or two when he'd had to snap his fingers to get Percy's attention because he'd been staring at Albie a beat too long.

Not as stealthy as he'd thought.

Des would just smile and shake his head, then repeat his order.

But Percy couldn't help it. Just seeing Albie across the paddock or in the stable, or God forbid, on his horse, Percy was lost to the sight of him. His heart skipped a beat every time and fluttered back to life. It made his breath catch, his blood sing.

He loved him more each and every day and still could hardly believe that this was his life. That he got to be his truthful self, that he did an honest day's work every day and could spend every night in the arms of the man he loved.

He almost wished his parents could see him now. Not in bed, of course. Not even with a male lover. But just how happy he was. How productive and hard-working he was. How he'd found a place where he was accepted and loved, with this group of misfits.

His new family.

Percy couldn't ever imagine being happier.

Until Albie found him mid-morning, mucking out stables, sweat dripping down his face, ignoring the flies and the way Ox kept trying to nudge him into the wall. Albie walked in, his short-sleeved shirt open at the collar, his skin glistening with sweat, and he was smiling like the devil.

Percy stood up straight, stretching his back, and wiped his forehead with the back of his hand. "What's that look for?"

"So, I was thinking . . ."

Percy found himself smiling right back at him. "About?"

"Well, I was thinking it might be time."

"For what?" Percy only now noticed that Albie was holding a folded letter.

"For you and me to go spend a day or two down on the lowland," he said. "Maybe find the best spot to build a hut."

Percy gasped. "You got it?"

Albie held up the letter, grinning, and he read the first few lines. "To the concern of Mister Albert

Bramwell. We acknowledge receipt of your application and hereby grant permission—"

Percy threw his arms around Albie and had to stop himself from jumping with excitement. "Albie! Do you know what this means?"

"Yes, we have an easement approval for a permanent right of passage through Crown land."

"Well, that, yes." Percy met his gaze. "But you're doing this. If you didn't prove yourself before this, you certainly will now. Not one person in these mountains will ever doubt you again."

His smile was shy and grateful. "Thank you, Percy. I couldn't have done this without you. Hell, I couldn't have even read this letter without you."

Percy wanted to lean up on his toes and press his lips to Albie's right there in the stable, in the middle of the day, but he didn't dare. But oh boy, how he wanted to . . .

"Will it be just you and me going down the mountain?" Percy asked, his voice low.

Albie seemed to understand exactly where Percy's thoughts had taken him. "Yes."

"We best have Elsie pack us adequate bread . . . and butter."

Albie grinned. "I've already asked."

THEY HAD an early lunch and were heading down the mountain with the summer sun directly overhead. As if the birds and insects agreed with Percy's mood, there was song all around them.

McAllister had made some headway with the fencing that now separated their land, though thankfully they'd had no repeats of missing children.

McAllister had left them alone too, which Percy was grateful for. How happy he'd be to hear that Albie would be utilising the bottom part of his land, diversifying his income, branching out, and being successful. Well, that remained to be seen.

Would Albie ever be a threat to McAllister's wealth?

No.

Not likely.

But Percy remembered how McAllister had wanted to buy Albie's farm. Made a deal of it. And maybe it wasn't about the land at all. Maybe it was just to prove that he could buy Albie's property—or any property for that matter—on a whim. That he could throw money at whomever he chose, like a sport.

But Albie had once mentioned that McAllister's property didn't include the river like Albie's did. And people like McAllister always wanted what other people had.

McAllister's property didn't have massive cliffs dividing it in two, either. He had more farmable acreage, flat rolling pastures. He'd always seen Albie's farm as lesser than his own.

Except for the river.

Access to water for livestock, for housing. Water was a valuable commodity.

Percy wasn't sure why he was thinking about that.

Something in the back of his mind.

"You're being quiet," Albie said. They were halfway down the mountain, meandering down the steep incline, ducking branches as they went. "Silence from you concerns me."

"Concerns you? Why?"

"You're either mad at me or you've got your thinking cap on, and either way, I'm in trouble."

Percy laughed. "I'm pleased to know that you've learned this. But if you have to know, I was thinking about what you're going to do to me tonight. By the campfire, under the stars. Not another soul for miles." He sighed wistfully. "How much butter did Elsie supply us with?"

Albie shifted in his saddle and cleared his throat. "You shouldn't say such things to me, or we'll stop right here."

"I wouldn't be opposed."

Albie shot him a look over his shoulder, half scowl, half warning. "We need to get to the bottom before dark. If we stop now, we might as well set up camp right here, and how would you propose we sleep on ground this steep?"

"Well, I don't have plans for sleeping much tonight."

Albie sighed. "Percival Collins, you are a dangerous man. Now I'll be thinking of nothing else for the remainder of the ride. Do you know how uncomfortable it is to ride with a . . . certain hardness."

Percy laughed. "Why, yes, Albert Bramwell, I do believe I am familiar."

Albie grumbled. "I'm sorry I asked."

"If it's any consolation," Percy added, "tomorrow I'll be the one who'll be sorry."

"I'll make sure of that."

Then it was Percy who shifted in his saddle, warmth pooling low in his belly, in his balls. And he was all of a sudden far too impatient for it. "Could we pick up the pace a little. Time's wasting."

THE LOWLAND near the river was just as beautiful in summer as it had been in winter.

There were flowers and tall grasses swaying in the breeze, and the sun was, thankfully, now getting low. The river was more a creek now, shallower than it had been when they'd been here to herd the horses, but it was still flowing, and boy, was it sure good to drink.

They found a good spot to set up camp not far from the water, under the cover of some trees along the old riverbed. Once the horses were settled, they collected some wood and dried grass, and while Albie started the campfire, Percy collected some fresh water from the river and sorted out their rations of food.

Percy rolled out their swag, getting their bed ready, and sure, he was hungry for food, but he was way hungrier for something else.

It'd been a week since Albie had taken him the way he liked the most. Sure, there'd been other ways to share their bodies, but what Percy ached for was to feel Albie inside him.

He almost pouted when Albie insisted they eat first.

"But I know you," Albie said. "Eating will take five minutes. What you want will take considerably longer. And I want to take my time with you."

Percy hated common sense and reasoning.

He sighed. "Fine, but this will be the quickest dinner we've ever had." Percy had never had much patience, and he had even less now that they were alone and were free to do as they pleased.

It felt like a gift they were wasting on unnecessary things such as food.

Dinner was bread toasted on the fire with cheese on top so it melted, and some of Clara's stewed fruit and tea from a billy. Percy was too impatient to enjoy any of it, and to make it worse, Albie didn't even seem to care.

So Percy played a different game.

He groaned when he bit into the cheese and toast.

Albie had laughed at first, but when he looked over to Percy, he made a show of licking his fingers and moaning.

Then Albie wasn't smiling.

So Percy moaned again, higher pitched this time, almost a whine, and he let his head drop back and he closed his eyes. "So good," he murmured.

Albie said nothing, so when Percy dared to open his eyes, he found Albie staring at him. Eyes dark by the flickering fire, his jaw bulging. "Percy," he warned.

"Hmm," he sighed. Then he licked his lips, teasing. "Do you have a problem?"

Albie's nostrils flared and he put his plate down real slow. Then, without a word, he stood up and stepped closer to Percy, grabbed him by the shirt, and dragged him backward to the bedroll.

Percy almost dropped his plate, barely managing to set it down at all before Albie pushed him onto his stomach and held him down with his weight.

"You are trouble," Albie mumbled gruffly, his lips at the back of Percy's ear. "You tease me all day like you don't know what you do to me."

Then he ground his erection against Percy's bottom. Percy spread his legs wider. "Oh, Albie, please."

"You know what you do to me," Albie bit out. "I want you every minute of every day. To see you covered in sweat in the stables, to have you tell me you want me when we're in our saddles for hours on end. Do you know how hard I've been all day?"

Percy raised his hips, sliding his hands underneath him to undo the buttons. "Take me, Albie. I need it."

Albie let out a shuddering breath, then his weight was gone. And Percy was just about to complain until he realised he was only reaching for something.

Butter.

Percy smiled as he slid his pants down over the swell of his arse. Then he closed his eyes, the fire dancing behind his eyelids, the heat of the flames not comparable to the heat burning inside him.

He let his mind wander as Albie got them ready, knowing what was about to happen. Knowing he was about to get everything he wanted. As if he were the cat about to get the cream . . .

Literally.

Then Albie was at his entrance. The blunt head of his cock pushing in, stretching and breaching. Percy cried out, no need to be silent. No need to be anything other than who they really were.

Albie froze, his body trembling. "Percy?"

"More," he said, raising his hips, spreading his legs. More of what, he wasn't entirely sure. More pain, more pleasure, more of whatever Albie would give him.

Albie pushed in deeper, harder, groaning loudly. "Oh, this is heaven," he whispered. "You take me to heaven, Percy."

Percy groaned as he took all of him, and when he

needed Albie to pull out a little, to move, to do anything, he remained still. He tried to roll his hips, growing desperate. "Albie, please."

Albie's hand on Percy's hip stilled him, and he pressed an elbow into Percy's back. "I want it too much," he said, his voice tight. "I'm scared I won't be gentle, and I don't want to hurt you. Oh, Percy."

"Have me however you want me," Percy bit out, unable to move underneath him. "Just move, please, Albie. Please."

Albie pulled out a little, the slide glorious, and then he pushed back in. Then he did it again, only he pushed back in harder. Then harder and deeper, over and over. It stole Percy's breath, the pain and the pleasure and everything he'd wished for.

Albie hammered into him, grunting and groaning, unrestrained and free of inhibition.

It was magnificent.

Albie's erection impaled him, and he drove into him as he held him down. And then he stopped, his breaths ragged. "I'm sorry," he murmured into the back of Percy's neck. "I can't control myself."

"Keep going," Percy urged. "Exactly as before."

Albie pulled back and slid in slower this time. He made a tortured sound, still breathing hard. "Can you endure it?"

"Always. Please don't stop. Not until you finish inside me, and maybe not even then."

Albie groaned out a deep, pained rumbling sound.

But then he began to move again. Maybe not as hard and fast as before, but somehow deeper and just as beautiful. The sounds he made, the grunts and the groans with every thrust, and the way he let out a cry as he came.

Percy loved the feel of Albie inside him. The heat of it, the intimacy. And taking his seed, it set something inside of him on fire. A sense of being owned, of being claimed.

He belonged to Albie in ways he couldn't explain.

It completed him.

He could have wept with the power of it, the emotions he felt. Tears filled his eyes and he let out a sob.

Albie pulled out of him quickly and turned him over. "Percy? What did I . . . ? Are you . . . ? Oh my—"

Percy laughed and wiped his traitorous tears. "That was perfect. When you give me your seed, Albie. There are no words to describe it."

This only seemed to confuse Albie. Embarrass him, even. "Oh, are you . . . ?"

Percy laughed again, and let his hand fall back to the ground with a thud. "I am very good."

Albie's brow furrowed and he made a fuss, pulling Percy's boots off, then his trousers, mumbling as he did.

Percy laughed again. "What are you doing?"

Albie scooped him up in his arms and held him. "I'm sorry I was rough. You deserve better."

"Could I have not deserved better with my boots

and pants on?" he asked with a laugh. He'd never been naked in the outdoors before. Percy rolled them over so Albie was now between his legs.

"I didn't want to soil your trousers, sorry," he murmured.

Percy cupped his cheek and leaned up to kiss him. "I love you, Albie. Don't ever apologise for taking me exactly as I asked you to have me."

Albie closed his eyes, wincing in the flickering fire-light, clearly not convinced.

Then Percy realised he rather liked how they were lying. He liked the feel of Albie between his legs, with his full weight on him, pressing against his half-hard cock.

He widened his legs, and found he liked it a whole lot more.

Then he brought his knees up, and Albie's cock slid against his slick hole. Percy gasped and raised his hips. "You could take me like this too," he breathed.

"I'm not sure I . . ." Albie winced again, rolling his hips, seeking the entrance. He went to his knees a little, gripped his half-hard erection, and guided it into Percy once more.

Albie put his hand beside Percy's head and dropped his head, shuddering as he slid all the way in. Sinking into the depths of pleasure.

Percy had never felt anything like it. Not this angle, not this position. He had no clue it could be like this. "Oh my god," he breathed.

"How can I want more?" Albie said, trembling with restraint.

Percy wrapped his arms around Albie and pulled him in for a kiss, moaning as their tongues met. Percy was so full of him, so consumed by him, and as Albie drove upward, rocking Percy in the best possible way, something sparked behind his eyelids.

Fireworks and gun powder and the most intoxicating drug he'd ever known, all at once.

He gasped and shook, trembling, and the grunting noises he made sounded feral.

Albie tried to pull back, but Percy clung to him, clawed at his back. "More. More. There. Again."

And Albie gave him what he wanted, needed, so desperately craved, until his body could take no more. One last thrust and Albie shot his seed deep inside him, and those sparks that had lit up behind his eyelids rained down and ignited the powder keg.

The pleasure that detonated inside him, Percy could not explain.

It didn't feel real. Couldn't possibly be real.

As if his body was possessed by pleasure, he fell apart with Albie still buried inside him. Convulsing, back arched, his cock shooting his seed between them. His legs trembled, his arms, and he lost all sight and sound.

So utterly high.

"Percy?" Albie's soft voice came back to him. "Are you . . . what was that? Are you . . . ?"

All Percy could do was laugh and maybe cry a little, but mostly laugh. His hands shook, his body didn't feel like his at all. But he'd never felt anything like it.

Albie's hand cupped his cheek, feeling his forehead, his neck. "Are you all right? Please answer me. What was that?"

Percy managed to open his eyes, catching Albie's concern in his dark eyes. "I don't know," he said with another laugh. "But we need to do it again."

———

THEY FELL asleep by the fire, Percy curled up safe and sound in Albie's arms. He'd managed to get his long johns back on, but it took a while for his body tremors to subside.

He got a new rush of jittery pleasure with each one, and he fell asleep happily knowing he had two rounds of Albie's pleasure inside him, feeling stretched and used.

Loved.

And he woke before the sun broke over the mountains, the early morning light softening the fields, the river.

It really was beautiful down here.

He left Albie sleeping, deciding to go clean himself up in the creek with some privacy. He stripped off his underwear and shirt, then sat fully naked in the water.

It was fresh and invigorating, easing any aches and stings, and cleaning himself in the process. He redressed, fixed the fire for fresh tea, then set about cleaning their utensils in the river.

With his long johns rolled to his knees and without his shirt, he waded downstream a little and set about doing his work. He tipped the old tea out, then rinsed the billy . . .

When something in the water caught his eye.

At first he thought it was just the sunlight glinting off the water, but then he realised it wasn't.

His heart raced with excitement and exhilaration as he reached into the water and snatched up a fistful of mud and pebbles. He shook out the dredge, turning his hand over to reveal some brown pebbles on his palm.

And a small nugget of gold, glinting in the sunlight.

He knew what this meant. He knew what this would mean.

What it did to his father.

"What is it?" Albie said.

Percy startled and instinctively closed his fist. He shook his head and swallowed hard, the excitement now a lump of dread. "Albie," he breathed.

Albie closed the distance between them. "What is it?"

He couldn't hide this from Albie. He just couldn't.

With a heavy, thumping heart, he held his hand out, revealing what he held in his palm.

Albie's eyes went wide, as did his smile, but when he looked at Percy, all Percy could do was shake his head. "I just found it. Just now. It was glinting in the sunlight under the water."

Why did his mouth feel so dry?

Albie studied him for a second. "Were you going to hide this from me?"

Percy shook his head quickly and thrust the nugget of gold into Albie's hand. "Take it. Have it. This stuff is poison. It will poison your mind, make you crazy, Albie. That's what happened to my father. He almost lost everything. He should have lost everything, if it weren't for my mother's family." He shook his head again, suddenly feeling ill. He pushed the heel of his hand against his stomach, and he was finding it hard to breathe.

"Percy," Albie whispered. "Calm down. Take a breath in." Percy did, and Albie breathed slowly with him. "That's it. Are you sure you're all right?"

He shook his head. "Albie, you can't let it ruin you. I won't let it."

"I would never," he said.

"All men think that. All men think they won't . . . They call it gold fever for a reason, Albie. It's ruined more men than it ever saved." He tried to lick his lips but his mouth was too dry.

Albie took Percy's arm and led him out of the water. "Come with me. Let's sit down."

They did that, Albie sitting beside him, until Percy

could breathe a little easier. "Sorry," Percy said. "I just . . . I panicked."

Albie gave him a soft smile. "You had a bit of a scare."

"I don't want to lose you," Percy said. "Not for gold; not for anything. You're a mountain man, a good farmer, as your father raised you to be."

"I'll never be anything else," Albie said gently. "And you're never losing me."

He turned his palm upside down, revealing the small nugget. It must have been two ounces, at least. It was pretty and innocuous as it sat there in Albie's hand, but Percy couldn't help but feel the weight of dread that came with it.

"You and I can look for more today," Albie said, and when Percy tried to protest, Albie put his hand up to silence him. "Just one half-day. We leave at midday to make it back to Alpine Falls by night fall, no exceptions."

Percy nodded quickly. That was reasonable, and fair.

"What about scouting out a site for a hut? Wasn't that the plan?" Percy asked.

Albie gave a pointed glance over the river, nearer to the valley. "There's a spot over there, far enough from the river should it flood. We'd need to clear some trees, make some fences, some holding yards."

"You still want to bring cattle and sheep down here in the winter?"

"Of course I do." He smiled at the gold nugget. "Percy, I don't doubt this could change everything for us."

"For us?" Percy said, panic building again.

Albie smiled at him. "For the farm. Us. Our farm."

Percy let out a rush of breath. "Oh." Then he shook his head again. "It's your farm, Albie."

They'd had this talk when Albie had mentioned putting Percy's name on the property deeds. He'd said it was the only way to recognise their relationship, and should anything happen to Albie the property would go to Percy, his partner.

Life partner, business partner, it was all the same, Albie had argued.

Percy had said no.

He couldn't let Albie do that.

And now here he was bringing it up again.

"Well, you found this," Albie said, looking at the gold. "So—"

"It's on your land," Percy countered. "That makes it yours."

Albie sighed. "Ours."

Percy didn't want to argue semantics today.

"Anyway," Albie said. "As I was saying, I don't doubt this could change things for us. We could make ourselves some serious money if we were to find any more."

Percy shook his head.

Albie held up his hand again. "I said if. That's a big

if. I know men have gone and lost their minds over it, Percy. And I promise not to let that happen to us. We'll cash it in and put it in the bank. We don't flaunt nothing. We'll be smart and buy things to make the farm better. Another bull, some more cows. More feed. A new saddle for Robert, new boots for Des."

"Will you tell them?" Percy asked, his eyes wide. That sense of dread was creeping back in. "There's no saying what they'll do. They might quit the farm to come looking, find their own gold."

"Not yet. I won't tell anyone yet."

"Ever," Percy said. "We keep this between us until we know for certain. There might not be any more. This could have been a one-off chance. And we'd have ruined lives forever."

Or there could be thousands just like it went unsaid.

Neither of them had to say that out loud.

"And we don't take it to Alpine Falls," Percy added. "Everyone would know before you were done folding your money."

"Our money."

Percy squinted his eyes shut. "Albie, I don't want it. I just want you. Nothing else."

Albie leaned in, giving his shoulder a soft kiss. "I'll have your name beside me on those title deeds one day, just you see."

Percy sighed, the fight in him gone. "It scares me,

Albie," he whispered. "The gold and what it does to a man's sanity. I've seen it before. I know what it can do."

"So we make a deal," Albie declared. "A promise, between us, right here and now." He held up the little nugget of gold, letting the sun hit it. "We will not let this rule us or ruin us. We can look only when we come down here to run cattle or if we need another night when it's just the two of us, if the weather's good. We keep this a secret until we both decide otherwise, but we don't keep secrets from each other."

"Agreed." Percy felt better immediately. "And whatever we find, we don't take to Alpine Falls. We take it two towns over if we have to. Like you said, we use the money to make the farm better. We won't let each other be blinded by this," he said, searching Albie's eyes. "I promise. You have my word, Albie."

Albie's smile was something special. "And you have my word, Percy. My promise to you, and my heart. You have that too."

Before Percy could be embarrassed, Albie looked out over the river and sighed before he slipped the nugget of gold into his pocket. "Let's forget about this for now and make some breakfast. Are you hungry?"

"Starving."

"I'll get the bread. You make the tea."

"Deal."

Epilogue
Ten Years Later

Time was a funny thing.

It moved in cycles, both fast and slow. Some days Albie could have sworn time flew by too fast, seasons merging into years far too easily. Some days working cattle and horses outside was so cold time seemed to stop altogether.

And then some days it seemed like just yesterday that he said a final goodbye to his father.

It had been ten years to the day that Albie had inherited his father's farm and signed the title deeds to his property. Ten years to the day that a thin and wiry blond man not much younger than him smiled his way into Albie's life.

And into his heart.

He wasn't so thin and wiry anymore.

Percy had filled out nicely. A strong man of almost thirty years now. His blond hair still probably a little too long, but those blue eyes still sparked with mischief, and his smile . . .

That smile still stole Albie's breath.

He'd never tire of it.

Never tire of waking up next to him, working alongside him.

And never tire of seeing Percy's name next to Albie's on the deeds to his property.

"Mr Bramwell, Mr Collins," Mr Flannigan said. "Congratulations."

Congratulations, indeed.

It had taken ten years, but Percy finally agreed to be partners.

Life partners, always.

Business partners, starting now.

"I'm sure your father would be very proud of your success, Albie," Mr Flannigan added. He gestured to them both in their nice attire, sitting across from him.

They both did look good today.

Clean suits, hair brushed.

A far cry from the kid that walked into this office ten years ago in his too-worn clothes, covered in dirt and sweat, full of grit and determination.

Well, the determination still remained.

They smelled a little better this time though.

"I would like to think he would be too," Albie said.

"Opening up the bottom parcel of your land was the right decision," Mr Flannigan added. "Made a few folks around these parts think about their land a bit differently. The men from Echo Creek, huh?"

Albie and Percy both smiled. "Yeah," Albie said, his heart so full it could burst.

Yes, running sheep and cattle in the winter down on the lowland had been the right decision. It soon became running sheep and cattle all year round, and the good townsfolk of Alpine Falls attributed Albie's slow-growing wealth to this decision.

They had no idea of the real reason.

No one did.

They'd found quite a few nuggets over the years.

More than enough to secure the future of Echo Creek. Enough to purchase good breeding stock, enough to buy shares in the stock market. Enough to never worry about affording their next meal ever again.

They hired more workers, making Des and Robert both leading foremen, and paid them handsomely for it. Even built them a house to share with their wives.

While Albie and Percy managed the property as a whole, they spent most of their time in the small house on the lowlands. They'd kept true to their promise. Their main priority would always be the mountain farm, but when they were alone and when time allowed, they did look for more gold.

It could have been so easy for Albie to neglect the farm and focus only on finding gold, panning, mining. But he remembered his father's love and pride in his farm, and he remembered the look of fear in Percy's eyes that day when they'd found the first nugget.

And he swore to himself he'd do everything in his power to never see that look again.

And Percy had been right.

They were now living the best of both worlds. Running the farm with enough money behind them to never have to worry again.

"How does it feel?" Albie asked him as they stepped outside of the lawyer's office.

The streets of Alpine Falls were busier these days. The town was growing, but a lot of familiar faces remained. "Morning," the chemist said, tipping his hat at them as he passed.

"Charles," Albie replied with a smile and a nod.

"Nice morning," he said as he went about his business.

Percy smiled out into the street. "It feels good, Albie," Percy finally answered. "I get it now."

"You get what now?"

"My name next to yours. It's not about the land itself. Not for me, at least. But my name next to yours."

Albie grinned at him, his heart full. "Exactly." Then he lowered his voice. "If we were wed and I were to die, you'd get the farm. This is just ensuring the same. And just so you know, if we could be married, I would."

Percy's cheeks flushed a little pink, and he swallowed hard. "Can we not talk about you dying, thanks. I won't have a word of it."

"Oh, I have no intention of it," Albie said. "I have a life with you to live first."

"Ah, Mr Bramwell," a familiar voice said. "Albie."

Albie turned to find none other than Williams walking to them. He appeared mostly dishevelled, and he had a cane now, after an intoxicated fall from a horse broke his leg. Ironically, not too dissimilar an injury to Des's. An injury Williams here had mocked Des for. Williams found himself fired from McAllister's and he'd come knocking on Albie's door, begging for work.

Only to have Elsie hunt him off the veranda with a shotgun pointed in his face, and for what he'd tried to do to Clara, Albie couldn't blame her.

Needless to say, he was not welcome.

That did start the rumour that Elsie and Clara were sharing the house with Albie and Percy, and Albie was happy for that rumour to run its course.

Let people believe what they will. It was more readily accepted than the truth would have ever been.

"Morning, Williams," Albie said.

"Not, uh, not looking for any more workers by chance, are ya?"

"No," Albie replied. "Sorry."

Not that he'd hire him even if he was.

"Shame," Williams said, squinting at the sun. "Say,

could you perhaps keep an ear out for anything, maybe put in a good word."

He would do neither.

"You could perhaps try the church," Albie said. He didn't like Williams at all, but he would never be as callous or cold as the likes of McAllister. Albie's father raised him better than that. "Maybe old Father Michael might need some ground maintenance work done. Or the school yard."

Williams nodded as if that was a good idea and went on his way. They watched him hobble off.

"You're nicer than he deserves," Percy murmured.

"I'd like to think so, yes," Albie replied with a smile.

"Percy? Percy Collins?"

Both Percy and Albie turned to find a woman with a small child at her side. She was well-dressed, a fine dress and hat, a purse in her hand. She had curls of blond hair around her ears and very familiar blue eyes.

"Marie?" Percy asked.

"Oh, it is you!" she cried, her eyes shining.

Percy collected her in an embrace, and Albie remembered the name Marie.

Percy's sister. One of them, at least.

She pulled back and dabbed tears from her eyes as she took him in. "Look at you," she said. "I've missed you. Where have you been? Where did you go when . . ." She dabbed at more tears. "I've missed you so much."

"I found myself here," he replied, then he looked at Albie. "This is Albie. He's my . . . partner. Business partner," he added quickly.

And damn, if it didn't give Albie's heart a stir.

Partner.

He held out his hand and gently took hers. "So nice to meet you. I can see the family resemblance."

Her smile was familiar too, but she quickly turned back to Percy. "You've clearly done well for yourself," she said. "Look at you. Oh, Percy."

"We have," Percy said. "Done well for ourselves. Cattle, mostly. Sheep, and the best stock horses around," he explained for people now watching. "How long are you staying in town for?"

She looked back down toward the train station. "We've only stopped momentarily, on our way to Sydney," she said. "Young Thomas here needed to stretch his legs. The ticket master said just ten minutes."

Percy looked at the boy and tousled his hair. He had a nephew . . .

"We best walk you back," Albie suggested, giving Percy some time with his sister.

They strode ahead, arms interlocked, and it warmed Albie's heart to watch. They saw them to the platform where they exchanged mailing addresses and promises to write.

"Echo Creek," she said, reading the name.

"That's us," Percy replied. "The men from Echo Creek."

That will always be us, Albie thought.

She hugged him goodbye, then he and Percy watched the train pull away, a horn and plumes of black smoke announcing its departure. And Percy stared after it for a long while.

"Percy," Albie said gently.

He turned, eyes a little watery. "Can you believe that?"

"She looks just like you."

"My baby sister."

"I'm so happy for you. You'll stay in touch. Maybe we can visit. She's more than welcome to visit us."

He nodded quickly and swallowed thickly. "She said our mother is well and our father is . . ." he shook his head.

"Oh, Percy. I'm sorry."

"No, he's not dead. He was incarcerated." He shook his head in disbelief. Just like Albie could barely believe it either. Then he leaned in and whispered, smiling. "He's a criminal, and my mother's two brothers threw him out of the house."

Albie put his hand to his mouth. Smiling didn't feel quite right. "Oh."

Percy laughed, but then he shook his head, sadly. "Gold fever," he murmured. "I told you it rots a man's brain."

Albie smiled and sighed at the warm winter sun. "Lucky we made that promise to protect each other from that."

Percy smiled up at him, slipping the folded note paper with his sister's mailing address on it into his breast pocket. "Can we go home now?"

"We sure can. To our home. It's half yours now, remember."

"I only did it to see my name next to yours."

"That's as good a reason as any," Albie said. They walked off the platform, men tipping their hats in their direction, ladies smiling as they walked the busy street. "Do you need anything else in town? From the store perhaps?"

"No," Percy said. "I've got everything I'll ever need."

Albie laughed, and he wore a smile the whole way home. They rode up the mountain, laughing and singing, telling stories and making plans, and the higher they got, the colder it became, the heavy mist settling in, dampening everything it touched. The smell of eucalypt and damp earth made him long to be home.

And when the rolling green field finally came into view, with the long drive to his house on the rise, Albie's heart had never been so full.

So happy.

Oh, how he wished his father could see him now.

"What's this?" Percy said, stopping at the gate.

There on the long wooden railing was the name Echo Creek, where Albie's name had been underneath it now for ten years. Another name was now etched in beside it, painted in white.

Echo Creek
A Bramwell and P Collins

ALBIE BEAMED WITH PRIDE. "I had Des amend it while we were gone. Do you like it?"

Percy turned to him, his eyes full of tears. "Albie. I don't know what to say."

"Say you'll open the gate."

He barked out a teary laugh and slid down off his horse. He opened the gate and Bandit walked through, only to race off without him, heading straight for the warm barn and fresh hay.

Albie laughed and laughed, but he slid down off Minnie, and let her do the same. She raced down the drive to the barn, leaving them both stranded by the gate. They could hear Des laughing as they got closer, and one of the farm hands followed the two horses into the barn.

Then he and Percy walked down toward the house, together.

As they always would.
As partners.
In business and in life.

The End

SMALL OUTTAKES

Three small scenes that never made the final cut. I was going to scrap them completely but thought my readers might like to see them anyway.

Enjoy.

———————

OUTTAKE ONE

[Albie and Percy are in bed]

Percy snorted but settled for a sigh. "I asked you before if you thought your father knew . . . Do you think your father would approve of us?"

Albie let out a deep breath. "Why are you wondering about such things?"

"I just . . . I don't know. I just wondered, is all."

Albie wasn't sure if there was more to it than that, but it'd been a long day and his eyes were fighting to stay open. "I've wondered this, and at first, I was sure he wouldn't. But now, I'd like to think it was he who sent you to me. He knew I'd need someone to love, someone to stand by my side. And if he's looking down from heaven right now—"

Percy pulled the blanket up. "I hope he's not."

Albie laughed. "He would see me happy, and he'd be like, yes, that's the angel I sent for you."

"An angel?" Percy snorted. "You don't need to flatter me. You have me already."

"It's not flattery if it's a fact." Albie stroked Percy's hair back from his eyes. "An angel just for me."

Outtake Two

Albie's main concern wasn't the wild horses, but more the fences to keep his cattle in and poachers out.

They'd need fixing.

A timely and costly exercise in futility perhaps, but needing to be done, nonetheless.

It was decided over dinner that, when the weather warmed up, Robert would go scouting for damage along the eastern fence line, and Albie and Percy'd take the northwest run. Only during the day, though. Sunup to sunrise. These cold nights weren't fit for sleeping outside, campfire or not.

Des would stay back and manage the farm. Albie knew Des didn't like it, but his knee wasn't up for such rugged riding for hours on end, and the truth was, Robert would be faster without him.

But more to the point, the work Des did around the house, the stables, the yards, was just as important. But Albie could see the frustration clear on Des's face.

A fact Albie made a point of telling him as he saw them out after dinner. Robert went on ahead, leaving Albie and Des to talk.

"Please don't be frustrated," Albie said. "The truth is I need you here. One other thing I inherited from my father was his trust in you, Des. This farm is my life and I wouldn't trust it in the hands of anyone else."

OUTTAKE THREE

"Dinner was nice. I was surprised," Percy said.

"About what? My cooking?"

Percy laughed. "No. Just how polite Des and Robert were. 'Please pass the bread'," he said, mimicking Robert's voice. He meant no harm, easy to tell by his huge smile and the light in his eyes. "It was nice. I guess it'd be an ugly sight if you didn't insist on their best behaviour."

Albie found himself smiling. "My father always insisted on proper table etiquette. It'd just be me and him at the table, but he'd make me sit straight, use my knife and fork properly, say please and thank you." The memory brought with it the familiar ache of grief, but there was a fondness too. "I think keeping the same tradition out of respect to my father seems the right thing to do. To keep whatever part of him alive." He frowned at himself. "That probably sounds foolish."

"No, it doesn't," Albie said. "If you make his memories and traditions part of you, then he's never really gone. And that's the greatest honour you can give him."

Albie was caught off guard by the emotion that hit him. The force of it. The weight of it. All he could do was nod.

The homestead fires were burning, the windows were golden, smoke billowed from the chimneys. It looked warm and inviting, and for a brief moment, Albie forgot he would never hear his father sing those old Irish tunes or smell his pipe by the evening fire again.

ABOUT THE AUTHOR

N.R. Walker is an Australian author, who loves her genre of gay romance. She loves writing and spends far too much time doing it, but wouldn't have it any other way.

She is many things: a mother, a wife, a sister, a writer. She has pretty, pretty boys who live in her head, who don't let her sleep at night unless she gives them life with words.

She likes it when they do dirty, dirty things... but likes it even more when they fall in love. She used to think having people in her head talking to her was weird, until one day she happened across other writers who told her it was normal.

She's been writing ever since...

---

nrwalker.net

ALSO BY N.R. WALKER

Merry Christmas Cupid

To the Moon and Back

Second Chance at First Love

Outrun the Rain

Into the Tempest

Touch the Lightning

EWB - Enemies With Benefits

Holiday Heart Strings

Bloom

TITLES IN AUDIO:

Cronin's Key

Cronin's Key II

Cronin's Key III

Red Dirt Heart

Red Dirt Heart 2

Red Dirt Heart 3

Red Dirt Heart 4

The Weight Of It All

Switched

Point of No Return

Breaking Point

Starting Point

EWB

Holiday Heart Strings

Bloom

SERIES COLLECTIONS:

Red Dirt Heart Series

Turning Point Series

Thomas Elkin Series

Spencer Cohen Series

Imago Series

Blind Faith Series

Missing Pieces Series

The Storm Boys Series

FREE READS:

Sixty Five Hours

Learning to Feel

His Grandfather's Watch (And The Story of Billy and Hale)

The Twelfth of Never (Blind Faith 3.5)

Twelve Days of Christmas (Sixty Five Hours Christmas)

Best of Both Worlds

Translated Titles:

Italian

Fiducia Cieca (Blind Faith)

Attraverso Questi Occhi (Through These Eyes)

Preso alla Sprovvista (Blindside)

Il giorno del Mai (Blind Faith 3.5)

Cuore di Terra Rossa Serie (Red Dirt Heart Series)

Natale di terra rossa (Red dirt Christmas)

Intervento di Retrofit (Elements of Retrofit)

A Chiare Linee (Clarity of Lines)

Senso D'appartenenza (Sense of Place)

Spencer Cohen Serie (including Yanni's Story)

Punto di non Ritorno (Point of No Return)

Punto di Rottura (Breaking Point)

Punto di Partenza (Starting Point)

Imago (Imago)

Imagines

Il desiderio di un soldato (A Soldier's Wish)

Scambiato (Switched)

Tallowwood

The Hate You Drink

Ho trovato te (Finders Keepers)

Cuori d'argilla (Throwing Hearts)

Galassie e Oceani (Galaxies and Oceans)

Il peso di tut (The Weight of it All)

Pieces of You - Missing Pieces 1

FRENCH

Confiance Aveugle (Blind Faith)

A travers ces yeux: Confiance Aveugle 2 (Through These Eyes)

Aveugle: Confiance Aveugle 3 (Blindside)

À Jamais (Blind Faith 3.5)

Cronin's Key Series

Au Coeur de Sutton Station (Red Dirt Heart)

Partir ou rester (Red Dirt Heart 2)

Faire Face (Red Dirt Heart 3)

Trouver sa Place (Red Dirt Heart 4)

Le Poids de Sentiments (The Weight of It All)

Un Noël à la sauce Henry (A Very Henry Christmas)

Une vie à Refaire (Switched)

Evolution (Evolved)

Galaxies & Océans

Qui Trouve, Garde (Finders Keepers)

Sens Dessus Dessous (Upside Down)

La Haine au Fond du Verre (The hate You Drink)

Tallowwood

Spencer Cohen Series

Thomas Elkin One

Lacuna

German

Flammende Erde (Red Dirt Heart)

Lodernde Erde (Red Dirt Heart 2)

Sengende Erde (Red Dirt Heart 3)

Ungezähmte Erde (Red Dirt Heart 4)

Vier Pfoten und ein bisschen Zufall (Finders Keepers)

Ein Kleines bisschen Versuchung (The Weight of It All)

Ein Kleines Bisschen Fur Immer (A Very Henry Christmas)

Weil Leibe uns immer Bliebt (Switched)

Drei Herzen eine Leibe (Three's Company)

Über uns die Sterne, zwischen uns die Liebe (Galaxies and Oceans)

Unnahbares Herz (Blind Faith 1)

Sehendes Herz (Blind Faith 2)

Hoffnungsvolles Herz (Blind Faith 3)

Verträumtes Herz (Blind Faith 3.5)

Thomas Elkin: Verlangen in neuem Design

Thomas Elkin: Leidenschaft in klaren

Thomas Elkin: Vertrauen in bester Lage

Traummann töpfern leicht gemacht (Throwing Hearts)

Sir

So Unendlich Viel Liebe (To the Moon and Back)

THAI

Sixty Five Hours (Thai translation)

Finders Keepers (Thai translation)

SPANISH

Sesenta y Cinco Horas (Sixty Five Hours)

Los Doce Días de Navidad

Código Rojo (Code Red)

Código Azul (Code Blue)

Queridísimo Milton James

Queridísimo Malachi Keogh

El Peso de Todo (The Weight of it All)

Tres Muérdagos en Raya: Serie Navidad en Hartbridge

Lista De Deseos Navideños: Serie Navidad en Hartbridge

Feliz Navidad Cupido: Serie Navidad en Hartbridge

Spencer Cohen Libro Uno

Printed in Great Britain
by Amazon

45645972R00229